Some ghosts ne

HAUNTED

When a Crow Indian acquaintance of Tomlinson's asks him to help recover relics stolen from his tribe, Doc Ford is happy to tag along—but neither Doc nor Tomlinson realizes what they've let themselves in for. Their search takes them to the part of Central Florida known as Bone Valley, famous primarily for two things: a ruthless subculture of black marketers who trade in illegal artifacts and fossils, and a multibillion-dollar phosphate industry whose strip mines compromise the very ground they walk on.

Neither enterprise tolerates nosy outsiders. For each, public exposure equals big financial losses—and in a region built on a million-year accumulation of bones, there is no shortage of spots in which to hide a corpse. Or two.

HAUNTED

RANDY WAYNE WHITE

BERKLEY BOOKS | NEW YORK

BERKLEY

An imprint of Penguin Random House LLC
375 Hudson Street, New York, New York 10014

HAUNTED

A Berkley Book / published by arrangement with the author

ISBN: 978-0-425-27516-0

PUBLISHING HISTORY
G. P. Putnam's Sons hardcover edition / August 2014
Berkley premium edition / August 2015

PRINTED IN THE UNITED STATES OF AMERICA

10 9 8 7 6 5 4 3 2 1

Front cover photographs: *House* © RGB Ventures LLC dba SuperStock / Alamy.
Beach © Slim Aarons / Getty Images.
Cover design by Nellys Liang.

Penguin
Random
House

For Pete

. . . and behold a pale horse: and him that sat on him was Death, and Hell followed with him. And power was given unto them over the fourth part of the earth, to kill with sword, and with hunger, and with death, and with the beasts of the earth.

—REVELATION 6:8

As a descendent of fallen angels, I cannot blame Darwin or the apes.

—S. M. TOMLINSON

This world is painted on a wild dark metal.

—PETER MATTHIESSEN, *Shadow Country*

AUTHOR'S NOTE

As always, this novel required research in various fields and disciplines. Before thanking those who kindly provided assistance, note that all errors, exaggerations, or misstatements should be blamed on the author or the exigencies of fiction. Boca Grande artist Shirley Cassady Goodwin provided inspiration daily via her watercolor interpretations of Florida. Mr. Steve Smith and the crew at Babcock Ranch of South Florida helped enormously by allowing me to observe and participate in igniting palmetto fields during a controlled burn—hazard reduction burning, as the technique is known. The Babcock folks were also very generous in sharing their expertise.

Florida's role in the American Civil War has too often been overlooked or trivialized by historians, but not all. While researching *Haunted*, I read several credible books on the subject, as well as diaries and papers made available through the National Archives. Thanks to the generosity of a personal source, I was also lucky enough to have access to logs and records of an organization that was active during that time period. In this novel, many liberties have been taken with historical fact, but it is my hope that Capt. Ben Summerlin's journal is accurate in tone, at least, and possibly hints at truths that, as of now, are unknown.

Over many years, encouragement was provided by my Iowa friends and teachers, Coach Bill and Sherry Freese, and Bill and Helen Wundrum. Dr. Joshua Sheridan, DVN, provided helpful (and chilling) research on behavior of chimpanzees. Also supportive were Mrs. Iris Tanner, the author's friend and guardian angel; my wife, Wendy Webb; my partners and pals, Mark Marinello, Marty and Brenda Harrity; my teammates Stu Johnson, Bill Lee, Gary Terwilliger, Don Carman, Judd Park Miller, and Victor Candelaria; and former classmates Barry and Cathy Rubel, Gloria Osborne, Norm Fiser, Bob Repp, Marv Esterline, Alan King, Kris Clark, Jackie Ray, Deb Votaw, Shirley Sharon Martin, Cheryl Moore, John Haines, Lon Hersha, Mike Gallutia, Ed Ott, Daryl Franz, Daryl Long, Steve Joyce, Chester Rutludge, Chuck Carter, Keith Hess, Cheryl Hitchcock, Stella Hinkle, Becky Durey Walls, Janet Dohm, Ron Collie. Once again, I owe thanks to Dr. Marybeth B. Saunders, Dr. Peggy C. Kalkounos, and Dr. Brian Hummel for providing expert medical advice. Special thanks to Capt. Bill

Bishop and Luciana Bishop Carbone, true Florida voices, and also to Brother Don Hensiak, Donald Wayne Hensiak, Joey Ann Kempson, Maggie Farley Bradfield, lovely Marla J. Martin, Ton Braciszewski, Kirsten Dickerson and Shane Traugott, Eric Pritzi, Sierra and Caiden Rainville.

At the Rum Bar on San Carlos Island, Fort Myers Beach, thanks go to Dan Howes, Andrea Aguayo, Corey Allen, Nora Billeimer, Tiffany Forehand, Jessica Foster, Amanda Ganong, Nicole Hinchcliffe, Mathew Johnson, Janell Jambon, C. J. Lawerence, Josie Lombardo, Meredith Martin, Sue Mora, Kerra Pike, Michael Scopel, Heidi Stacy, Danielle Straub, Latoya Trotta, Lee Washington, Katlin Whitaker, Kevin Boyce, Keil Fuller, Ali Pereira, Kevin Tully, Molly Brewer, Jessica Wozniak, Emily Heath, Nicole English, Ryan Cook, Drew Fensake, Ramon Reyes, Justin Voskuhl, Anthony Howes, Louis Pignatello, and John Goetz.

At Doc Ford's on Captiva Island: Lovely Julie, Capt. Mario, Steve, Dominic, Nick, Clark Kent Hill, Kristin and lovely Adalynn Hill, Chef Greg Nelson, Chef James King, Alexis Marcinkowski, Amy Charron, Cheryl Erickson, Erica Debacker, Heather Walk, Holly Emmons, Isabel Garcia, Julie Grzeszak, Karen Bove, Larissa Holmes, Matt Ginn, Sarah Ginn, Shelbi Muske, Nick Hopkins, Thayne Fugal, Jon Calupca, Alexa Mozes, Hope McNulty, Ashley Foster, Chad Chupurdia, Daniel Flint, Dominic Cervio, Stephen Day, and Greg Barker.

Finally, I would like to thank my two sons, Rogan and

Lee White, for helping me finish, yet again, another book.

—Randy Wayne White
Telegraph River Gun Club
Babcock Ranch

1

IN FLORIDA, HUNDRED-YEAR-OLD HOUSES HAVE solid walls, so I guessed wrong when I heard my friend Birdy Tupplemeyer make a bleating noise downstairs. I figured she'd snuck a man into her room, which was unfair of me, even though Birdy admits to being free-minded when it comes to romance.

On windy October nights my imagination prefers love to spiders, I guess. That is my only excuse.

I was in a hammock on the second floor in what had once been a music room. Birdy, who lacks camping experience, had chosen a downstairs room for her air mattress because it was closer to the front door.

"I'd have to hang off the balcony to pee," she had reasoned, which made sense even before the wind freshened and the moon rose. The house was abandoned; no electricity or water, and the spiral staircase was in bad shape. I myself, after too much tea by the fire, was debating whether to risk the balcony or those wobbly steps when, through the floor, I heard a thump, another thump, and then a mewling wail that reminded me of a cat that had found companionship.

She's with that archaeologist, I thought, and buried my face in a pillow, but not my ears—a guilty device. My curiosity has always had an indecent streak. I also had a reason. That afternoon we had met Dr. Theo Ivanhoff, an assistant professor with shaggy black hair: late twenties, khakis low on his skinny hips and wearing a Greek fisherman's cap. He was on the property mapping artifacts from a Civil War battle that had taken place before the house was built. Theo had struck me as an aloof know-it-all and a tad strange, but it had been a month since Birdy's last date so her standards had loosened. Later, by the campfire, the two of us sitting with tea and marshmallows, she had shared some bawdy remarks including "hung like a sash weight" and "Professor Boy Toy," referring to a man only a few years younger than us.

Naturally, I felt supportive of my friend, not alarmed. Until I heard: "My god . . . what *is* that?" which could have meant any number of things.

Guilt battled my curiosity. I turned an ear to the floor just to be on the safe side. Then shattering glass and a shattering scream tumbled me out of the hammock and I was on my knees, feeling around for a flashlight that had tumbled with me.

Birdy's voice again, more piercing: "Bastard . . . get off."

Panic, not passion. I ran for the stairs. Thank heavens I was barefoot, so I knew it was a flashlight I kicked across the room. Bending to grab the thing, I clunked my head, then stubbed my toe going out the door. In the hall, the flashlight's white beam bounced among cobwebs and a dusty piano while Birdy screamed my name.

"Hannah . . ."

I hollered back, "I've got a gun!" which was true, but the gun was locked in my SUV, not in my hand. Then I put too much weight on the banister as I catapulted down the stairs—a brittle pop; the banister fell. I spiraled down a few steps on my butt, caught myself, then raced the banister to the bottom. The banister won. I shoved it aside and was soon standing outside Birdy's door, which was locked. That scared me even more.

I yelled, "Birdy . . .?" and pounded.

"Get in here!"

"Open the door."

"It's jammed! Oh . . *shit*, Hannah, hurry."

I wrenched the knob and used my shoulder. The door gave way on the second try and I fell into the room, which was dark but for moonlight reflecting off broken glass on the floor. I got to my feet and, once again, had to hunt for the flashlight. My friend, dressed in T-shirt and shorts, had her back to me and was dancing around as if fighting cobwebs or in the midst of a seizure. "Get it off, get it off!" she yelled, then winced when she turned, blinded by my arrival.

I lowered the flashlight, relieved. I'd feared an attacker, but she was alone. I rushed across the room and put a hand on Birdy's arm to stop her contortions. "Hold still," I had to tell her twice while I scanned her up and down. Finally I stepped back. "I don't see anything."

"It was in my hair."

"*What?*"

"How the hell should I know?" Birdy added some F-bombs and bowed her head for an inspection. I used my free hand, the light close, to comb through her thick ginger hair, which was darker at the roots, Birdy saying, "I was almost asleep when something landed on my face. Something with *legs*. It crawled up my forehead, then stung me on the neck—I'm sure there was more than one. I tried to run, but the damn door wouldn't open."

"Where on your neck?"

I moved the light, but Birdy hollered, "Finish with my hair first!" That told me the sting could wait.

"Probably a palmetto bug. They don't sting, so you probably imagined that."

"Imagined, my ass." Birdy pulled her T-shirt up, ribs showing, a petite woman addicted to jogging who didn't get much sun because of her freckles and red hair.

I checked her back and down her legs. "Where's your flashlight?"

"Goddamn bugs on my face, I must've dropped it or something. I don't know. I'd just found the switch when one bit the hell out of me. Anybody would have lost it after that."

I said, "That explains the broken window."

"What broken window?"

Birdy Tupplemeyer is a high-strung, energetic woman,

but normally steady in her behavior, as you would expect of a deputy sheriff with two years' experience. I had never seen her so upset. "You didn't hear the glass break? You must have thrown that light pretty hard. I'm glad you weren't waving your gun around when I came through the door."

I bent to check the back of her neck, but first took a look around the room, seeing glass on the pine flooring, the shattered window, a moon-frosted oak tree outside, and my friend's air mattress, a double-wide with cotton sheets, her overnight bag open in the corner, clothes folded atop it.

"My pistol's under the pillow," she countered. "Don't worry about getting shot. Worry about the damn bugs—this freaking room is infested." She shuddered and swore.

I pushed my flashlight into her hands. "I'm not a nurse. Check inside your own pants."

Light in hand, Birdy pulled her shorts away from her hips, then disappeared down her baggy T-shirt, the shirt glowing like a tent until she reappeared. "For once, I'm glad to be flat-chested. Those sons of bitches sting. Here . . . look for yourself."

She lifted her head, the light bright on a welt that was fiery red on her freckled throat. My heart had stopped pounding, but now I was concerned.

"Give me that," I said, taking the light. "Does it hurt?"

"Burns like hell."

"Is it throbbing?"

Birdy heard the change in my voice. "Do you think it

was a spider? I *hate* spiders. Maybe I should go to the E-R. What time is it?"

"Stop squirming," I said, but that's exactly why I was concerned. I grew up camping, hiking, and fishing in the Florida backcountry with my late uncle, Capt. Jake Smith, who became a well-known guide after being shot and then retiring as a Tampa detective. More than once, Jake had told me, "People are the most dangerous animals on earth. Everything else, avoid it and it will avoid you."

Jake's long list included creatures that scare most newcomers and keep them snug and safe inside their condos: snakes, sharks, alligators, panthers—and poison spiders, too. The only dangerous spiders in Florida are black widows, brown widows, and, possibly, the brown recluse, although I have yet to see a recluse for myself. The widow spiders tend to be shy and seldom bite unless you mess with them or happen to slap at one in your sleep. I've seen many, often living in colonies on porches of people who have no idea they are there. Their spiky egg sacs are unmistakable. Which is why, when camping, I prefer a screened hammock to a tent.

This was something I hadn't explained to Birdy. She had grown up wealthy in a Boston suburb so was nervous from the start about sleeping in a house that had a dark history and was fifteen miles from the nearest town. Never mind that her Aunt Bunny Tupplemeyer, a Palm Beach socialite, had hired me to spend a night or two in the place and record the comings and goings of strangers. The woman's reasons had to do with the million dollars she had invested in river frontage that included the old house—a house she wanted torn down. Birdy was along to keep me company and, as mentioned, was currently not dating, so had chosen adventure over depression rather than spend her Friday night off alone.

She started to panic again. "What if it was a poison spider? Shit, I should have slept in my car." Being from Boston, she pronounced it *kaahr*. She checked the time. "It feels like midnight, but it's not even nine-thirty. I know a woman doctor I can call—she's a gyno, but, hell, I'll just lie about where the damn thing bit me."

I touched my finger to a speck of blood on her neck. "It's a sting, not a bite, but you'll be fine. A spider would have left two little fang marks. I've got some first-aid cream upstairs."

"*Fangs*? Jesus Christ, my Beamer, I should've crashed in the backseat. Those bastards are probably in my bed right now, screwing like rats and hatching babies. Smithie"—her nickname for me—"we can't sleep here. My Aunt Bunny, that conniving bitch, is to blame for this."

She was upset, so I discounted her words. "It was a wasp, most likely," I said, and, for the first time, shined the light at the ceiling above the air mattress. Immediately, I pointed the light at the floor, but too late.

"Oh my god," Birdy whispered, "what was that?"

She yanked the light from me. Plaster overhead had broken, showing rafters of hundred-year-old wood so dense with sap that they glowed where it had beaded. But there were also glowing silver eyes. Dozens of eyes attached to black armored bodies with claws and curled tails. They were scorpions, some four inches long. Stunned by the light, one fell with an air-mattress thump, righted itself, and scrabbled toward us over clean cotton sheets that were tasteful but not as practical as a sleeping bag.

Birdy screamed so didn't hear me say, "It's okay, this kind isn't dangerous," then nearly knocked me down running for the door.

2

My lineage includes many aunts and uncles, some noteworthy, most not, but I have yet to refer to a family member with the word Birdy used to blame her aunt for the presence of scorpions in Florida.

The word struck me as unreasonable. On the other hand, it also comforted me regarding my tolerance for a mother and at least one aunt—the third Hannah Smith in our family—whose behaviors have ranged from man-hungry to just plain crazy.

My mother, Loretta, and my late Aunt Hannah, being a mix of both.

It is true, however, that Mrs. Bunny Tupplemeyer, a Palm Beach widow, was the reason we were here.

Birdy, whose actual name is Liberty Grace, had invited me for a weekend at her aunt's beach house, then a cocktail party at a penthouse apartment that was downtown, close to shopping, at the corner of Ocean Boulevard and Worth. It was a tenth-floor saffron high-rise not far from the Kennedy compound, I was told. The Opry mansion, with its gate and carved marble fountain, was farther down the beach.

This was two weeks ago.

I grew up on the Gulf Coast of Florida but had never been in downtown Palm Beach. Condos and shops possessed a gilded indifference, the streets edged with royal palms from Prohibition days. Residential areas were screened by towering hedges and a muffled Rolls-Royce hush that warned of money and double standards.

"Relax," Birdy kept telling me in the car. "Just be yourself. If the Great Dame starts interrogating you— and she will—just smile and compliment her jewelry. Or bring up astrology. She loves guessing people's signs. While she's boring you with that, signal the staff for another martini. Dame Bunny likes them icy cold."

Dame Bunny, that's how my friend referred to her wealthy, socialite aunt.

There was no need for me to relax because I wasn't nervous. I'm a light tackle fishing guide who deals with wealthy clients day after day in a small skiff around Sanibel and Captiva Islands, although I live across the bay on the island of Gumbo Limbo. I've learned that the rich are no different than the rest of us when it comes to tangling lines, or whoops of delight when a big fish jumps, or when their bladder demands a bucket and a moment of privacy.

Birdy was the nervous one, not me.

Odd, I thought. She had summered in Palm Beach as a girl and during college. Her mother, Candice, had been a Palm Beach debutante prior to graduating from Wellesley, then joined a commune near Aspen, which, I was told, had only solidified the family's Palm Beach–Boston ties.

"To people with money, politics are more of a fashion statement," Birdy had explained.

But when I'd spent some time with her Aunt Bunny, I understood why my friend was nervous. It was at the cocktail party. I had escaped to the balcony. An Italian banker, after backing me in a corner, had been a little too touchy-feely for comfort. My hostess noticed and followed me outside, a martini in one hand, a cigarette in the other.

"Tired of Victor, the sex-starved poodle?" she asked, sliding the door closed. Then looked me up and down, noting the simple gray shift I wore belted at the waist, my leather flats and a lavender scarf I had bought at Pulitzer's just down the street. "With your legs," she added, "I'm not surprised he's sniffing around. But you could stand to lose a few pounds, darling."

I ignored the insult out of respect for my drunken elders. "He said his name is Vittorio," I replied. "I asked him to spell it because of his accent."

"Made him spell it," the woman repeated, fascinated I would bother.

"It's a good way to remember names. He was polite enough, but I wanted to see what the ocean looks like from out here. Very nice place you have, Mrs.

Tupplemeyer." On the Gulf Stream, miles away, tankers the size of buildings drifted, the sky blacker, it seemed, than a dark night on Sanibel.

The woman stood beside me at the marble rail and flicked ashes. "Smart girl."

"Pardon me?"

"His wife was watching. She's one drink away from making a scene. You've got enough size, I don't think even Rita would try the slapping, hair-pulling thing. But who knows? She drinks absinthe, the real stuff, and sniffs cocaine to stay thin." A pause. She blew smoke into the night and pivoted. "My niece says your family has quite a history in Florida. That you know people I wouldn't know—locals."

Hicks and rednecks is what she meant.

She continued, "She also told me you shot a man a year or so ago. Damn near killed him. Is that true?"

I pretended not to hear and asked about a bracelet on her wrist that glittered with scarlet stones.

"Don't change the subject. Any woman who can pull the trigger, I find that damn impressive. But I'm unclear about exactly what it is you do. Are you a fishing guide or do you run an investigation agency?"

I said, "Both, ma'am, but mostly fishing. The shooting incident, I'd prefer not to discuss." Then looked at the stars and commented, "I didn't read my horoscope today. What about you?"

The woman fell for it, but only momentarily. "There's an astrologician I use, she's excellent. The summaries in newspapers are silly garbage. I have her card, if you want."

Astrologician? The word had a scientific ring but sounded phony.

She continued, "Back to what I was saying . . . Liberty told me you were on a case when it happened. The shooting—a sexual predator or some such scum—that you shot him in the pelvis. Self-defense, so you weren't prosecuted. In fact, you got some kind of award from the local police department. I admire a woman with that kind of spunk. I can think of a dozen men I'd love to shoot and that includes my late husband. Abe was his name. In my world, marrying a man for money doesn't justify verbal abuse."

She expected a reaction. I looked at the ocean instead.

"You used a pistol, according to Liberty. She said you had no choice. The man would've killed you. What I'm hoping is, you shot him in the pelvis because you were aiming at his balls. Am I right or am I right?"

I stepped back and said, "Good lord!"

The aging socialite, her chiffon gown of gold hanging from her shoulders, lowered her voice. "Honey, you can tell me anything. I've done things that would curl your hair. Why? Same as you. We're both survivors."

My ears were warming. I tried to hold it in but couldn't quite manage. "I want to get up early to see the Flagler Museum, Mrs. Tupplemeyer. I think I should leave before you confess to any more crimes."

"That offends you?" She put her hand on my back in a comforting way but also to guarantee I would listen a while longer. "It's not like I asked if you were sleeping with my niece. I wish you were. But I happen to know she's totally heterosexual." The woman paused to smoke. "What about you?"

I created some space between us. "Are you about done asking nosy questions?"

"*No*. Can it hurt so much to open up to an old woman? I'm interested. I don't care if you're gay or not. Trust me, I've had worse things than a firm young breast in my mouth. It's a matter of personal taste, the way I see it." She smiled, surprised by the double entendre. "By god, I ought to write that one down."

"Why don't you do that?"

"Don't be snide. There's a chance we can do business together and I have a particular job in mind. So I'm interested in who you are."

She reminded me of Loretta, my manipulative mother. I settled down in a sullen way, doomed to participate. I said, "I was dating a marine biologist. We even talked about marriage, but he travels too much. Now I'm dating an airline pilot and an attorney—a special prosecutor—but just for something to do. I enjoy my women friends, but sharing a bathroom or a bed isn't part of my makeup."

"Good for you—I'd ride a bus before I'd share my bathroom. You say this biologist, he claims he travels too much?" The socialite's raspy laugh chided *What a bullshit excuse*. "Good riddance to him, then. You'd be living in a condo that hosts happy hour and allows children. Liberty has god-awful taste in men, too. And, let's be honest, neither one of you are beauty queens. Can you believe my airheaded sister named her that?"

I said, "Beg your pardon?"

"Her name, dear—Liberty Grace. It sounds like a slogan for herbal tea." The woman turned to look through the glass, where, among chatty guests, two men in blazers had cornered Birdy, who was holding a drink and wearing a blue cocktail dress that brightened her ginger hair.

I said, "I think she's cute. And she certainly has good taste in clothes." Then took the offensive. "As names go, Bunny is a heck of a lot stranger than Liberty, if you ask me."

"I didn't ask. Or are you just being snotty?"

I replied, "I'm *interested*," mimicking her.

The woman glared for an instant. Then a slow smile. "Yes . . . I can see you doing it—shooting a man right in the balls. Okay, then. Bunny is an old nickname. In Palm Beach, it's a sign of acceptance, especially for a New Yorker named Eve Katz—that's me. I got the name Bunny at boarding school"—her smile became sly—"because I enjoyed boys. You know, had fun hopping from one bed to another. Small tits and a hellacious sex drive, those are the only things Liberty inherited from me—so far. There!" Smoky laughter. "That's something I didn't even tell Abe—him with his donkey pecker and rooster strut. Can we retract the claws now?"

Her reference to farm animals threw me for an instant, so it took a beat to remember that Abe was the husband she'd wanted to shoot. I said, "You should thank your schoolmates. Your nickname could've been a lot worse."

"Oh, it was, dearie, it was. *Bunny* was for social

functions, but it stuck. That's why I worry about Liberty. She's been man-crazy her entire life. Which is fine for recreation. But she's going to inherit my money, which makes her a target."

Because Mrs. Tupplemeyer had mentioned business, I said, "I'm a poor choice if you're looking for a bodyguard. And you're forgetting that Birdy is a trained law officer. I'd be willing to bet she has a gun in her purse right now."

"*Really?*" Surprised but hopeful, the woman turned to peer through the sliding doors. "Do you think she'd do it?"

"Shoot a man? She goes to the target range once a week. I doubt if she could miss something that big."

"No," the woman said, "I mean pull the trigger. Trust me, every bachelor in that room sees a bull's-eye on her ass when they look at her. Or what passes for an ass. I own a derringer, but was never able to get drunk enough."

"Drunk enough to fire," I said to confirm.

"Of course. On several occasions. And the one time I did drink enough, I spilled the goddamn bullets in the sink and the maid refused to call a plumber."

I cleared my throat. "My advice to you, ma'am, is give that gun to your niece. She's too smart to mix alcohol and bullets. What I think is"—I hesitated, wondering if I should say it—"well, I think you've got anger issues, Mrs. Tupplemeyer. And you drink too much to own a firearm."

"Anger issues?" The woman threw her head back and laughed, then noticed her martini glass was empty. "I *like* you, Hannah Smith. How about stopping by in the morning? By *morning*, in Palm Beach, we mean *noon*. There could be a nice retainer if you help me with a certain problem." A studious pause. "You're a Gemini, aren't you? Early in June, with Leo rising. I bet half of you still feels guilty about that pervert you shot—but your better half wishes his nuts were in your trophy case. Am I right or am I right?"

I didn't know what to say to that. When I finally did respond, it was with caution. "I'm not going to shoot a man for you, Mrs. Tupplemeyer, if that's what's on your mind."

The woman, opening her cigarette case, said, "Call me Bunny. Oh . . . and would you mind getting me another martini? *Cold*—tell one of the servers. I've got other guests to attend to."

MRS. TUPPLEMEYER—I couldn't bring myself to call her Bunny—had her slim, handsome attorney explain the details to me. Not at her apartment. His Palm Beach office was at the corner of Hibiscus near the arts center, marble statues and a fountain outside.

Birdy came along. Her Aunt Bunny didn't arrive until we were almost done.

The attorney, his sleeves rolled up, pulled two chairs close to his computer and opened a county tax map that showed land parcels west of Lake Okeechobee, closer to Labelle than Arcadia, in central Florida. He zoomed in.

"Mrs. B—your Aunt Bunny—she's part of an investment consortium that purchased this section of land, a little over six hundred acres. It's north of the Caloosahatchee River between Arcadia and this little town, La-belle." He touched the screen. "Are you familiar with the area?"

"She is," Birdy said, deferring to me.

My friend was correct, but that didn't make me un-usual. On a map of Florida, the Caloosahatchee River is difficult to miss. It crosses the state west to east, Fort Myers to St. Lucie or Palm Beach, depending on how a boat chooses to exit Lake Okeechobee on its way to the Atlantic Ocean.

"Why do you ask?" I asked the man.

He talked a while about the complexity of investors combining properties into a single parcel for develop-ment. "What it comes down to is," he said, "Mrs. B is on the hook for approximately one hundred acres of mostly cattle and timber that runs along this creek." He touched the screen again. "The creek—actually, it says 'Telegraph River' here—it runs into the Caloosahatchee, which is starting to boom. On the other side of the creek, there are a few small-time ranchers, a fundamentalist church or two, and a mom-and-pop RV park. But development is coming to the area. So far, so good."

He looked to confirm we were following along. "Bunny, she's a damn smart woman. I know she did her homework. Unfortunately, she also let her friends—certain associates as well—talk her into committing to this project before she came to me. A project like this, you need to do a thorough analysis before you write a check."

A country club community with a strict covenant to build million-dollar homes on five-acre lots is what the investors envisioned.

Birdy jumped ahead. "How badly is my aunt getting burned?"

"A quarter million, so far," the man said, "plus a second payment of a million dollars is due next month. *Unless* we can find a way to turn this around. No, actually, Mrs. B needs to bail out because, if this project does happen, it'll be years down the road. And here's why."

The screen changed. Now we were looking at an abandoned two-story house, a roof of rusted tin, windows boarded over, and a strange-looking cupola built higher than the chimney. The chimney was brick, the cupola sided with clapboard. Once upon a time, it might have been the main residence of an elegant estate.

"Is that a water cistern?" I asked, meaning the cupola. I'd never seen anything like it. Or so I thought, until he explained that the place had served as a school after a foreclosure in the 1940s. The belfry had been added to house a bell.

"Mrs. B and the other investors knew from the start this house is protected by Florida Historical Properties laws. That wasn't a problem. They could've thrown a fence around the place or restored it as sort of a community capstone. A communal park—picnics on Fourth of July, like that. The house was built in 1890 by a man from Virginia who raised cattle. Charles Langford Cadence. Which is a very marketable name—Cadence Estates or Cadence Greens—lots of possibilities. Has a nice ring, doesn't it? The previous owner was a Brazilian who planted exotic trees for timber. Now the property has some of the most beautiful mimosas and other hardwoods you've ever seen. The combination made the house well worth saving."

The attorney swiveled to me. "Have you heard of the place?"

I said, "I think so, but I can't remember the context. The Langfords were early Florida cattlemen. But Cadence isn't a common name here . . . Or I could be confusing the two."

"I meant the house," he said. "About four years ago, a hack reality show called *Vortex Hunters* did a segment on the place. And the idiotic lien holders played along. Lots of eerie night footage and contrived research about murders and suicides, and negative energy—that sort of thing. It's true that Charles Cadence was murdered or committed suicide way, way back—the TV show hinted that his wife killed him or hired a Florida gangster. A later owner also died there. But—"

"Was this during Prohibition?" I asked. I was interested because I'd read that mobsters from New York and Chicago had operated out of the area. I mentioned Al Capone, but drew a blank on other names.

The interruption derailed the attorney, but he handled it with patience. "No, I think the TV writers invented their own gangster. He was a Bonnie-and-Clyde type. A guy who'd been raised in the swamps, knew how to live off the land—that was their angle—which is why the cops couldn't catch him. But, as I was saying—"

"I bet it was John Ashley," I said.

"John who?

I repeated the name but didn't explain that John Ashley had been a real person. He had murdered and robbed and traveled with a girlfriend. I knew about Ashley because he had been born near Sanibel and there were rumors concerning him and one of my great-aunts.

"Ashley . . ." the attorney said, trying to recall, then decided it was unimportant. "The point is, show me a hundred-year-old house where someone *hasn't* died. That would be unusual. Television cares about ratings; screw the facts. So they staged a reenactment—the psycho gangster, blood on the walls, children screaming— all that sort of nonsense . . . But we're getting off topic. Here's the real problem . . ."

The man clicked open another file while Birdy aimed a sarcastic grin at me. "A haunted house. Let's do a sleepover. We can make s'mores and sing 'Kumbaya.'"

From your lips to God's ears—a favorite expression of an old fisherman friend, Cordial Pallet. Little did we know.

The computer screen changed. Multiple photos: a rusted cannon partially exhumed, a close-up of several clay tobacco pipes, a brass button stamped CSA, chunks of spent lead, a rusted stirrup that appeared too tiny for a man's foot.

CSA: Confederate States of America.

The attorney explained, "These were found on the property. Mostly near the creek and the house, but some other sites, too. Turns out, they're all Civil War period. Before the state will issue permits, due diligence requires a long list of surveys—flora and fauna, water quality, that sort of thing. In this case, an archaeological survey turned up the things you're looking at. From what I've read, there were only five or six significant battles in Florida. North Florida, mostly, so I can't blame Mrs. B for not anticipating the mess she's now in. But here's what put the brakes on the whole project." He reached for the mouse and clicked again.

A human skull, jaw missing. Like the cannon, only partially exhumed. Close-ups of three brass buttons stamped with eagles. Then another excavated spot containing two skulls, a human pelvis, and several femurs, the bones black from age or fire.

Birdy, who has a master's in law enforcement and a minor in archaeology, sat forward. "Oh my god."

The man, however, was fixed on my reaction. I told him, "So far, this is interesting. Some of my relatives fought in the Civil War—for the North and the South. And John Ashley, he was famous in this area. No, *infamous* would be the word."

"Part of your family is from the North?"

"No. All Floridians, but it wasn't unusual to be on different sides. And one of my great-uncles was a blockade-runner. His papers are stored in my mother's attic. I'll dig them out, if you want."

The attorney said, "I like the way you think," but my friend, Birdy, didn't get it.

I explained. "Back then only a few hundred people lived in this part of Florida. It's possible my great-uncle knew Charles Cadence. The Brazilian, too, maybe. When we get home, I'll see what I can find." I paused, then asked the man, "Why are you looking at me like that?"

He knew more about me than he had revealed, that's why. Embarrassed, he glanced down, jotted some notes on a pad, and said, "Let's not get ahead of ourselves," then talked about the photos. "Archaeologists now suspect the acreage owned by Mrs. B was the site of a battle that historians thought took place near Orlando. Brief but very bloody. Or that they've found a battle site that didn't make the history books. More of an extended skirmish than a battle, they think. Their guess is extrapolated from the number of artifacts found over X amount of surface area—some sort of damn formula they use. Worse, they also suspect the house might have been built on or near a field cemetery."

The man sighed and said to Birdy, "No way your aunt could've seen this coming. They've brought in a supposed expert. Until his team's done, the development project is dead in the water. We're talking years, not months—possibly never."

Birdy asked several questions before I said, "I still don't understand what this has to do with me."

The man opened a drawer and placed a file on the desk. "Because Mrs. B asked me to, I did a search on you.

I've confirmed that you're a state-licensed and -bonded private investigator. But with almost no experience, from the number of reports you filed with the state."

"I never claimed otherwise," I replied. "It was my uncle's agency."

The man nodded and waited.

"My uncle was a sheriff's detective before he started chartering. He had wealthy fishing clients who hired new staff every season. They often needed background checks done, so it was a handy license to have. I worked in his office during junior college, which I didn't finish—as I'm sure you already know." The last part came out sharper than I intended.

"No need to get defensive," the attorney said. "You're a friend of the family. We trust you. So Mrs. B wants you to help with an idea I came up with. It's a long shot. But the more I think about, maybe not such a long shot after all." He swiveled around, opened the folder, and handed us each a sheet of paper. "This will help you understand."

The document had to do with real estate laws.

Disclosure laws vary from state to state, but Florida does not require sellers or agents to disclose homicide, suicide, deaths, or past diagnosis of communicable diseases to buyers. However, Florida law does forbid Realtors from selling "stigmatized properties" without full disclosure. A stigmatized property is defined as a structure or parcel of land where real or rumored events occurred that do not physically affect the property but can adversely impact its monetary value . . .

Several phrases were highlighted in yellow. The attorney recited them without having to refresh his memory by looking. "Real or rumored events that *can* adversely impact a property's value. Note the wording. Think about the *Vortex* episode. A lot of people saw it. Presumably, there are potential buyers and neighbors, too, who actually believe the property is *stigmatized*. Haunted, cursed, bad karma—the house scares people, in other words. The seller didn't disclose that to me or Mrs. B at closing. He also didn't disclose the fact that a Civil War battle took place there, that it's possibly even the site of a field cemetery. Did he know or didn't he? Well, the fact is, it doesn't matter. The seller sure as hell knew about the TV show. Superstitious baloney or not, I'm convinced this is Mrs. B's way out."

Pressing his point, the man scooted closer. "If this gets to court—which it won't—we don't have to prove the place is haunted. All we have to prove is there are rumors or events that adversely impact the property's value. The seller didn't disclose those facts at closing. Hannah, that's where you come in. You're from an old-time Florida family. Locals are more likely to talk to someone like you. The small-time ranchers, the mom-and-pop campground people, anyone who lives nearby. I want you to talk to them. See what they have to say. And you're a—I hope you don't mind a bit of chauvinism here—you are a very attractive woman. And the lead archaeologist is a man."

The attorney saw my expression change so was quick to add, "Don't get the wrong idea. Because of the federal

Antiquities Act regarding graves—we're getting into le-
galese here—I'm not privy to what the archaeologist
finds. But he might talk to you, even let you take pictures. That would be a nice little addition to the case I'll
present. Do you have a good camera?"

"A friend just loaned me a Canon with a good lens," I
said, meaning the biologist.

"Perfect. They don't have to be professional quality,
but we need lots of close-ups. A cell phone wouldn't do."

I glanced at Birdy, who shrugged her approval. "I'd
love to see the place. And if it helps Bunny, I can go with
Hannah on my days off."

The attorney nodded. *Good.* "I've already advised
your aunt not to pay next month's installment. We'll put
it in an escrow account. If need be, she'll write off the
quarter-million loss, but it saves her a million dollars in
cash and further assessments down the road."

Birdy asked, "You just came up with this?"

"I've been working on it for several weeks. Last night
your aunt called me, very excited. Even as smart as she is,
she follows her horoscope, as you probably know. She
told me *a transecting connection*—some type of astrology phrase—was predicted for yesterday. I forget exactly.
She believes the connection is you, Hannah. I was dubious until"—the attorney's eyes shifted to mine—"well,
until I read about your background. Now I see it as a
stroke of good luck. We'll win the case either way, but
what you provide could be helpful—if you're willing."

I felt uncomfortable being the center of attention but
also was unclear about a few things. I asked about the fee

and how much time was required and what exactly he and Mrs. Tupplemeyer wanted me to do. Then, "What about the other investors? You said they're friends of hers. Are they pulling out, too?"

He pursed his lips, cleared his throat. "I'm the one who found a loophole in the real estate laws, but I'm not paid to advise them. We're much better off keeping everything under the radar."

The attorney looked at Birdy, then me, to confirm we understood his meaning. "Trust me, in Palm Beach people know the rules when it comes to money. Business is business. They'd do the same to your aunt in a heartbeat." Then he smiled. A man who could afford to have his teeth capped and wear an expensive silk tie of blue on this Monday morning, the second week of October.

Which is why, a week later, Birdy Tupplemeyer suffered the shock of scorpions falling on her face and ran out the door, screaming.

3

I TOOK ANOTHER LOOK AT MY FRIEND'S NECK
and said, "I was wrong about the Benadryl, it's in my
SUV," then went down the porch steps, through the
trees, limping a little because of my stubbed toe. A stone
wall, a gate and *No Trespassing* signs hadn't protected
the old house from vandals, but a chain had forced me to
park outside the gate.

That's where I spotted the man. He was watching
Birdy from the shadows: tall, swoop-shouldered in a
hoodie, only his head and torso visible above the four-
foot wall.

My breath caught. I stopped. *The archaeologist?* I
wondered but wasn't sure. He was focused on Birdy, who
was pacing, waiting for me to return with the first-aid kit
I'd thought was upstairs in my bag. Why the man hadn't
noticed me leave the porch, I could only guess. Maybe

trees and hanging moss had absorbed my shadow. Maybe it was the way darkness shifted from milky blue to gray. It was a thick October night with wind, clouds drifting across a moon that would be full in two days and bright enough that I didn't need my flashlight.

There was another possibility: That afternoon, the archaeologist had been smitten by Birdy, with her lean body and her minor in archaeology, but he had ignored me after a contentious exchange.

The assistant professor had insinuated that Florida's role in Civil War history had more to do with profiteering than patriotism. When I objected, his coolness toward me had bloomed into dislike.

My feelings hadn't suffered any. Kindergarten through high school, I was a gawky beanpole of a girl, so the inattention of men is nothing new. I have grown into my body, however, and my confidence has improved. Being ignored by an oddball archaeologist was no big deal, even though Theo was decent-looking in a dark, loose-jointed sort of way.

Birdy had enjoyed their flirting. Traded barbs and puns, with her sharp wit. Ivanhoff had obviously found her attractive. A *fixation*—was that a term that applied to Peeping Toms? I didn't know. Nor was I certain it was the archaeologist. The shape was tall enough, but there was no Greek fisherman's cap and no sign of a walking stick. Dr. Theo had carried one, carved cypress, which I considered a foppish affectation. Birdy, in her current frame of mind, had claimed it was a phallic symbol that hinted at the man's availability. Which had seemed silly but humorous in a girlish, sleepover way, but wasn't fun now, standing alone in darkness, separated from a stranger by fifty yards of weeds, trees, and a stone wall.

I stood, glancing from Birdy to the man, watching him watch her. Then he crouched, perhaps aware I had disappeared from the porch.

Finally he saw me. Straightened to his full height and turned his back. Did it in a nonchalant way to pretend I wasn't there or that he wasn't spying. In my hand was the key to my SUV. I pressed *Unlock*. The flashing lights startled him but weren't bright enough to confirm his identity. The man stretched as if bored and ambled toward the river, which was down the road, through the trees and down a bank. His sneaky behavior irritated me. It also gave me courage. I angled toward the road, the stone wall between us, and shined the flashlight. When the light hit him, he was too far away to reveal details. And he walked faster. I hollered, "Who are you?"

He didn't turn. Instead, he hunkered down low and jogged toward the trees with an odd limping stride as if he had a bad leg.

That spooked me. The archaeologist didn't limp. There was an unhealthiness about this man's behavior and his lack of body control. And I'd been right: he was wearing a hoodie or a cape on a night that was cool and dry, not cold.

From the porch, Birdy called, "Are you talking to me?"

I hollered back, "Go inside."

"What?"

I said it again, my hand on the gate.

She yelled, "Are you kidding? Not without shoes and a blowtorch, I'm not."

I had taken the time to put on jeans and a denim shirt of copper red but had yet to retrieve my friend's clothes from her room.

When I get her clothes, I'll pack her gun, too, I decided, then hurried to my SUV before remembering something else: hidden under the backseat was another gun—a stainless 9mm that Birdy had wanted to see because it was custom-made, a very rare model. It had been left to me by my Uncle Jake. I'd fired the weapon only once in my life and had no desire ever to use it again.

Take the pistol or leave it in the SUV?

I left it behind.

BIRDY SWALLOWED a Benadryl but refused to dress until I had searched every inch of her slacks, blouse, and shoes to prove there were no scorpions hiding there. I had done the same for myself but not as carefully.

She was cutting the timing close, although we didn't know it. The archaeologist would soon surprise us by rapping on the door.

"Poison crabs," Birdy said and made a guttural sound of disgust. "That's what they remind me of. Crabs with stingers. And bristly legs. One of those bastards ran right up my forehead. Like tiny robots—they remind me of that, too."

I didn't see a connection between scorpions, crabs,

and robots but let her talk while I rubbed Benadryl on her neck, the sting mark swollen but displaying no red lines to suggest she needed a doctor. No constricted breathing either. "Does it still hurt?"

"Son of a bitch, if I was a better shot, I'd go in there and shoot every one of them."

Several boxes of shells would be required to complete the job, but I didn't say it. I had returned to her room alone, scorpions on the floor and walls, too, not just the rafters. If they were in the walls, they were in the rest of the house, but I had closed the door as if that would keep us safe.

Something else I did: checked every window I passed to confirm it was nailed shut, no sign of the peeping man outside. And I had retrieved Birdy's semiautomatic pistol from beneath her pillow. Her overnight bag, which lay open on the floor, was another matter. Examining clothing and extra shoes would take time. Her bag was the only reason she had agreed to return to the house.

We were by the fireplace in the parlor now, where I had been told not to build a fire but had anyway. The slow flames softened the hiss of a Coleman lantern in the middle of the floor. No furniture in a space with twelve-foot ceilings and marble-manteled windows and a chandelier too high for teenagers to steal. Cobwebs and dust, a cigarette pack crumpled in the corner with beer cans, in a house that had been built by a Virginia cattleman. Charles Langford Cadence, a man who had been murdered or had shot himself.

I had done some research since we'd met with the attorney, which is why I knew a lot more about the property. I also knew that John Ashley, the gangster, *might* have done the killing. An old newspaper clip I found rumored that he was guilty, but Ashley was legendary in the region by that time and legends are rumor magnets.

On the other hand, John Ashley was a proven killer. Between 1914 and 1924, he had terrorized Florida and the Bahamas. He and his gang—which included a girlfriend named Laura—had robbed trains and banks and murdered innocent people. They became international outlaws when they raided the Bahamas, killing several and hijacking shipments of rum.

After each heist, Ashley escaped into Florida's interior. The TV show was right about that: he had grown up in the Everglades and could live off the land. The wild country between Palm Beach and Fort Myers was familiar to him. There was no evidence he had murdered cattlemen along the way, but Ashley had been charming and talkative. He was certainly aware that Charles Cadence had built a grand house on the Telegraph River—and had married a much younger woman, a beauty named Irene.

In 1928, during a hurricane, the Lake Okeechobee dam burst. The torrent swept over central Florida and killed nearly two thousand people—probably more. Many bodies were never recovered or identified, but the Cadence house survived. The same year, a Chicago developer bought the property but was left penniless after the stock market crash. The next two owners also went broke. The tax debt was satisfied by foreclosure and the house was converted into a school. Children of farmers and cowhands attended, but the school was closed abruptly after only six years.

Why?

The Internet didn't offer an answer. My best guess was that around the same period, a disease called deer tick fever caused a panic in the Everglades. A bounty was placed on deer—animals that played no role in spreading the disease, as it turned out—but Florida's deer population was decimated anyway.

I discovered two interesting journal entries from a lady who *might* have taught at the school. If true, it was my introduction to a ghost or apparition that was associated with the Cadence house in later years—*the woman on the balcony*, I came to think of her. Or *young Mrs. Irene Cadence*.

In January 1939, the teacher wrote: "I am much vexed by the tantrums in recent days of otherwise good children who are from good homes. Today, Mary, a subdued girl who earns fine marks, excited the class when she ran outside, pulling at her hair and screaming. She did so without cause and despite the frigid weather. This incited other children to follow, some who claimed to hear a woman crying on the balcony. I blame this on deer fever, not the tragedy said to have occurred in this house. Girls at a certain age are sensitive and such stories impress deeply. Mary's temperature, however, was normal when we finally calmed her and warmed her near the fire . . ."

Another entry, dated February 1939: "Five children

have now been sent [home] by a blistering of the skin, mostly of the hands and wrists but thrice in the appearance of blisters or carbuncles on their faces. A painful tenderness near my cheek warns that I, too, have been infected, as do recent nightmares. How wretched the screams of that poor woman on the balcony! We expect a visit from Dr. Hansen of Ft. Myers most any day now . . ."

The producers of *Vortex Hunters* had found these same lurid tidbits. I confirmed it by downloading an episode entitled "The Malediction of Cadence Place." Most of it was sensational nonsense but did include some history that was useful—especially a few facts about Charles Cadence's wife, Irene. That's how I knew she'd been considered a woman of great beauty with skin the color of "parchment" and raven-black hair.

The house had remained empty until the 1960s, when it was remodeled by an artist—a member of New York's avant-garde and a friend of LSD proponent Dr. Timothy Leary. One December night, he fell from the balcony and died. The coroner's report listed alcohol and "other drugs" as contributing factors.

I had shared this information with Birdy. She had delighted in the stories because they were fun to hear, the two of us alone in the empty house, but she wasn't frightened—until now. I lifted her chin and asked, "Does it still throb?"

"Like I got jabbed by a hot needle. The thing crawled from my cheek into my hair—I can still feel it. What I need is a mojito and a bath. How far's the nearest hotel?

I bet they have a bar." She finished buttoning her blouse, the starched collar unusual for camping, but it looked good, the way it framed the angles of her face.

I said, "On the bright side, we don't have to worry about palmetto bugs."

"Enough with the palmetto bugs. They're cockroaches, only bigger and they can fly," she said. "Just a nicer name. I hate roaches, too. In college, there was a garbage strike and roaches took over our dorm. Middle of the night, a girl would scream, I didn't even wake up, it got to be so common. That was before I switched to law and moved out of the liberal arts wing, which had a lot of flaky people to begin with." Birdy paused. "Cockroaches, scorpions—I'm not sleeping in that room anymore, so forget it. Just wait until one bites you."

I knew we needed another hammock and a box of bug bombs if we were going to spend a night or two in this place. Bunny Tupplemeyer's attorney had said overnighting wasn't a must but could be useful. He had decided that evidence the house was *not* haunted would help prove his claims were based on law, not superstition.

From the SUV, I'd brought canvas chairs and she sat—but not without first flipping the thing to check for visitors.

"They sting, not bite," I said, while I filled a Ziploc with ice from a cooler that contained tea, bottled water, and a few yogurts. "When I was ten, maybe twelve, one nailed me on the thumb while I was stacking firewood. Then, a few years ago, I picked up a tarp and got it in the palm of my hand. Ice helps. Try this." I handed her the bag.

"Did you cry?"

"I wanted to."

She said, "Hardass. I should've known."

"No, it's the way things are on the islands." I was referring to the house where I had grown up and where my mother, Loretta, still lives, in a little fishing village, Sulfur Wells, across the bay from Sanibel and Captiva Islands on Florida's Gulf Coast. Birdy had been there often enough that I didn't have to say the house was older than the house we were in. Or that it sat on an Indian pyramid built of shell. "Outside, mostly, we find little reddish scorpions, but no worse than ant bites. The big black scorpions, like those in there"—I tilted my head toward the hall—"they're common on the shell mounds. Burns like fire, I know, but the pain goes away if you don't have a reaction. I've heard they came from Cuba or Mexico on the Spaniards' boats, but I don't know that's true. Loretta doesn't like them, but she hates cockroaches worse, so you learn to get along. You never find cockroaches in a house that has a scorpion."

"You're telling me you grew up living with scorpions?"

"It's not like I kept them as pets."

"But they're there. In your house, I mean. Right now, not just years ago."

"Loretta's house, yes."

"Incredible. My mother, the queen of nonviolent hippiedom, would freak out. Call in the napalm or set the house on fire. That woman won't even eat eggplant because it's sliced like steak. Did she ever get bit?"

"Loretta? Once that I know of. It was hiding under the toilet seat. She came running out with her skirt around her ankles, mad as a hornet. First time I ever heard her use the F-word. Plus some other words I was too young to recognize. That woman has a mouth on her."

Birdy laughed, her spirits improving.

I borrowed my Uncle Jake's philosophy to counsel her. "Don't bother them, they won't bother you. Cockroaches are a different story."

She nodded at that and stared into the fire. Finally said, "It snowed in Boston today, but here I am sitting with little Miss Hannah Sunshine and nursing a scorpion bite. I could sure use a mojito. If you ever talk me into camping again, I'll bring a couple of pitchers."

It wasn't true that I'd had to convince her, but I conceded, "A mojito sounds pretty good right now."

Birdy reached for her flashlight, which I'd found in a pile of glass. She used it to check the ceiling for the umpteenth time, the crystal chandelier frosted with cobwebs and dust, moonglow through the main window. Next, the walls, as if searching for enemy snipers. Then she switched the light off and placed it on the floor near her pistol—the pistol holstered, no belt—and refocused on the fire, finally relaxing a little as the Benadryl kicked in.

"How long you think before we can go through my suitcase?"

We? I almost asked, but guessed that half an hour was a reasonable period. I had dragged her bag into the hall and sprayed it with mosquito spray. Deep Woods Off! was the only thing I had to convince scorpions there were better places to hide.

Birdy muttered something while craning her neck, then said, "This must have been a beautiful house back in the day. Weird. Build a place like this out here in the middle of nowhere. Lonely as hell, too, especially for the guy's wife. What was her name?"

"Irene. Irene Cadence. She was seventeen and he was forty when they married. Irene wasn't quite thirty when he died. I couldn't find what happened to her after that—nothing factual anyway. According to the TV show, she went insane, haunted by guilt or loneliness— that sort of stuff. But they made that up, had to. It was their way of explaining why a teacher and her students claimed they heard a woman crying up there." I pointed up to what had once been a music room. It opened through French doors onto a balcony that faced east and a line of trees along the river's bank.

Birdy said, "She probably went stark raving mad out of boredom. Wouldn't you have hated to be a woman back then?"

I replied, "My aunts and grandmothers were—sons were a rarity among the Smiths. My two great-aunts, Sarah and Hannah, they had it rough, the way they lived—this was the early 1900s. About the same time this house was built. They raised their own food, chopped firewood and sold it. Not together. I don't know why, but they went their separate ways." After a moment, I smiled. "Sarah and Hannah didn't have much luck when it came to *finding* men either." I hadn't mentioned the Peeping Tom. Talking about men was a way of working into the subject without causing a panic.

Birdy asked, "That old book you brought, it belonged to one of your aunts?"

I don't know why I was surprised she had paid attention to what I was reading earlier. She was a trained sheriff's deputy after all. "It's a journal I found in Loretta's attic," I said. "Remember me mentioning my great-uncle to the attorney? I went through his papers."

"Her attorney's gay," Birdy said, "but he still had the hots for you. You didn't notice?"

I was flattered but stayed on topic. "The journal belonged to my Great-great-uncle Ben Summerlin. Maybe three *great*s back—from the late 1800s. It was in a box I found when I was about thirteen or fourteen, but I still haven't managed to read it all. A lot of pages are stuck together like they got soaked. Or maybe just age. And he used abbreviations—old-timey sort of language. Code sometimes, too. He was a man who didn't enjoy writing, you can tell. If one word would do, that's what he wrote. 'Captain Summerlin,' people called him. He was a cattleman and a blockade-runner. He owned a forty-foot sharpie, *Widow's Son*. And a dory named *Sodbuster*."

"A what?"

"Sailboats. They weren't big, but not so small either. They didn't draw much water."

"Why'd he name them that?"

"He didn't say . . . or I haven't gotten the right pages unstuck. There's no telling how people name boats."

Birdy said, "In cowboy movies, *sodbuster* is what the bad guys call farmers, isn't it? Interesting name, I guess."

I had found a journal entry a lot more interesting than that, which I had already shared with Birdy without naming the source. It mentioned a box of coins my long-dead uncle had lost after being chased by Union soldiers. He had run his dory aground and scuttled it.

100 silver dollars gawn, he'd written with an ink quill pen some months later. The date: December 1864. Jettisoned, hidden, or stolen, the journal had yet to reveal.

Birdy, remembering, asked, "What would a hundred silver dollars be worth now? Captain Summerlin, I like his name."

"Two or three thousand dollars," I said, "depending on their condition. I looked it up on the Internet. Silver dollars is how they paid cattlemen in those days, Union and Confederates both."

"He sold to both sides?"

"Some did," I said, and let my eyes move around the room. "This had to be a good area for cattle. That's not much of a river out there, but I bet it was like a highway in those days. Captain Summerlin might have mentioned it in one of his later entries. Not by name, but the location seems about right." Then I tried to get back to the subject of men by asking, "That archaeologist we met, Theo Ivanhoff, did he seem a little strange to you? In an odd, sneaky sort of way?"

Even when she is yawning from Benadryl, Birdy's brain works faster than most. "I knew you didn't like him. That's why you bit his head off when he went on a talking jag—all because of your uncle the blockade-runner. There had to be a reason. You're usually so polite."

She was right about the professor. I didn't like him.

"I wasn't mean about it, I just corrected him," I replied. "I'm glad to hear you say *talking jag*. I thought you were hanging on every word. That man doesn't know when to shut up."

"No," Birdy said, giving her hair a flip. "I was picturing him in the shower. I bet you were, too." Said it in a fun, devilish sort of way, her mood back to where it had been before a scorpion landed on her face. "I've got forty credit hours in archaeology. Might have majored if the guys were better-looking. Theo's a five, ordinarily, but he is a solid twelve on the King Tut scale."

The timing was right to discuss the man I had seen peeping. I started to say, "Oh, I forgot to tell you. When I went outside to get the first-aid kit—"

Three soft raps on the door interrupted me.

"Who the hell could that be?" Birdy said. "Probably teenagers getting a jump on Halloween." She reached for her pistol. "Stay here. I'll go."

4

DR. THEO IVANHOFF WAS TROUBLE. I SENSED IT, and, before the night was done, he would prove it by trying to sneak a wedge between Birdy and me. Instigate an argument, play one off the other—I had seen this method before.

Even with her sheriff's deputy instincts, Birdy seemed oblivious. The two of them had archaeology, an empty Friday night and loneliness in common. She liked the shape and size of the man, I suppose.

Softened by firelight, Theo was decent-looking, I had to admit, but in a way I consider feminine, like a sheik in a silent movie. Smooth skin, gaunt, his hair combed back just right, and dark eyes that were more alive for the angles of his face. But the angles were slightly off, pinched like a ferret, a man who sniffed his opponents before deciding how to behave. His clothing was a warning, too, the way it demanded attention: black jeans, a black collar-less shirt buttoned tight, no belt, no socks, his billfold on a chain like he'd just climbed off a Harley or out of bed. Add a white collar, he could have passed for a priest vacationing in Hawaii.

When Theo noticed me staring, he said, "You're still not convinced it wasn't me. Are you?"

I had told Birdy about the peeping man while I observed Theo, but there had been no reaction, just amused patience. Like I was a child. I said, "The nearest house is two miles on the road to Arcadia. The main road is half a mile—more, I'd say—but your trailer's close, right there by the river. Don't sound so offended. You'd think the same if you saw what I saw."

He had the irritating habit of hooting "Well, now!" a cartoonish signal of victory or discovery. He used the device before saying, "You don't know anything about this area, do you? If you don't mind walking, I can take you to where forty people are camped not more than a mile from here. Or get in my canoe, there are houseboats hidden in some of those bends, the trees so thick you couldn't spot them from the air. I said it wasn't me. Now, in essence, you're calling me a liar."

In essence—an educated man who draped words like fashion scarves.

Birdy said, "She's not accusing you," then swiveled in her chair to me. "Anyway, he wasn't breaking any laws."

"This land is posted," I said. "Why didn't he stop when I asked who he was?" I turned to Ivanhoff. "You had to get written permission to stay here, didn't you?"

Theo, settling back now that I was on the defensive, said, "The investment group *invited* me. I didn't have to ask."

I should have expected that. Earlier, he'd spent twenty minutes telling us how important he was, saying, "Federal law requires they bring in an expert before they cut down every damn tree for miles and build houses. Or whatever cardboard community they're planning. But they can't touch the place until I say it's okay. I've been here a month and I'm in no hurry. The so-called lead archaeologist only stops by on weekends—and only if his arthritis isn't acting up, the old prick. Recceology's not his strong suit, so I'm the person actually in charge."

Recceology was the study of battlefields, he'd explained. Civil War battle sites had to be mapped before they could be bulldozed. Even minor skirmishes, like the one that had taken place here, between the house and the river, in 1864 or '65. Theo hadn't said what his actual work was, though, nor had he invited us into the areas he had cordoned with rope. Three areas, about a quarter acre each. There were dirt mounds and sifting screens, signs posted by the government that read *Federal Antiquities Site. Access Prohibited*.

Theo had done some probing, too, by asking Birdy, "What kind of development does your aunt have in mind? Condos or a planned community? They're keeping it all hush-hush, which is just stupid. They're better off if I know."

I didn't trust the man but found some of what he had to say interesting. The same with his references to the nearby RV campground and houseboats, because those were the people I needed to speak with. Then I made a mistake by asking, "You're what's called a *ricky-ologist*? Are there other Florida sites you've excavated?"

An expression of contempt flared while he corrected my pronunciation, then he had expounded on his expertise. Twenty minutes, we'd stood there listening.

I didn't want to risk another lecture now, so I cut the man off before he could start, saying to Birdy, "I bet your aunt's insurance company considers trespassing a crime."

"The grande dame of Palm Beach," she said to Theo. "My aunt's just an investor, not the owner. Well . . . this part of the acreage is assigned to her, I guess. But we don't arrest people for trespassing unless there's a complaint." Taking the middle ground before taking sides. Then she tried to dismiss it, saying, "A week before Halloween, a place like this is bound to attract some weirdo visitors. Drunken kids, the UFO types." Birdy caught herself before adding *That's why we're here.*

Theo eyed her for a moment. "You're right. That's why the RV park's full." Then turned his sights on me. "Why do you call her Birdy when her name's Bertie?"

Birdy warned, "Because she wants to," and continued with what she was saying. "The house has a reputation— all that paranormal baloney, so who cares? I say we find a hotel and get a drink. It's still early and, let's face it, we can't sleep in a house full of scorpions."

Theo, who claimed he'd stopped by because he saw fire flickering in the windows, was sitting cross-legged on the floor, his Birkenstocks beside him. Size fourteens, was my guess. He'd already told us he had rum and tequila in his camper—hinted he had some grass, too, but shut up fast when he learned my friend is a sworn officer of the law. I expected him to repeat the invitation a few times before trying to cut Birdy out of the herd. That was his intent: cause a spat, or sufficiently offend me, and it would be just the two of them. Scorpions, however, interested the man. He sat up a little straighter. "How many have you seen?"

Birdy told him what had happened.

Theo, getting to his feet, said, "I can get rid of those, no problem. I've got just the stuff in my camper. While we're at it, I'll introduce you to the mysterious stranger Hannah saw."

Birdy, annoyed, said, *"What?"*

"I knew who it was from the start."

"Why didn't you just come out and tell us?"

Theo grinned, "You wouldn't have believed me," while he threaded a foot into his Birkenstock, which he used as an excuse to throw an arm around Birdy for balance, having fun with the situation while he hopped on one foot. "Seriously, you tell me about a hunchbacked guy with a limp and I say, 'Oh yeah, that's the Roswell Man—half human, half alien—he's a nice guy,' what's your reaction going to be?"

"That you're full of shit," Birdy said.

"Exactly, but it's true. His name's Tyrone. The RV park, carnival people, they've wintered there for years. He takes walks at night because of the way his face looks.

I'm not making this up. That's how he bills himself, *Roswell Man*, the place in New Mexico where his mother was probed—you know, *screwed*—by an alien."

Birdy said, "Oh, *please*."

"That's Tyrone's act, for christ's sake. Or sometimes he's a *chuman*—half chimp, half man. That's the scientific term, by the way. He's got posters on his walls."

"*Chimp-man?*"

"*CHU-man*. He has some kind of skin condition, like scales instead of skin, but it sort of looks like fur. There are country hicks willing to believe anything, apparently." After a beat, Theo added, "Maybe Hannah's heard of him."

I held my temper but countered, "I didn't say he was hunchbacked," while Birdy staggered beneath Theo's weight, laughing, no longer annoyed.

The good-looking archaeologist hooted into her ear, "Well, now!" and flashed me a look to sharpen what came next. "I love proving amateurs wrong."

WHEN THEO WENT inside his pop-up camper, Birdy whispered, "The guy's a total prick."

It had taken him a while to get the door open. And when I'd asked, "Where's your car?" he had snapped at me, "A friend's using it—is that okay?"

No, it wasn't. The camper sat alone in a clearing, the trailer tongue on a cement block. It caused me to wonder: *Is the place really his?*

Birdy was suspicious, too. "His girlfriend probably has the car. Or wife. Let's play along and see who we meet at the RV park. Are you okay with that?"

So far, but I feared she was rationalizing a way to spend more time with Theo and enjoy the strong rum and Cokes, which his long arm now presented us from the door. The door closed, Theo saying, "Gotta find some stuff and powder my nose, ladies. Make yourselves at home."

I took a sip. "I can't imagine the sort of life a person has calling himself Roswell Man. Makes me sad even to think about. In grade school, there was a boy who had skin so scaly, he finally stopped coming. Real scales—a medical condition that was incurable."

Birdy made a cooing noise to empathize, but her mind was on the night sky. "You know . . . camping might be the way to go out here. Even with this moon, the stars are bright."

I said, "Supposedly, the condition gets worse with age. *Ichthy* . . . I can't quite recall the name, but it's *ichthy*-something. An *ichthyologist* studies fish, which has to do with scales, that's why I remember. It's a terrible disease for a child. I had a problem with acne in my teens and thought it was the end of the world. I always went out of my way to be nice to that boy."

"Pimples?" Birdy acted as if that was funny until she noticed me glaring. "Sorry, forgot about your temper," she said, then lowered her voice. "Somehow Theo guessed you're here to prove the ghost stories are bullshit.

That's why he's passive-aggressive. He doesn't want the property developed, so he sees you as one of the bad guys. Not in those words, he's too smooth. Or thinks he is."

Theo and Birdy had done some whispering while they walked ahead of me through the trees, through the gate, down a one-lane asphalt road to the Telegraph River, which didn't look like a river because it was so narrow, cloaked by moss and shadows.

I took another sip: Coca-Cola on ice, but mostly rum. "Your aunt is more interested in legalities than the truth. You could have told him that. She doesn't care about ghosts any more than she does asbestos or mold."

"Hell with him. Always keep men and crime suspects guessing. He's pompous, that's all. When I told him Dame Bunny has a million bucks invested in this project, he shrugged it off like it was no big deal. But he is kind of amusing."

Replying to Birdy's tone, not her words, I said gently, "If you want him to take you out for a drink, that's okay. I've got work to do." I had left Capt. Summerlin's journal on the mantel, hoping the hot, dry air would loosen some pages.

Birdy exhaled a derisive "Hah! What, he's been here only three weeks? Like he owns the place already. He's not even the lead archaeologist on this project. Notice how he glazed over that?" A moment later, she added, "But he is young. And he does have an interesting face."

I thought, *Uh-oh.*

A small generator, quiet as a sewing machine, surged,

brightening the lights, while we waited, including a yellow bug light hanging from a limb near a charcoal grill and a fire pit and a hammock strung between trees, but the kind made in Mexico, not a jungle hammock with netting like mine.

Birdy considered the outdoor orderliness of the place, the little pit and potted plants, before observing, "He's made a comfy little nest for himself, hasn't he?"

I said, "If it's actually his."

When Birdy replied, "Oh, please," I again thought, *Uh-oh.*

Theo ducked out the door, carrying a sack and an oversized light with a battery pack. "Let's deal with your bug problem first," he said.

We returned to the house.

I WASN'T ENCOURAGED by the man's spider-killing technique. Inside the house, Theo built the fire higher and closed the fireplace flue. I had already lugged Birdy's suitcase, air mattress, sheets, and a pillow into the room, pausing to smash a few scorpions en route.

Birdy was behaving unusually girlish, even with a 9mm pistol in her purse, a Glock loaded with hollow-points. She stayed on the porch until Theo called her in.

"Chrysanthemum resin," he announced, opening the bag. "It's a trick I learned from one of the campground regulars. Mosquitoes and chiggers were driving me nuts until I used this. She's an amazing woman—studied with some tribe in the Amazon. A regular witch."

He sifted a handful of powder into the fire, the flames blue-edged when they flared, but then were smothered by more powder.

"You're studying witchcraft, too? You could be a psycho, for all we know." Birdy was flirting again—or was she?

Theo enjoyed the humor. "Half the women in the RV park claim to be witches. And not just the carnie women. I don't care what they are as long as there's something they can teach me. Natural remedies are a hobby. Early battlefield surgeons, that's all they had. One of my favorite professors used to say that alchemy is chemistry's Dutch uncle. But it's medicine's grandfather."

He emptied the bag. Smoke boiled into the room. A pleasant incense odor at first, like a burning mosquito coil that was soon overpowering.

"Hurry up, I want to check something," he said. "Where were you sleeping when you got stung?"

Birdy had covered her nose and mouth. "You can burn the place down, I wouldn't go back in that room."

"You'll get a kick out of this, promise." He appealed to me. "Hannah?"

I said, "If we don't suffocate first," and walked toward the hall, Theo behind me carrying the light, which looked high-tech, a rectangle of LEDs with a battery pack.

When he turned it on inside the room, the darkness became eerie blue velvet with a glowing fringe. "Ultraviolet light," he explained. He held the thing like a shield and entered, panning it across the ceiling.

I have seen scorpions under ultraviolet light before, but always with cheap flashlights or neon tubes, nothing like the unit Theo carried. The ceiling, the walls, glittered with emeralds. The room moved, its skin alive. When several clattering green comets fell to the floor, Theo stomped them with his Birks.

"Scientists don't understand why some insects react to UV light," he said, backing away. "That's why I brought this. When we come back later, we'll know if they're gone or not."

I called to the hallway, "Birdy—you need to see this."

No, she didn't. The three of us went coughing out the front door. The smoke, or holding my breath, caused me to feel oddly separated from my body, a slight buzz that added a blue corona to my flashlight's beam.

On the steps, Theo explained to Birdy, "Pyrethrum is the active ingredient in the resin. How are you feeling?"

"Like the only time in my life I tried mushrooms, sort of . . . nice. How about you, Hannah?"

"I think he should have warned us," I replied. I needed air so kept walking.

"Pyrethrum isn't dangerous. It was one of the first insecticides. Persian soldiers depended on it. I wish you'd have seen those scorpions under UV. We use it a lot in the field, but for finding bone fragments and pottery shards, not insects. They fluoresce, too."

Birdy's girlish streak vanished, but only I realized it, knew it because she used his remark as an opening. "In Guatemala, my professor would have killed for a lab-grade UV light. I did three weeks on a Maya project there. I'd love to see the techniques used by someone who really knows what they're doing."

Theo stopped as if to return to the house. "Then let's go back."

"No, I mean the archaeological applications. I want you to show us your dig site. It's on the way, isn't it? And you're already hauling that light around."

Theo balked, saying it was late.

Birdy used psychology by addressing me. "Most people don't understand how disappointing a dig site can be. You can excavate for years and not find anything significant. Poor Theo's been here only for a few weeks, so I totally understand."

Theo, who was leading the way, turned to block our path. "That's not the reason."

Birdy pretended to empathize. "You never told us the name of the lead archaeologist. Is it too late to call and ask permission? I'm a cop. I understand the chain of command."

It worked.

After a detour, Theo used a flashlight to guide us under a rope onto the dig site. Mosquitoes greeted us from the shadows while a night bird screeched, its wings black against the moon.

A sudden thought stopped me—or paranoia caused by the smoke. I let the other two go ahead, but they backtracked. Birdy asked, "Something wrong?"

"I left the journal on the fireplace mantel," I said. "What if the house burns down?"

Theo snickered at the improbability. "She keeps a journal?" *Journals were for teenagers.* It was in his tone.

I shot back, "If you have a question, it's faster to ask me directly. No, I don't keep a journal—well, I do, a fishing journal, but that's for business reasons. I was talking about something else."

"Oh, you're a fishing guide, too, huh? Along with being an expert on history." Taunting me now.

Birdy told him, "Back off, boogaloo. As a matter of fact, she is."

Theo grinned. "Oh?"

"Hannah is fifth- or sixth-generation Floridian. She's named after a great-aunt who chopped wood for a living. Look up Hannah and Sarah Smith—they're in the history books. But it's her *uncle's* journal. He was a blockade-runner. What was his name again? Captain Summerlin. But I forget his first name."

My friend, by intending to bruise Theo's ego, had let a confidence slip. The man's attention zoomed. He stared at me. "Captain *Jake* Summerlin?"

Theo was referring to another distant relative who had exported cattle to Cuba, not Ben Summerlin, who had expanded beyond cattle into blockade-running and also dabbled in rum. The error allowed me an out.

"A different man," I said. "I'd better go back to the house."

The expert on Civil War battlefields didn't believe me—or didn't want to believe me—but his demeanor changed. "Hannah and Sarah Smith," he repeated.

Birdy started to say she would return to the house with me, but Theo interrupted. "Well, now! I think we got off to a bad start, Hannah. I didn't realize you're related to the Summerlins and the old-time Florida Smiths. Seriously, *Sarah Smith*?" Then he proved his knowledge of history by explaining to Birdy, "She was the first woman to drive an oxcart across the Everglades. This was back in like 1910, 1911."

The temptation was to correct him—the first *person* to do it—but I remained cautious because Theo, I realized, wanted to get his paws on Ben Summerlin's journal. So I played dumb. "Was she really?"

Theo saw through my lie. His certainty was in an absurd bow, a gentleman deferring to a lady's reticence. He checked the time while his mind retooled. "You know . . . instead of rushing, why not wait until morning? I've got three excavation sites going. And UV light works just as well in sunlight. Really spectacular, what you'll see."

He suggested we freshen our drinks and go straight to the RV park. "I'm late, as it is. There's a Civil War hobbyist—he's giving me some kind of award. And don't forget about Tyrone."

"I don't need to meet Tyrone," I said. Truth is, I didn't want to intrude on a stranger who walked around at night to avoid gawkers.

Theo ignored me. "Have you ever used ground-penetrating radar, Bertie? Tomorrow, I'll show you how to operate one of the best units made."

My friend, as if enjoying a sudden estrogen spike, replied, "That is so sweet. But if we go to the campground, will we still have time for a drink later?"

I was thinking, *The journal—I should go back and get it?*

I didn't.

A mistake.

5

WHAT THE PALM BEACH ATTORNEY HAD DE-
scribed as a mom-and-pop RV park wasn't. The strangest
combination of people I'd ever seen inhabited the other
side of the river, down a private road where campers and
RVs were nestled near dockage for boats and canoes.

According to Theo, getting there would have taken
twenty minutes by car, so we walked. Followed him
across a defunct railroad bridge, the moon behind us.
Every few minutes, I looked over my shoulder, worried
the old house was ablaze, but the sky remained a steady
onyx-silver above the trees.

We exited a path onto the private road. Two signs were
posted. One was a warning to those entering the campground: *No Rednecks, Gypsies, Boom Boxes, or Close-
Minded Nabobs. Cash Only.*

Nabobs? I could guess what the word meant.

The other sign was smaller, posted at a gated gravel drive:

SLEW VACCINE AND HERPETILE

TRESPASSERS RISK ENVENOMATION

BY APPOINTMENT ONLY

The signs were stenciled in red, made by someone with an ego.

Theo confided, "A processing lab, supposedly," and didn't look back.

My mind was on the journal in the house that was fuming with vapors, the front door padlocked, not that I was comforted by that. Thieves could easily break a window or shimmy up to the balcony and through the French doors.

Birdy said, "Gypsies," as if she found that interesting yet disapproved. "I know 'Herpetile' means snakes, but is slew the owner's name or slew as in swamp?" She turned to me. "That's another word for swamp, isn't it?"

Theo had been talking nonstop but tolerated the interruption. "Call it anything you want, it's still a snake farm. Can you imagine milking snakes for a living? The guy has to be twisted. Or hung up on the money thing."

"I doubt if hospitals care one way or the other," Birdy replied.

"Oh? I guess you'd like handling snakes—you know, real thick, long ones."

Theo thought that was funny. Birdy didn't. So he tried another approach. "I do what I do because I love it. I have a commercial pilot's license, too, but it's my life, you know? Jesus . . . dealing with reptiles all day sounds sort of freakish to me." Odd, his response—a mix of contempt and hubris.

Birdy picked up on that. "Three weeks here and you haven't met the owner?"

"'By appointment only,' the sign says, but I've seen the place from the outside. There's not much, three buildings and an old Land Rover. One of the classics, though—an old Defender, like in the jungle movies. At least we'd have something to talk about—if I bothered."

I was thinking, *This man is nuts,* while Birdy asked, "Did you try calling?"

"Businesses don't take calls anymore. It's all Internet-driven. There's money in raw snake vaccine, I don't doubt that. But, from those signs? He's got to be a pretty strange animal."

Finally Birdy agreed. "A pompous prick, is what he sounds like. 'Envenomation'—why not just say poisoned?"

Theo replied, "Because they are two very different things," sounding like a pompous prick himself. "It's not like the RV park gets a lot of traffic. A dozen trailers and a few tents, is the busiest I've seen it. And that was yesterday." Then he resumed talking about the man he was supposed to meet and the award he was receiving—a subject I had tuned out ten minutes ago.

Birdy's patience was also wearing thin. She interrupted to say her sheriff's department had brought in an expert on Florida Gypsies, part of a continuing education program.

"Why would anyone care?"

"Someone bothered to put it on a sign," I countered. "Why do you think, Birdy?"

"The place could be sued for discrimination, is what I think. Gypsy is considered a racial slur. The accepted term is the Romani people. Or Roms. Carnivals attracted them to Florida way, way back. Most went legitimate. Assimilation, that's what happens to most ethnic groups. But not all, and the ones who've stuck to the old ways can be very bad news. Dollarwise, it's incredible the amount of crime they get away with."

Theo again. "Yeah? But back to what I was saying—"

I blocked him. "What else did the expert say, Birdy?"

My friend continued, "Traditional Roms only marry among themselves—arranged marriages, usually—and they still pay dowries. Can you imagine? A few—not all, of course—but some think cheating an outsider is a badge of honor. They work in packs. Con games and fraud. Fortune-telling from the carnival days is still a favorite gambit, but now it's high-tech. Seriously—a *billion*-dollar business. In Lauderdale, they just busted a fortune-telling ring. Like twenty people, all with the same last name. Cops confiscated boxes of electronics: eavesdropping and surveillance gear, stolen hard drives. And then there are the simple cons: bogus house repairs or yard work. Some pass themselves off as Hispanic. Like a pretty Latina home health-care nurse, she goes in while her brothers rob old couples blind."

Theo said, "Profiling and stereotyping nonwhites—does your department offer courses on that, too?" Then tried to make it into a joke. "I'm *kidding*. I know law enforcement is tough. So you're an intelligent woman, very attractive. Why did you choose such a crazy occupation?"

Birdy threw it right back at him. "Because I like handcuffing men who are twice my size but ten times as naïve—which is probably why they make half my salary."

Theo said, "Ouch," in a humorous way. "Do I have time to apologize before you do the Miranda rights thing?"

Birdy laughed at that. *Damn*.

"The woman who sold me the chrysanthemum resin? Just a warning—don't tell her or anyone else you're a cop."

We had rounded a bend: pop-up campers and RVs set apart in clusters, three fires and a tent, people gathered tribally in separate halos of light.

Birdy asked, "Is she a Gypsy?"

Theo, back in control, said, "You'll see what I mean when we get there."

THREE WOMEN, all with long gray hair, two wearing tie-dyed dresses, looked up from a bong they were passing around, happy to see Theo until they noticed us. Their smiles flattened. The bong vanished under the table. The table held a plate of cookies, burning incense, and a battery-powered candle that flickered in its plastic chimney.

Birdy whispered to me, "Except for the chubby one, they could pass for my mother. Throw in a tofu turkey and it's my pain-in-the-ass childhood all over again. Let's make this quick."

Woodsmoke, incense, and reefer, the odors clung to the clearing. Trees screened all but a circle of sky. Opposite us was a domed tent and an RV camper. Two men sat playing a board game by lantern light. Theo called, "See you in a minute," as we passed them. One man waved and the other said, "Righty-o!"

It was probably the Civil War hobbyist he had mentioned. I liked the older man's looks: solid, grandfatherly in slacks and gray hair. But he and his friend were outsiders, segregated by space and a lack of shade. Others here were different. I could see it in the furtive looks, felt it in the air. Nearer the river was a van and more pop-up campers, all attached to vehicles that had towed them. Except for a CBS house—*Office* on a sign out front—and one trailer, an old single-wide on blocks, the roofline curved like the lines of an aging Cadillac. A small wooden porch held it to the ground.

Tyrone and the park manager are the only full-time residents, Theo had told us.

I didn't want to linger on the image of a man with scales, so I replied to Birdy, "I'm thinking I should talk to the owner of the vaccine place or whoever runs it. I don't see how a bunch of weekend campers can help."

"Hipster-genarians," she muttered, meaning the three women. "The Butterfly Generation is turning into moths."

I said, "I wouldn't bother him tonight, of course. To-morrow, I'll look up the number—Theo has to be wrong about his phone being unlisted. Don't you think we're wasting our time here?"

"I bet they're all high as kites," my friend said. "Look at their expressions—sixty-year-old flower chicks hoping to score some good lovin' from Theo. Very, very groovy until we show up."

"Don't be mean," I whispered.

We stopped while Theo approached the women, arms outstretched to symbolize a group embrace. One stood to hug him. She also planted a serious kiss on his lips, her eyes shifting to check us out. Smug, her expression, this sixty-year-old woman braless but fit enough to look pretty good in an exotic muumuu, a hibiscus behind her ear. "*You're* late," she pouted and pressed her body to Theo in an extended hug, then stepped back and ignored us from fifteen paces.

Birdy, not whispering, but not loud, remarked, "If I make it to menopause, please have my vagina sutured. Or just shoot me if I get that desperate."

"Keep your voice down," I said, "she might beat me to it."

The women stared with fixed smiles while the attractive one hooked an arm around Theo's waist. "Who are your friends, Theo? Shame on you for not warning them."

Theo, instead of inviting us over, sounded nervous when he asked, "About what?"

"Their clothes. Or, at least, you could have warned me."

As if we hadn't heard, he held up a finger and called, "Give us a sec, okay?"

Birdy spoke to me from the side of her mouth. "Do you believe this? Turn up your hearing aid, Granny."

"It's your fault," the woman told Theo. "They're dressed like sales clerks, not for star channeling—you know, kicking back under all this space. Tell me they're not totally straight." She glanced over. "Starch and mall outlets—whew—it clashes with, you know, the vibe we're trying to achieve."

"Achieve a vibe?" Birdy whispered. "Star channeling? Oh my god. And check out that dress—they've got Target stores in the jungle someplace."

"Definitely a bitch," I agreed. The word was out of my mouth before I realized it.

Birdy said, "There's hope for you yet," and walked toward the table. I started after her but stopped for no reason other than a strange sensation blooming within me: a sudden wariness of the verbal sparring that awaited. I didn't know these women. I didn't want to know them. What was I doing here?

Paranoia. Mild, but it was there in my head.

Too much rum, plus that smoke, I thought. Or was it the smoldering bong beneath the table? Reefer and incense and woodsmoke swirled, the dusty air corralled by shadows, the moon sliding westward. The moon seemed the only familiar and trustworthy thing for miles. My eyes swung from Birdy to the activity around us. Three campfires, the biggest near a cluster of trucks, men and women milling, drinking, talking, too far away to decipher words. People who did a lot of this, set up in campgrounds, miniature homes bolted to their trucks, always ready to move at a moment's notice.

Gypsies? I wondered. Until Birdy's summary, I was unaware that Gypsies lived in Florida.

You're being unfair. That came into my mind, too, and it was true.

A camper door opened, a woman the size of a child stepped out. She walked with the quick, muscle-bound strides of a dwarf—"Little people," I corrected myself. Another miniature woman joined her. In her hands, a basket of something, while her friend, head bowed, lit a cigarette . . . or a joint.

Not Gypsies, carnival workers, I realized. Suddenly, I felt more at ease. Like the moon, carnies and circus performers were familiar. Not commonplace, but they fit in because it is true that Florida's their traditional wintering place. Just across the street from where my mother lives, and where I grew up, is a colony of gingerbread cottages known as Munchkinville. Supposedly, carnival folks built them years ago. When I was a girl, my uncle would take me to Gibsonton, which is on the Myakka River near Tampa and north of Sarasota, where there is a trapeze-and-clown academy. I had enjoyed those trips, usually by truck but once by boat. We'd seen elephants being washed along the river and caged monkeys. We ate at the Giant's Restaurant and toured shops and a post office that provided a special mail slot at dwarf level because so many little people lived nearby.

I had met the "Werewolf-faced Lady," who was very

kind, although shy, and clean-shaven during the off-season. I'd had my photo taken with the sweetest little woman you can imagine, despite her age and fame. "Miz Margaret," I had called her. Ms. Margaret, only three-feet-something tall, had been the "Flowerpot Munchkin" in *The Wizard of Oz*, one of my all-time favorites. She'd also played other roles in the film, wearing different costumes throughout. On the day we'd met, a back ailment was causing her pain, but she had brightened like a rose for the camera while I'd knelt beside her and managed a smile of my own.

Margaret . . . Margaret *Pellegrini*. It took a moment to recall her last name. And a news story, a few years back, that reported her death at age eighty-nine. I'd been in middle school when we'd met. For no rational reason, I suddenly wanted to fill in the blanks. It was at least fifteen years since I'd seen her. How had Ms. Margaret's life gone during the intervening years? I wondered if it would be rude to intrude on the two tiny women across the clearing who stood alone near a fire sharing a joint, not a cigarette. Even stoned, they would certainly know the name Margaret Pellegrini.

"Hey . . . Smithie . . . are you okay?" Birdy, who looked out of place in her slacks and stylish blouse, stood next to Theo, who was a foot taller, while the three women gabbed among themselves.

I felt better but wanted to keep moving. "I'll be right back," I told her.

Don't abandon me was the look on her face.

Theo called, "Hey . . . first, I want to introduce you

to three honest-to-god witches. Or 'sorceresses,' they prefer. All from Cassadaga, so it's got to be true."

Thanks to my mother, I knew that Cassadaga was a village in central Florida founded by an old-time spiritualist. The place is still known for witches and fortune-tellers.

Instead of laughing at Theo's claim, the women puffed up in importance, bored, but willing to indulge the good-looking archaeologist.

"The correct term is *Magissas*," the heaviest of the three warned when I was close enough. "From the Greek. And we don't shake hands."

Fine with me. I forgot her name and the name of the other woman within seconds of hearing them. The lean, attractive one was Lucia. Lucia, with her sharp, aggressive eyes, said, "I *do* shake hands," and we did, but she caged mine with her fingers and wouldn't let go until I pulled free.

"Don't be offended," she said, "it was actually a compliment," then explained to her friends, "This one has some beasties bottled up inside her head—I'll tell you later."

I said, "*Excuse* me?"

Using her eyebrows, she communicated with her friends: *See what I mean?*

"Lucia picks up on"—Theo grinned at the woman— "what did you call it? Through skin contact with certain people, Lucia says she can splice into their thoughts, sense past traumas or health issues. Neuro-communication . . . no, -*cognation*. No, neuro-cognition, that's it."

Birdy didn't approve. "You have a P-H-D but still believe that sort of crap?"

Lucia, speaking to Theo, said, "I'm used to it," then addressed Birdy. "I don't bother to prove myself unless I find an interesting subject—a person with enough spiritual layers to teach me something. The habitually unevolved . . . simpletons, them I avoid. Theo?" The woman waved away the question Birdy was in the middle of asking. "They're your friends. I don't want to upset you. But if she wants proof, I'll give it to her."

There was a dreamy, superior quality in Lucia's voice that would have been more effective without the nasal whine.

My read on the situation: The assistant professor didn't want to be in the middle. He had been bedding Lucia, despite her age, but tonight had his sights set on a younger woman, even though she was a cop.

Theo tried diplomacy. "Whatever you say. But, first, I didn't tell you this but Bertie and Hannah have the keys to the old Cadence mansion. They're sort of camping there tonight and—"

"They're *what*?" the women at the table asked simultaneously. Envious, not incredulous.

Theo said, "Bertie's aunt bought the place."

All three straightened, a reflexive deference to my friend's new importance. One of them asked, "Have you heard the weeping bride yet? I've spoken to her many times."

She was referring to Irene Cadence—the woman on the balcony. I didn't believe it, of course, but couldn't help asking, "What did she tell you?"

Theo drowned out my question. "They're doing the sleep-in-the-haunted-house thing, but a scorpion stung the hell out of Bertie a few minutes ago. That's why I brought the girls to see you." He addressed us. "These ladies know more about herbal medicine than anyone I know. Scorpions, the ones here, aren't supposed to be dangerous, but—"

"They can be damn dangerous," Lucia warned and got to her feet. "Where did it sting you?"

Birdy said, "If I needed a doctor, I'd call one, okay?" Then weakened. "What do you mean *dangerous*?"

"Stung you where, dearie? It's important."

"Well . . . on the neck. It was throbbing but doesn't hurt much now. Do you mean *dangerous* as in a *delayed reaction*?"

Lucia, in Mother Teresa mode, came around the table. "Let me have a look. How close to the jugular? Judy . . . we'll need a poultice."

Both women stood from the table, wobbling some, concerned but obviously stoned.

Birdy, lifting her head, asked me, "What do you think?"

I was disappointed the woman hadn't answered me about Irene Cadence but said, "You're doing just fine already. A poultice wouldn't hurt, I guess, as long as they don't ask you to swallow or smoke something. What kind of poultice?"

Lucia, who was my height, gave me a cutting look . . . returned her attention to Birdy's neck and touched a hand to her necklace, a pendant hidden beneath her dress. "Ask her to *swallow s*omething? I'm not surprised to hear you say that. But I don't practice violence against living things."

I said, "It pays to be cautious."

"Yes . . . but it doesn't pay to be rude. Suspicion is always rooted in guilt. Yours is anyway. Dearie, I *know* what you did."

Birdy's eyes squinched into slits. "What's that supposed to mean?"

Lucia shrugged. "I'm seldom wrong about these things," while her eyes stuck to mine: hard eyes that appeared silver by battery candlelight but were probably green or blue.

"If you're accusing me of something, come out and say it."

Theo tried to intervene. "Of course she's not."

"I already know the answer," Lucia said, "why would I bother?"

The man I shot—that's what she meant. Impossible . . . yet I sensed it was true. For the second time that night, I said, "*Excuse* me?" which, so far, was the cleverest response I could manage.

Lucia smiled, but the smile flattened before she dropped the subject. "Diviner's root and camphor and whatever else the girls come up with. A poultice will draw out the poison—something I learned while studying tribal medicine. That's why I'm worried. The poison"— she lifted Birdy's chin again—"it's so damn close to your brain. But of course it's up to you, dearie."

The abandoned house—the Cadence mansion, Theo

had called it—that's what this was about. Lucia's sudden warmth was her way of getting a look inside. Never mind how she had guessed I'd shot a man. No . . . not guessed—it was a trick. Don't we all carry secret guilt inside? Lucia was a manipulator. She had used a fortune-teller's device. I realized it. Did Birdy?

Yes . . . she did. Birdy took a seat, her back to the pic-nic table, and waited. She pretended to listen to Theo while Lucia snuck the bong away and carried it inside. Every few seconds, Birdy and I exchanged looks. Each time, her expression sent a message, but I prolonged the exchange to be certain.

Lucia is a fraud. I know it.

That was Birdy's message.

There was a second message: *Get lost.*

Liberty Tupplemeyer wanted to do some police work on her own.

Speaking to Theo, I said, "Keep an eye on her, you mind? I'm going to introduce myself to those women."

He was confused, then followed my gaze. "Oh . . . the midget twins. They're always so stoned—don't be sur-prised by anything they say."

It wasn't a warning, he was worried. The archaeologist didn't want me speaking to the locals.

I told Birdy, "I'm not going far," meaning I would be watching her, too.

6

BEFORE I COULD LURE THE TINY WOMEN INTO A conversation about Ms. Margaret and Oz, the man awaiting Theo's attention lured me into a conversation about old bottles and the Civil War. His RV was closer to where two witches and a . . . and *Lucia* were preparing a poultice, so I let him convince me to sit for a while.

Another reason: Tyrone's trailer was on the path and I'd seen a face appear at the window. Possibly checking if it was safe to go out or simply peeping at women again. For me, hanging close, waiting for Birdy, was more comfortable.

After shaking hands, I said to the older gentleman, "Yes, please, cold tea would be nice." His name was Belton Matás. Adjusting the gas lantern was Carmelo, a hard-looking man, early thirties, with a vacant smile.

"I'll get it," Carmelo said and hurried to an Igloo

cooler next to a tent. Something about his eagerness suggested that his mind was stunted.

Mr. Matás had waved as I walked past. I'd assumed he was waving at me. In fact, he had been signaling Theo that they were still waiting. It was one of those silly social errors I make too often. But the man put me at ease, saying, "You're even lovelier up close. Please, sit. Do you live nearby?"

On the table, instead of a board game, were maps and a few books. I explained about the old house while I settled into a canvas chair, then said, "Theo—Dr. Ivanhoff—told us about the award he's getting. But he didn't say what it's for."

Carmelo, from the cooler, called, "More wine, Mr. Matás?" He spoke the name with a Spanish inflection.

Belton Matás, a blank expression on his face, asked, "Award?" then bought a few seconds by telling Carmelo, "A bottle of water, please." He waited until he'd opened the bottle, taken a sip after miming a toast. "Dr. Ivanhoff had to be talking about someone else. We've exchanged a few e-mails, but I didn't meet him until this afternoon." He addressed Carmelo. "Help yourself to another beer, my friend."

"Thanks, Mr. Matás!"

The older man watched him go. "Carmelo's a local and not very bright. But there's an honesty about people like him I find endearing—plus he knows this river like the back of his hand. And please, dear, call me Belton. I've given up correcting him."

"He works for you?"

"Almost a week now. I'm what you would call an am-ateur historian–slash–self-published author"—a nod at the two books—"which is another way of saying I'm a retired bum. But it's better than dehydrating in some home for old farts." He smiled, the lantern reflecting off his glasses. "Excuse my language."

I touched one of the books. "May I . . . Belton?" It felt okay using his first name.

He placed his hand on the book to delay me. "I didn't write these. I brought them as—" Carmelo had returned, realized we were talking, so sat cross-legged near the tent. Belton suggested he find a cushion, asked if Car-melo wanted snacks—there were peanuts in the RV—before he returned to the conversation, saying, "Where was I?"

I asked, "Are you writing about the battle that took place here? I wish someone would. I couldn't find a word about it on the Internet."

The man was way ahead of me. "Fascinating, isn't it? That's why I came down from Richmond. Carmelo, he's got what they call a bass boat and we've been up every creek and canal north of the Caloosahatchee. Maybe I should explain. The Caloosahatchee is a bigger river—more of a canal, really. It runs from—"

"I'm a fishing guide not far from here," I said, giving him a pat on the wrist to apologize for interrupting. "Mostly out of Captiva Island. I fish the mouth of the Caloosahatchee some, but I've never been farther than the locks above Fort Myers. I'd love to read one of your books."

Belton, a roly-poly man in his late seventies, was delighted. "Carmelo," he called, "I've met my second native Floridian in a week."

Carmelo gazed at the moon while he chewed peanuts. "That very cool, Mr. Matás."

I hadn't said I was born in Florida, but it was okay. I have a slight accent, I've been told, the Florida accent being milder and different than others who are raised in the South. I continued to listen, after a glance at the picnic table where, within shouting distance, the two witches and Lucia tended to my friend. But where was Theo?

Belton noticed, picked up on my uneasiness. "People come and go here. It's worse than a bus station."

"It's an unusual place," I agreed.

That gave him confidence. "At the risk of offending, I'll just come out and say it. Three nights here is more than enough for me. I don't mind people using drugs, it's none of my business. But the smell is so strong, I think everyone goes a little crazy after sundown."

"A little earlier, I felt sort of strange myself," I said. "But I did have a rum drink."

"It's not your fault. Something's in the air. Night before last, I made a wrong turn—didn't see the *Serpentarium* sign—and this *animal* came charging out. I'd swear to God it was a chimpanzee or, I don't know, some crazy person in a costume."

I sat forward. *"What?"*

"It couldn't have been, I know. I'd been driving for

twelve hours, so it was probably a big dog—a Saint Bernard or mastiff. Something that size. Then an old man with a flashlight came out, screaming at me. Have you ever tried backing up a rig like that in a hurry?" He meant the RV camper.

"Did the man threaten you?"

Belton, on a roll, didn't hear the question. "Then, last night, the gentleman who lives there"—he indicated Tyrone's single-wide—"went galloping off when I said hello. It was dark, I must have surprised him. Truthfully, I felt like running myself when I got a look. Today, I found out he works in a sideshow. But when you're unprepared for a face like his—my lord."

"His face is that . . . unusual?"

"It was dark. I don't want to be cruel, but . . ." *Yes* is what Belton was implying.

"It can't be an easy life for him," I said. "Is he a tall man?" I was wondering about the Peeping Tom.

"Hard to say, but I can't get out of here soon enough," he said and cleaned his glasses, his expression humorous. "If I want to get high, I'll hop into a nice dry martini. And you'd be welcome to join me. Hannah, I think we might be the only normal ones around here."

I laughed, but it was nervous laughter as I sipped my tea. "What time were you supposed to meet Theo?"

"We left it open." Matás looked at his watch. "Only ten o'clock. Feels later. Tomorrow at one, he's going to show me around the dig site. Trust me, he took some convincing. Dr. Ivanhoff is . . . well, let's say he has a very robust ego." The man stopped to think about something, then snapped his fingers. "That award—I know what he was talking about. A historian friend in Atlanta gave me a box to deliver. He didn't say what it was. Research material, I assumed. I'm sure that's what Dr. Ivanhoff was referring to."

I said, "Oh." My mind was on Theo, but not because of an award. I was connecting his absence with the journal I'd left behind.

I stood to go. Belton's face showed disappointment. "Not yet—there's something I want to show you. Carmelo, bring that box of bottles."

"Bottles?"

"They can be quite valuable, you know. This afternoon, we found a bunch that are circa Civil War period. I think you'll find them interesting. Or . . . am I boring you?"

I said, "I've got a small collection myself." Which was true—snorkeling the bays around Sanibel and Captiva, my Uncle Jake and I had found bottles and crockery that dated back to Spanish times. Matás asked for details. He appeared delighted by what I had to say. Even so, I was uneasy about leaving Birdy alone. Finally I said, "Excuse me for a minute," and walked toward the picnic table to check on her.

Birdy saw me. She attempted a long-distance message by setting her jaw, with a slight swing of the head. I didn't understand until she added a private thumbs-up, did it in a forceful way that told me she hadn't been drugged or poisoned and wanted more time with the witches. When Theo reappeared from nearby trees, I was convinced.

I turned back, interested to see what Belton Matás had discovered.

BELTON—I was comfortable saying his name now—pulled the lantern closer and chose a map, which he flattened. "This afternoon, Carmelo led me to a spot not far from here—the guy's fished and hunted this country since forever." He placed a thick finger on the map, which was actually a satellite photo. It showed a chunk of land, miles and miles of wetlands, cypress and grazing pasture, and a curling ribbon of blue that was Telegraph River.

"This map doesn't narrow it down much," I said.

"I'm afraid it'll have to do for now," he replied—being cautious, which I could appreciate. I wouldn't have asked a fisherman exactly where he had caught such and such a fish. Bottle hunters deserved the same courtesy.

"I don't blame you." I smiled and focused on the satellite image. The river, hidden by trees, was seldom visible as it snaked south toward the Caloosahatchee River, but a telltale swath of green traced its path. The river's headwaters narrowed into the creek where we had crossed the railroad bridge, but neither the campground nor the old Cadence house were large enough to see. North of us were more wetlands and swamp, all undeveloped. Miles of nothing, fenced cattle range and wilderness preserve.

I said, "You were smart to hire a guide. I wouldn't

want to get lost in this area. But why were you hunting bottles?"

Belton heard glass clattering in the tent. "Carmelo! Please try not to break another one." Then a patient pause before he replied to me. "Think of it as amateur carbon dating. Find a bottle embossed with a date—let's say, 1860—you can be absolutely certain it wasn't placed there in 1850. Obvious. But let's take it a step further. If the bottle is buried under a few feet of muck, whatever lies in the same strata can be linked to a similar date. Give or take a decade, of course. And the type of bottle: groups of men drink rum and ale, babies and old people need medicine. Bottles were rarer back then but still disposable. They had a shelf life." He looked up. Carmelo was carrying a Tupperware box that clanked.

I enjoyed the next few minutes inspecting dozens of glass shards and several unbroken bottles. One was a rectangular medicine flask, *Sassafras Tonic* embossed above the manufacturer's mark and location, *Vicksburg, Tenn.*

"Confederate?" I asked.

"Not necessarily. It's not dated, so I have to research the maker. The bottle is seamed"—he held it to the lantern—"it's flat-based, so it could have been made after 1865. I try to stay objective, but"—his smile was more like a wink—"I think you're right. And here's why."

From a separate box, he placed a green translucent bottle that was heavy-lipped and out-of-square. "Pontilied" is how he described the bottom, which was sharply concave. The front was embossed:

XXX
PORTER ALE
WALTHAM, MASS.

"Check the back," he suggested, then watched, having fun because I was interested.

Before the glass had hardened, a date had been etched: 1864. The color and shape were so unusual, I said, "I'd love to photograph this."

"You're a photographer, too?"

"Just learning. A friend loaned me a camera with a lens that's good for low light. It sees colors most people don't."

"Drink enough of this Porter Ale, you'd see all kinds of things," he grinned. "And someone did."

From the same box, he removed a dozen shards that were similar. "They had quite a party. Or stayed in one place for a while. This came from just downriver—a mile, I'd say."

I scooted closer to the lantern and held up the bottle: thick green glass; air bubbles trapped within—air from the lungs of a long-dead craftsmen. I said, "This is more like art. What I appreciate most? Besides you and Carmelo, the last person to touch this might have been a soldier during the Civil War. It creates a sort of closeness, you know? Makes me wonder about him. Was the man lonely? Did he survive? I once found part of a Spanish demijohn that gave me the same feeling, and—" Suddenly, an unexpected thought popped into my head.

"Is something wrong?"

I held the bottle out for him to take. "What about fingerprints? I shouldn't be touching this if the soldier's prints might still be—" I stopped again, shook my head, and laughed. "What am I saying? They didn't know about fingerprints back then. I'm usually not so dense."

Belton Matás didn't consider me dense. "There's no way to match them, but fingerprints on one-hundred-and-fifty-year-old glass isn't silly. I've found thumbprints in handmade bricks from that period, ceramics, all sorts of things. You're actually very perceptive."

I asked a few questions. He asked about the old house. "Why not sleep in a hotel?" I offered a partial truth: My friend's aunt owned the property and wanted to know if rumors had turned the place into a sideshow attraction.

"The only one way to find out," I explained, "is to stay there for a night or two and keep notes. Plus, being this close to Halloween, we thought it might be fun." Which had been true—until the sun went down.

"Fascinating," he said. It was a word he used to nudge my story along. The whole time, through his thick glasses, he studied me with pleasant approval that could have been mistaken for fondness. Soon, he nodded as if he'd made up his mind about something and said, "Carmelo, please bring my briefcase. I want to show Hannah our map."

Carmelo was surprised. "Your *map*?"

"You heard me."

There were already maps and satellite photos on the table. Belton saw my confusion and, after hesitating, pat-

ted my hand in the same friendly way I had patted his. "I
consider myself a good judge of character, young lady.
I'm going to show you where we found these bottles.
You enjoy history. You seem to know something about it.
No"—I had started to thank him—"this is to my advantage, not yours. I want your opinion on some photos I
took. However, I will ask one favor in return. It has to do
with—"

From the RV, Carmelo interrupted, "Should I take my
boots off, Mr. Matás?" He was standing at the door, the
door open.

Belton made the sound people do when frustrated
but patient. "*Always*, Carmelo. That's the rule. Oh, and
please bring the magnifying glass. It's on the desk."

He turned to me. "It has to do with Dr. Ivanhoff. I've
met some fine archaeologists. I've also met one or two
who are egocentric thieves and their position gives them
a license to steal. I don't know the man. Until I do, I'd
like you to keep this just between us."

"Sure," I said. Already, I was hoping to be invited
along on his next bottle expedition. However, I also reminded myself, *You don't know this man any better than
you know Theo. Take it slowly.* Which is why I didn't offer
collateral in the form of information about my uncle, the
blockade-runner.

Carmelo placed a briefcase on the table: leather and
tarnished buckles. Belton removed a laptop, which he
opened, then a cardboard tube that contained another
satellite photo. As he arranged things, I looked at more

bottles. They had been rinsed but not cleaned. Muck and sand clung to the inside. They had a distinctive odor familiar to me.

He noticed. "What are you thinking?"

I took another sniff. "Sulfur. Where I grew up, well water tastes like this. My mother still prefers it. Not as strong as the smell of mangroves or some spots in the Everglades. That could be because you rinsed them. Otherwise, I'd guess you found these underwater."

Raised eyebrows, a boyish pretense of shock on his face. He slid the photo in front of me. "I think *you* might be the witch. Have a look."

The satellite photo could have been shot from a helicopter, the details were so clear. It showed a river switchback, cattle pasture on the west side, which might have been part of the old Cadence estate. To the east were old-growth mimosa trees—feathered leaves gave them away—then dense cover, brambles and palmettos and bayonet plants. Stamped into the chaos was a vague rectangle, a pile of bricks or rocks at one end. A squarish pile of something else was nearby and the faintest hint of pathways, one through trees to the east and a narrower path that vanished before it got to the river.

"Use this." Belton handed me the magnifying glass.

It didn't help much. After a while, I sat back. "There was a house here with a chimney. Not a big house. Maybe an outbuilding or two and fencerows. This is what I can't figure out." I indicated a spot on the photo. "It looks like a stack of bricks. Part of the chimney, maybe, after it fell, but that doesn't seem quite right." I tried the magnifying glass again.

No need. Belton pulled his chair around and used the computer, which neither of us could see until he dimmed the lantern, its hiss dropping an octave. Moths fluttered, one hammered against the screen. He swatted it away and opened a file while our eyes adjusted.

"I don't know what it is either," he said. "If it was smaller, I'd think some kind of brick oven. Now I'm thinking a root cellar, a cool place to store things. It's coffin-shaped but too big for that. And why would anyone build a crypt way out here anyway? It's eight-by-four and at least five feet deep, with an arched cover that's falling in. But still solid. The bricklayer who built this really knew his trade."

Right away, from the photo, I knew what the structure was but let him click through more images, Belton saying, "Carmelo shot deer there as a kid and remembered the foundations of what had been a house. Yesterday afternoon, on the river—he's got an electronic fish finder on his boat—we passed over something interesting on the bottom. That's why we went back today."

Carmelo, listening to every word, said, "I'm a good shot. And lotsa big fish."

My attention sharpened. "But you weren't fishing."

"No, of course not," Belton said. "There's a deep spot there. Almost fifteen feet deep, which is unusual in a river this narrow, and he happened to mention hunting. Then he remembered the house, so I said let's have a look. I didn't expect much. But isn't that the way it always happens?"

Carmelo moved to a spot on the ground while Belton opened a new photo. Vines curling through its bricks, the structure was rectangular, shaped like a loaf of bread. The vaulted cover had collapsed, but enough bricks remained to form a graceful arch.

"It's a rain cistern," I told him. What I wanted to ask was, *What did you find on the bottom of the river?*

Belton concentrated on the photo. "Are you sure? Hannah, I've seen photos of cisterns from that period. They're usually big wooden barrels held together with iron hoops."

I said, "People used bricks if they knew how to do it. I've seen cisterns the same shape in Key West and some other places. How far is the house from the river?"

"Only fifty yards or so. They had plenty of water."

I said, "Not if you had to carry it in a wooden bucket. That's far enough back to avoid flooding, but they would've needed a cistern. Fifty yards is a long walk through heat and mosquitoes." Then I did ask about what they'd found in the river, but indirectly. "Is the boat equipped with a fish finder? Or an actual bottom-reading unit? One is a lot more detailed and expensive."

"Hannah Smith, the fishing guide," Belton reminded himself. Cautious again. No . . . he was suspicious.

I said, "I'm not interested in catching bass. I'm wondering what might have sunk there during the Civil War. Why else would you be interested?"

"Why, indeed," the man said. On his face was a mild

smile. He seemed to be waiting for me to elaborate. I was tempted to come right out and tell him that Capt. Summerlin had scuttled a boat somewhere in the area—possibly this river. My great-great-uncle's journal had yet to reveal details.

But I, too, have a suspicious streak, particularly when it comes to strange men. So I reached and pulled a map of Florida closer. "Explain to me why Union troops would be this far south?"

"Ale bottles from Massachusetts," he said. "Smart girl. But that's no guarantee the beer was drunk by Union soldiers."

"Maybe not. But soldiers from the North would've come by boat. You can carry a lot more supplies in a boat than on horseback. Bottles of beer are too heavy to carry more than a few on horseback."

That was only a partial explanation. I knew Union soldiers had been here because the attorney had shown us photos of their uniform buttons. Belton Matás sensed I was holding back but played along by offering an overview of the Civil War—or started to—when I noticed Birdy walking my direction.

I got to my feet. "I think my friend's ready to go. Can we talk tomorrow?"

He stood at gentlemanly attention and signaled for Carmelo to stand, too. "My pleasure, Miss Hannah Smith. But how about this? Come with us in the morning and I'll show you where we found the bottles. Carmelo has to get gas for the boat first—that means driving to a gas station—so how about nine-thirty?"

I didn't want to bring up Theo's name or the plans we'd made. "It would have to be later. I wouldn't want to hold you up."

"Let's say noon, then." His eyes found Birdy. "Invite your friend along."

"That's nice of you. I'll ask her on the walk back."

"You didn't come in a car?"

"We were told it's faster to come across the old railroad bridge."

Belton cleared his throat. "Some advice from an old man: I wouldn't wander around here alone at night."

That caused me to look at Tyrone's double-wide. No reason, I just did. Once again, there was a face at the window, a shadow that watched Birdy approaching or watched me. I felt sadness for the person inside, not fear. I held up a hand and waved to acknowledge his existence.

The blinds snapped closed . . . then opened. A single hand polished the window in slow motion, two brief strokes—a reply.

The blinds closed.

7

FROM THE WAY BIRDY SUDDENLY WENT QUIET, I knew we would be sleeping in a motel tonight, not the house, so I beat her to it, saying, "Let's find a place in Labelle and come back in the morning with bug bombs. We'll set them off before Theo shows us the dig site. By evening, it'll be okay to sleep."

Birdy, her mind somewhere else, said, "Huh? Oh—I can't. You know I work Sunday mornings, so I can't stay tomorrow night." She peered ahead, unsure of something. Several steps later, she took my arm and whispered, "Someone's coming."

"Where?"

"A person. See?"

No. The moon was to our left. Enough light pooled on the road so that we didn't need our flashlights, but not enough to make out details. When I reached for my flashlight, Birdy, voice low, ordered, "Don't. Keep moving," then slipped the purse off her shoulder; a purse that contained a semiauto pistol loaded with police manstopper rounds.

"Whatever you say," I replied—both of us whispering—but then changed my mind when I saw movement near the sign we'd seen earlier: *Slew Vaccine and Herpetile.*

I planted my feet, which dragged Birdy to a halt. "Mr. Matás pulled in there by accident the other night and a big dog or something charged his car. I don't want you to shoot someone's dog."

Her purse was open but she hadn't taken the gun out. "I wouldn't—unless I had to. Even out here, dogs should be on a leash." She thought for a moment. "What do you mean *or something*?"

I said, "Shush," because details were emerging from the trees. It was a person carrying something heavy, a formless shape that breached the entrance to what Theo had described as a small, modern facility. The object looked like an oversized trash can; the person, male, was wide-shouldered, strong, but as short as a child. He squatted, placed the can by the road, then reversed his course, walking with the odd teeter-totter strides of someone who is muscle-bound or on stilts. There was a gate. He pulled it closed behind him.

Birdy gave it a long, uneasy minute before saying into my ear, "A dwarf. That's another dwarf . . . isn't it?"

I sniffed the air flowing toward us, a light breeze from the north. Garbage . . . fermenting fruit . . . and a fecal musk that forced my head to turn.

Birdy's, too. "My god, what's that stink?"

I said, "Mr. Matás could have been wrong about the dog. At first he said it was something else, maybe a—" I hesitated.

"A what?"

"At first he thought it was a chimpanzee."

"A *chimp*? Jesus Christ, how do you confuse a dog with a chimp?"

I shushed her again. "That was his first impression. It was dark, he was in that rental RV of his. Then an old man came out, yelling, and Mr. Matás is close to eighty himself. Anyone that age would've been confused. Now he thinks it was one of the large breeds like a Saint Bernard."

"A chimp!" She reached into her purse. "Those things are monsters. Did you read what a chimp did to that poor woman? She had to have a face transplant." Birdy had her pistol out, a flashlight in her other hand. She stood taller to scout ahead. "Come on, let's have a look."

"A look at what?"

"Footprints. The road's mostly sand. That'll tell us. Special permits are required to keep dangerous pets. I'll have the owner's ass if there's an illegal chimp roaming around here at night."

I said, "A person who makes snake vaccine probably knows more about permits than either one of us. Let's go back and ask someone to drive us."

She kept walking. "Then whoever owns the thing can, by god, show me the paperwork."

I grabbed her arm, but Birdy remained focused on the

gate. "Stay here, if you want. Tell me you didn't read about the woman who had her face chewed off."

"You are *off duty*. And what if the dog or whatever it is bites? Call your office and tell them about this once we're safe and in the car. Let's get a few deputies out here." Another tug, but it was the wrong thing to say.

"I *am* a deputy sheriff," she reasoned, but spoke to herself. "Off duty or not, I'm still an officer of the court. Let's at least look for tracks." She pulled away and walked toward the drive, pistol at her side.

I followed along. The sign posted at the driveway glittered with yellow reflective tape, oaks formed a cavern above. Cicadas buzzed a seesaw chorus until we were near the mouth of the drive, then suddenly went silent.

Birdy stopped. "That thing has to weigh a ton." She was referring to the trash can. It was industrial-sized and stuffed with pruned tree limbs, pieces of furniture, and broken tile. "It would take both of us to lift it."

"Seriously—let's come back in a car."

"Stop worrying. This is what I'm trained to do." Pistol ready, she continued walking.

I didn't share her confidence. In my pocket was an LED flashlight, small but dazzlingly bright. It was a gift from the biologist I had dated, a man who, I suspected, had traveled to many dark places and was particular about light. When I switched it on, Birdy said, "Wow, that helps," but then crouched and said, "What the hell was *that*?"

The light had spooked something in the bushes to our right. We heard the heavy crunch of breaking limbs. The noise started at ground level, then seemed to ascend higher into the trees.

I whispered, "Let's get out of here."

Instead, Birdy hollered toward the driveway, "Sheriff's Department. Come out and identify yourself." With the pistol pointed at the ground, she walked toward the whip and crackle of branches.

I couldn't run off and leave her, so I used the flashlight—painted the tree canopy and tracked the sound—but was always a second behind. All we saw were moving branches and a cascade of falling leaves. I stabbed the beam ahead at a massive oak. I hoped to intercept whatever it was. When I did, the tree exploded with a thumping, squawking cloud of birds . . . birds the size of vultures.

Birdy, the cop, ducked and said, *"Shit,"* while I kept the light steady.

That's what I thought they were—vultures—until one soared toward me, its clumsy wings struggling to stay airborne and follow the others, who also appeared too large for flight. The birds scattered overhead. The sound of falling rain pattered around us, then they regrouped and crash-dived toward the river while I chased them with the flashlight.

"What the hell!"

I responded, "My heart damn near stopped!"

"Are they pelicans?"

"Turkeys," I said. "Wild turkeys. My lord, they scared the fire out of me."

Birdy took a deep breath and made a whistling sound.

"I hope you noticed not once did I point my weapon at them. That's training—wait until you've identified your subject."

My reply was equally off topic. "My uncle took me turkey hunting two or three times, but this is the first time I was ever close enough. There had to be at least a dozen. Wild turkeys, they're very smart."

We went back and forth like that—nervous talk—until I saw a glob of gray goo on my shoe that matched a streak of gray on my jeans. Birdy noticed something on her shoulder . . . then in her hair. She touched it and sniffed. *"Bird shit."* She made a queasy noise.

"Turkey shit," I amended, my vocabulary still out of control while my beating heart slowed.

"What a night. First, a scorpion bites me, then my hundred-dollar blouse gets turd-bombed. A foot of snow and Boston is sounding pretty good right now." Birdy found hand wipes in her purse, then proved my instincts right by adding, "No way in hell am I going to bed without a shower. We either get a hotel or I'm following you home. What time is it?"

It was ten-twenty, which I told her while my brain settled and began to work again. I wanted to believe my flashlight had tracked turkeys clattering through the trees. But I didn't believe it. The turkeys had been roosting. Something else bothered me: I had smelled fermenting fruit and garbage, not limbs and broken furniture. To confirm the incongruity, I swung my light to the trash container ten yards away. It was piled high with wood.

Birdy sobered. "Yeah . . . let's check for tracks."

"*Why?* That's not what I was looking for."

"Stay here, if you want."

I couldn't do that, so only muttered, "Lucia must've slipped a crazy pill into your drink."

I dreaded what we might find but felt better when Birdy knelt by the can and used her index finger to trace a deep impression in the sand. "It was a man wearing shoes," she said. "See? He turned around here—the tracks aren't as deep—and walked back to the vaccine place. Size seven or eight in ladies' shoes, I'd say. Tiny for a man, so he's short but wide and strong as hell."

"*Sandals,*" I corrected her, "no heel prints." I wanted to share my friend's relief but couldn't muster the conviction.

Birdy sensed it. "Chimps don't wear sandals *or* heels. Let's find a Holiday Inn."

"After I get Captain Summerlin's journal," I replied.

WHAT WE FOUND was better, the River's Edge Motel on Old County Road 78, just across the bridge from La-belle, a pretty little town with a friendly cowboy flavor. The motel had large, clean rooms that overlooked the Caloosahatchee River and a dock where three trawlers and a houseboat were moored among smaller boats.

"Screw sleeping with scorpions," Birdy said after she had showered and joined me on the porch. "I like this place. How about we book two rooms for the week and bill my aunt? It's only thirty minutes to the old house and no more than forty for me to get to work on Sunday morning. That way, I can stay tomorrow night."

I agreed it was a nice motel but was in a foul, suspicious mood. "There's less chance of being robbed, at least, or people snooping," I said. I was referring to what I'd found after returning to the Cadence house. The door was still padlocked and Capt. Summerlin's journal was on the mantel, but not exactly as I'd left it. I'm particular about how I place things. Right away, I knew. The box lid was sealed; I'd left it ajar so air could circulate. Further proof was a torn page and new cracks in the binding; the cracks could have been caused by flattening the book to photograph the contents.

Birdy, whose room was three doors down from mine, said, "We're off duty. We've got clean sheets and bathrooms, so stop with the paranoia. What you need is a drink."

There was no nearby bar to provide mojitos, so we'd bought a bottle of red wine at a 7-Eleven, a store not known for fine wines. That didn't seem to matter at eleven-fifteen on a Friday night, the two of us eager for a shower and beds to sleep in.

I replied, "You said yourself that Theo disappeared long enough to break in. I don't trust him. Was he still hitting on you?"

Birdy, fussing with her buttons, nodded. "He put his hand on my ass. I told him it was a little early in the game for heavy petting, but maybe after the doctor took his cast off."

"That's all you said?"

"Threatening to break his arm wasn't enough? Besides, being a pompous prick isn't a deal breaker with me. Not if he's got nice bone structure and nice hands. Did you notice Theo's? Kind of delicate for a man his size."

"There's a word for that kind of behavior," I told her. "Are you sure the witches didn't drug you?"

Birdy smiled, "Hold that thought," and returned with the wine and two glass tumblers, the River's Edge being a mom-and-pop motel with kitchenettes and cupboards fully stocked. She poured the glasses, handed me one, then offered a toast—"To separate bathrooms"—before telling me about her time alone with Theo and the three women.

"They knew that my aunt sent us. And she knew way too much about me for it to be a series of lucky guesses. I'd like to say I don't believe in paranormal powers, but . . ." Birdy sipped her wine, made a face, and said, "God, this is awful."

"You're talking about Lucia?" I asked. "What did she say?"

Birdy sniffed her glass and focused on the dock, where the trawlers were buttoned up for the night but the houseboat's windows were bright. On the roof deck, two long, lean silhouettes listened to Garth Brooks, the music softer than male laughter. "I bet those men have an extra cold beer or two. If there's a God in heaven, maybe even some decent tequila and a lime."

I replied, "It's too late to go begging drinks from strange men. Answer my question." I was tired—another reason I wasn't in good humor. This was the first chance we'd had to talk because Birdy had followed me in her BMW rather than leave one of our vehicles unattended at the Cadence place.

"You've got a prudish streak in you, Smithie."

"It's a good thing one of us does. Maybe this wine needs to breathe a little. Tell me what happened while we wait."

"C-P-R and a respirator can't change vinegar into merlot. How much did you pay for this?"

I said, "About the same as a gallon of gas. Now, tell me what happened."

What happened was, Lucia had done a good job of proving—in Theo's words—that she could *splice into the thoughts* of certain people, especially those who also had psychic gifts. That made Birdy an especially difficult subject, according to Lucia, an insult my friend fumed over while explaining, "I don't know how the bitch did it. She told me things about my childhood that no one—I mean, *no one*—knows. I've gone over and over it in my head. It's an act, a fortune-teller's act, but how did she do it?"

I had a theory. Bunny Tupplemeyer had confided secrets to her *astrologician*, a person who wasn't trustworthy. It was guesswork on my part and a serious charge that might offend the socialite if she heard. So I let my friend talk.

"The clever thing was, Lucia didn't come right out and state such and such happened at whatever age I happened to be at the time. She would make a statement, then ask leading questions, like, 'You have a scar on your lower abdomen, the right side. Children have their appendix removed, but I don't see an operation in your past.' You know, talking in that superior tone of hers. Then comes the question, but she already knew the answer, I'd bet on it. She asks me, 'What happened when you were fourteen years old?' No, she says, 'What happened, *dearie*.' The way she uses that word, it's like a razor with a smile."

Birdy hated being called dearie, but had tolerated it, just as she had tolerated the other women fussing over a poultice made of herbs wrapped in cheesecloth. Theo had sat cross-legged on the picnic table, watching, not saying much except to marvel over Lucia's accuracy

I asked, "What about the scar? Was she right?"

"I was sixteen, not fourteen—see what I mean? Even her mistakes are convincing. It's a technique."

"Yeah, but how did it happen?"

Birdy talked over me. "Same with asking questions. Remember her crack about your guilty conscience? She knows you shot someone, I think."

I said, "I thought about that on the way here," but still withheld my theory.

"Lucia is smooth. The questions make her routine more believable. You know, force people to participate. It allowed her to manipulate me into giving answers that, like I said, she already knew. Maybe not the specifics, but close enough. Very professional. But how the hell does she do it? Oh"—Birdy snapped her fingers—"and there was something else. I'd bet that Lucia and Theo have known each other for a lot longer than three weeks."

She sniffed her wine again. "Tell the truth, do you think he's screwing her?"

"Theo and Lucia?" I asked, but decided it was wiser to take a guess about the scar. "You did something really stupid when you were sixteen, didn't you? That's why you won't say."

"The way Theo would chime in, it was almost like he was working as her shill. That would be a deal breaker for me. The timing, a sort of patter they had going." Birdy ruminated over Theo's behavior but finally answered, "I wouldn't call getting a kiss from David Ortiz stupid."

I couldn't place the name but said, "You've got to be kidding."

"Nope, but it didn't start out as fun as it sounds. I was at Fenway Park and fell over the railing when I stretched too far for a foul ball. Next to the dugout is a sort of camera pit and I landed on a field keeper's rake—seven stitches—but Big Papi was right there and swept me up. I'd do it again in a heartbeat. I'll show you the ball he signed."

She was a Red Sox fan. I knew she was talking about baseball but had to ask, "What about David Ortiz? Why did he kiss you?"

Birdy, amused for some reason, replied, "I didn't say *he* kissed *me*" and laughed but was watching the houseboat. The two men were lounging while a new song floated over mown grass and a hint of distant jasmine. She gave the wine another try, then dumped it. "They're probably locals—fishermen, maybe. So they might have some good stories about the Cadence place. That could be helpful." She let that settle, then asked, "Do you know anything about country music?"

I knew what she was working up to. "They're playing Garth Brooks—but don't you dare go bothering them this late." She had called me prudish, which I am not, so it felt okay to play the role I'd been assigned—until I proved her wrong. And I would.

Birdy stood and straightened her collar, prettying herself up. "Is he popular?"

"Think of David Ortiz in a cowboy hat," I said. Then I swung over the railing so that I was the first to introduce myself to the men on the houseboat.

8

BIRDY WAS RIGHT. THE CADENCE HOUSE WAS well known in Labelle. The same was true of people who lived near the house—including a neighbor who was said to be insane. But the rumors were so dark, they were of a whispering nature, and it took work to pry those stories free.

The men were locals—nice guys—but they weren't fishermen, despite the houseboat. They were honest-to-god cowboys—a claim I would have doubted if they hadn't been so modest when describing their jobs. Copenhagen cans in the pockets of their Hawaiian shirts and rodeo photos inside the boat added to their credibility.

Cow hunters, they called themselves. That was persuasive, too. It's what Florida cowboys have always been, called because in a state that's mostly swamp, not open plains, more hunting than herding is required. They kept horses at a stable north of Labelle and hired out to cattle ranches, but sometimes used four-wheelers if they didn't have to rope or chase strays.

Brit and Joey—one not as tall up close, but both men lean with calluses and dark tans. Joey, who was at least six-four, had Seminole hair and high cheeks so appeared to be part Indian. Brit was more talkative, but even he preferred sentences of four or fewer words. *I believe so . . . That's what I've heard . . . Could be, ladies.* That's the way they spoke, reserved, but perceptive enough to read the situation correctly: *Two women, after a hard day, had come seeking a cold drink, but nothing more. Oh . . . and one of the women was a deputy sheriff, so watch it.*

Their easygoing manner changed, however, when I mentioned the Cadence house, then skipped ahead to ask, "Do you know anything about the vaccine company? Slew Vaccine and Herpetile? It's right next to the RV park."

Genial hospitality was displaced by an invisible door. The door could be opened or slammed, depending on how things progressed. Brit, suddenly cautious, asked, "What about it?"

I said, "Well, we got quite a scare tonight. I could have sworn we saw a big chimpanzee on the property. We were walking the road near the entrance and there it was."

Birdy leveled a look at me to remind me, *Chimps don't wear sandals.*

It didn't matter. Brit sidestepped the question anyway.

"Babcock Ranch is near there—ninety thousand acres. We do a lot of work for Babcock, but all they run is cattle and sod. No monkeys, I've ever seen."

I let him see I was amused by that. "But you know the place I'm talking about?"

"There's a Church of God down the road my folks used to attend. Or I could be confused about what you're asking."

Another evasion.

Joey tried to help out. "You grow up in Labelle, there's not a crossroads between here and Sebring we haven't rolled through a stop sign or two. But that's not the same as knowing a place. The name might be familiar. Were you hoping to see snakes instead of monkeys?" A slight smile when he asked but dead serious while he waited.

I said, "We expected not to have the fire scared out of us. I would like to speak with the owner, but not tonight—and not tomorrow either—if there are wild animals roaming around. A phone call would do. If you know his name, that would help."

Now they were suspicious. Brit, with a shrug, suggested I try the phone book, then asked his Seminole-looking partner, "What time's it getting to be?"

Ten minutes, tops, we'd been there. I hadn't even squeezed a lime into the weak vodka tonic I'd requested. I squeezed it now and, after an uneasy silence, asked, "Did I say something wrong?"

Joey resumed the role of a gentleman host. "Course you didn't. The Cadence place, there's a lot of stories we heard as kids. In high school, too. There's nothing wrong with stories, but what a man keeps on his property is his own business. Circus animals in Florida, there's nothing new about that around here"—his eyes found Birdy— "but maybe the laws have changed. Either way, it's none of *our* business."

Birdy's questioning look transitioned into surprise. I understood. He had just hinted that, yes, chimps— monkeys of some type—might be found at the area. He had also refused to snitch on neighbors, even though they lived thirty miles away.

Birdy got it, too. "We didn't go there to spy or arrest the guy. Hannah wants to meet the owner for business reasons."

Brit said, "Oh?"

"Yeah. She's . . . well, she's collecting stories about the old Cadence house. Like you said, it's got quite the history. There was a TV show a while back, they did a piece. Maybe you saw it. That's the sort of thing she's after, which means interviewing people who know the area. Like the stories Joey mentioned."

Voice flat, Brit said, "News reporters. Sure."

It was a question, not the statement, which Birdy decided to answer. "No, like I told you, I'm a sheriff's deputy. But I'm off duty, just tagging along. Hannah's the one who has to keep notes and do all the work." She turned, her eyes asking, *Should we go?*

We were sitting on the aft deck of the houseboat, an orange crate between Birdy and me, while the men leaned on the railing. I wasn't ready to leave, so I put down my drink and looked from Brit to Joey in a frank way. "Let's back up here. It was rude of me to pry and I apologize. I don't tolerate people snooping into my life. No reason you should either."

The modern cow hunters seemed to appreciate that. After a cue from his partner, Brit said, "Already forgotten."

That wasn't true, I could tell. "I'm not a journalist either. I want to be clear about why we're here. I am getting paid to collect stories about the Cadence property, but the job doesn't include being nosy about your neighbors."

I waited, expecting one of them to ask, *Paid why?* They didn't. The invisible door, I realized, had opened a tad, but the next move was up to me. I said, "Truth is, I inherited a part-time investigation agency from my uncle and this is"—I had to think back—"only the fifth job I've had that requires fieldwork. Mostly I'm a light tackle guide out of Sanibel and Captiva."

"A fishing guide?" Brit asked the question, but both were skeptical.

I said, "October's my slow time, which is why I'm doing this. Fly-fishing is what I prefer, but I'll take just about anything that comes along. Except for peak tarpon season. I'm fussy about clients during tarpon season. Last year, I booked more than two hundred full days, plus some casting lessons. And the Lauderdale boat show, two years in a row, I've done demonstrations for Sage fly rods."

They asked a few questions to test me, then asked a

few more because they were convinced it was true and they both enjoyed fishing.

"My uncle was a guide," I said. "It's a hard way to make a living. He told me, 'Some weeks, you think you'll get rich, but you never do. And some weeks, you think you'll starve, but you never do.' That's the way fishing is, so I keep the agency going on the side. I hope I've explained myself."

Brit, while reassessing Birdy's legs, said, "Yep."

Joey said it, too—"Yep"—but added, "We get tarpon up here sometimes. Bass, of course, and snook you wouldn't believe."

"I'll remember that when my bookings pick up. Right now, I'm focused on what I'm being paid to do. If you remember stories about the Cadence house, I'd sure like to hear them—unless it's too late, which I understand."

Joey, for some reason, gave me a private wink after catching my eye. Then said to Brit, "You're the one who loves to talk. Tell 'em some of the things we heard back in high school. Bore the ladies while they enjoy their drinks."

That broke the uneasiness. We became a chatty, sociable little group, although increasingly quiet while Brit told stories of murder and madness and a woman who could be heard weeping from the balcony on moonlit nights. I got out my spiral notebook and asked questions. But had the good sense not to pry when Brit, after eyeing me, said, "I'd be careful walking that area. There's an ol' boy there some say is slap-ass crazy—and not in no fun way. Monkeys would be tamer. If I knew it was fact, I'd say his name, but I try to avoid gossip."

Birdy assured him, "We can take care of ourselves," while I finished a drink I hadn't planned on finishing. It was nearly one when we stood to leave. They insisted on walking us back.

I hadn't anticipated that.

There is a natural pairing process when four people exit a dock: Birdy and Brit led. That was expected. I'm used to following extroverts in such situations. I felt no awkwardness until the pairings were further defined by the distance that separated our rooms, Birdy's room being three doors down from mine.

Brit followed when she turned left. I veered to the right and felt a sudden tension, figuring Joey would follow. So far, both had been respectful and polite, but these were two high-testosterone men. They rode horses and carried guns, as they'd told us, and often had to sleep rough with nothing but mosquito netting and the stars. Nice guys, true, but this was a rare weekend in town for them. The advantages of two single women sleeping in separate rooms had to be on their minds.

Pointless, my worrying. When I reached the door, I was alone. My escort was standing, lanky and long, in the moonlight, a discreet distance separating us. I felt relief at first, then it stung my ego. Three doors down, a latch clicked. Birdy, for our benefit, warned Brit, "Okay, but just for a minute," then they both disappeared into her room.

I had to say something. Inanities such as "Thanks for a nice evening" had already been exchanged, so I decided to soften my escort's disappointment. "I still have some work to do," I explained from the railing.

No need for that either. He had already started toward the dock but did manage to reply, "Good luck," over his shoulder and wave.

He's married or real, real tired. That's what my ego decided. Then reminded me, *You're not interested anyway.*

True enough. Even so, I felt a spark of girlish redemption when the man stopped, thought for a moment, then turned. "Do you drink coffee in the morning? I get up awful early, but you're welcome to drop by."

"Coffee or hot tea," I answered. "Either's fine, but how early's early?"

"Before sunrise. I gotta have my horse trailered by six." A pause before explaining, "Brit's off 'cause of his fire-starting class. So I'm working alone."

He sensed me smiling. "Is that funny?"

I said, "If Brit's learning how to build a fire, I suppose it is."

"The boy could use some help in that area, too. But this is a state certification thing. Ranches do a lot of controlled burns to clear out undergrowth. I could explain it to you over coffee."

I already knew about burn backs yet it made me feel better. "I appreciate that, Joey. If I'm up, I'll knock on the hull. Do you prefer Joey to Joe?"

"Either," he said, "but not Joseph. That was my father—according to Mom." Dark laughter while he added, "That man got around a lot, but never *stuck* around, if you know what I'm saying."

I replied, "I'm sorry to say I do."

"His last name was Egret. Like the bird. If I wasn't used to the darn thing, I'd think about changing."

"Joe Egret," I repeated softly.

"And you?"

"Plain Hannah Smith. Your name sounds familiar for some reason." It was true. Joey Egret . . . Joseph Egret . . . it was attached to some person or memory in the back of my mind.

"Same with Smith," Joey said. "Nothing plain about that name . . . *Captain* Hannah."

Laughter, and he was gone.

AT ONE-FIFTEEN A.M. I gave up trying to sleep and settled back with my great-uncle's journal. Written on the cover was:

> Receipts & Expenditures
> Benjamin F. Summerlin
> Master/Owner Vessels for Hire
> Widow's Son (40' Sharpie)
> Sodbuster (24' Dory)

The first entry that referenced the Civil War was twenty pages in:

13 August 1861 (Habana, Cuba): $3 silver for a new hat mine being stoled by a drunkard on Duval St. War—he says the dumb bastards finely dun it & the Greys has

kilt thousands at a place called Bull Run but the Blues
won Pensacola & kilt only 100. These numbers do not
seem right to me. I have been learning my Spanish
rather than risk Yankees for neighbors . . .

Captain Summerlin had been a candid, insightful
man. The book smelled of incense and smoke after sitting over the fireplace—chrysanthemum resin, Theo
claimed—a scent so strong it made me wince. Hopefully,
the thing would air. It had already benefited from the
dry heat. New pages could be separated with the help of
gentle pressure or a fingernail.

Not all, though.

Spiral notebook at my side, I started at the beginning,
after reinspecting the fresh cracks and newly dog-eared
pages. It was a leather-bound volume produced by Wilm-
ington Maritime of North Carolina. Designed for book-
keepers, not a seagoing cattleman who cared more about
numbers than spelling. Captain Summerlin had used it as
a ship's log and a notebook and also a place to doodle.
On the inside cover were clumsy attempts at birds, a dol-
phin, and what might have been a cow.

On the next pages were sketches of women. Much attention had been devoted to their hefty breasts and hair,
but no effort made to adorn them with clothing, let alone
the kindness of a nose that resembled a nose. They all
beamed back at me, however, with cheery, inviting smiles.
Two wore flowers where Eve would have worn them.

You lecherous old man, I thought yet smiled. The
sketches breathed life into my long-dead relative. He

wasn't old when he'd taken pen in hand—early thirties, which was my own age. He had found a way to entertain himself when he was alone. No harm in that. Better still, the sketches proved that indecent thoughts weren't new to our family's bloodline.

That alone provided some comfort after the thoughts *I* had been battling.

No wonder. I was lying in the chill of a wall air conditioner, wearing only a T-shirt, while Birdy and her cowboy guest did god-knows-what just three rooms away. The marine biologist was on my mind. Officially, we had stopped dating, but he was still an occasional late-night visitor—a *welcome* visitor—and it had been a while since he had come tapping at my door. He was out of the country or I might have called him to talk.

Restless didn't accurately describe my current state of mind.

I had no physical interest in the airline pilot or the attorney I'd been seeing. No commitments either. There was no reason in the world I shouldn't replace my sleeplessness with harmless conversation if, say, someone within walking distance was also awake—aboard the houseboat, for instance.

I was rationalizing. I knew it but didn't care.

So far, I had refused to allow myself to go to the window and check. Captain Summerlin's bawdy sketches, however, seemed to grant full permission. I laid the book aside and opened the curtains: a light was still on in an aft cabin of the boat.

Joe Egret. I thought the name softly, trying to nail the

connection. The window didn't provide sufficient motive, so I cracked the door and used my ears: trilling
frogs and wind cloaked the river's silence, but Garth
Brooks would have been easy enough to hear. There was
no music.

Damn . . . damn it to hell.

I felt free to say whatever I felt because I was alone.
Several sharp comments later, I decided, *Instead of complaining, do something productive.*

I returned to the journal.

Theo—or someone—had found the entry about the
missing hundred silver dollars. I was certain because the
book opened naturally to the place as if it had been but-
terflied open and mashed flat. That angered me, angered
me enough to push biologists and cow hunters out of my
mind.

Men—nothing but trouble.

Yes, they were, especially with none around to show
an interest in me.

I turned the air down, got back in bed, and tried to
put myself in Theo's place if he had, indeed, copied entries from the journal. The Civil War and the missing
silver dollars would have been his only interest. So I referenced dates and tried to create a bare-bones time line
that might point me to where Capt. Summerlin had scuttled his dory, then buried or hid or dumped a box of
coins.

Back and forth between the pages I went. First, I had
to work out the man's abbreviations and odd spellings.
At times, he inserted numbers for letters which seemed a

form of code. I soon gave up trying to figure that out. Then I focused on content. Between August 1861 and December 1862, only three of the forty-some entries mentioned the war. These were vague or sardonic references to shortages of salt and coffee, and a jab at the Confederate Navy's inability to take St. Augustine. Between 1863 and 1865, however, the war received more of my great-uncle's attention.

What had changed?'

The answer, I decided, was in a file on my laptop, which I had already summarized in longhand after stringing my hammock that afternoon:

From the war's start, Florida's 140,000 residents had mixed sympathies. The Union depended on locals to control Key West, Tampa, Pensacola, and Jacksonville. Only 14,000 Floridians joined the Confederate Army.

In 1863, the Battle of Vicksburg changed everything. It closed the Mississippi River as the South's main supply conduit. That left only Florida to provide cattle, salt, and other staples of war. Cattlemen and mariners, whatever their sympathies, were caught in the middle. The Union had to cut off supplies. That meant killing Florida's cattle where they stood and controlling waterways. It sparked the cattle wars and salt wars of inland Florida. Blood began to flow.

The Caloosahatchee River, which connected two oceans (aided by a short overland trail), was a major prize. The Union took Ft. Myers at the mouth of the

river. But control of Ft. Thompson—an outpost near
Labelle—varied. There was heavy fighting, especially
near Tallahassee, Jacksonville, and also at Lake City
where 10,000 troops engaged. After six hours of
fighting, 3,000 lay dead.

By 1864, the Cattle Wars had shifted and hardened
sympathies. Union sympathizers formed a unit called
the Florida Rangers. Those who sided with the South
formed the 1st Battalion "Cow Cavalry." Men without
politics but who owned boats and cattle could get rich
if they wanted. Or they could risk their lives by aiding a
cause they hadn't believed in from the start.

A few cow hunters and captains did both. Even for
them, times were hard. Beef on the hoof was valuable,
but worthless without salt to cure and preserve the
meat. In the end, it was salt, not gunpowder or gold,
that controlled the fates of Florida and the South.

After I'd reread the summary, I sat back, wondering
about the accuracy of what I'd written. *Salt* . . . Such a
common item. My eyes moved to the kitchenette, where
a plastic shaker sat on the counter. For me, a dollar would
buy a year's supply. Not during the Civil War. Salt was
mentioned in historic references, but it was Ben Summerlin's journal that proved its value in a world without re-
frigeration. Those same entries also provided clues to
where he might have scuttled his dory *Sodbuster*—and
why he was on the run from Union soldiers.

I yawned, glanced at the window, then buckled down
to copying the entries, but used ellipses to skip over

sentences that did not apply. When Capt. Summerlin omitted a location or date, I included a question mark. When his writing was illegible, I noted that, too. The code he'd used began to make sense: the first letter of a word followed either by hyphens that approximated the number of letters the word contained or sometimes by a number. Because of the man's poor spelling and his whims, translation required guesswork. S with three hyphens could mean *sail* or *seed* or *salt*, while S4 was a profanity—*shit*. I chose words that seemed to fit but added a question mark when dubious.

The temptation was to jump straight to the scuttling incident in December 1864. But I stayed on task, determined to finish entries from 1863 before turning out the light.

7 August, 1863 (Sanybel): The Blues has blowed up rum stills from Pensacola to Key Marco without no whimpering but has now burnt all saltworks along the coast. This will win them a bullet from many if a chance given. Shooting cattle aint won them no friends nether. Nor will their looting gerillas when they come ashore drunk . . .

21 August: Thank the Lord for green turtle meat cause of the fix we are in. Damnt if I know how to make salt & who does cause salt is like breathing air. Them that do know quick find the attention of the Blues & whatever dynamite needed. This is because saltworks is always built on the coast which is handy but aint smart. Men such as Captain Gatrell &

brothers has been studying this matter & we will meet soon.

12 September, 1863 (Sanybel): Yankees from Juseppa Island found salt pans on La Costa Beach & threatened hanging. Damnt spies is among us. I will never again run away after such sneaky business as this. Acourse the Yankee bastards accused me with nary proof. Prove this in court I told their snot nosed lieutenant. I am both judge & jury which you would do well to remember sir, he says. Addressing me as sir saved the snot nose a licking for I will not tolerate rude behavior from them sech as he. As to my expenses for them salt pans & other supplies, they are as follows . . .

24 February, 1864 (Key West Turtle Kralls): News is that pony horses is sellin for $2000 in Confederate paper but you kant buy a hogshead of salt for 10 times that. This was tolt to me by a Yankee officer at Ft. Taylor. He come aboard to inspect for contraband but cut things short after asking about the name Widow's Son. He had never seen a 40' sloop bilt of yeller pine & rigged with leeboards that can be razed in shoal water. I'll bet she's fast, he reckoned. I gave him the handshake & says, She'll float on fog & nary cut a mark.

It is a smart name I chose cause 18 demijohns of rum was stowed among cigars & molasses under the man's feet. But no salt. Even Habana aint got no salt.

15 April, 1864 (Old Tampa): Off loaded molasses & seen the worst with mine own eyes. People muddy as

hogs is digging up floors of meat houses & leaching salt that has leaked into the soil. They shovel dirt into hoppers & fire the mess with a blacksmiths furnace. Cheesecloth is dear so it is rank burlap they use as a filter after water boils. 50 people stand in line for a days filthy work & come away with a cup of something that grinds like sand in the teeth but has the tang of salt. Damnt this war & damnt an ocean that won't part with its salt unless you're a drowning man. Or own a furnace the size of a steam engine for rendering . . .

19 April (off Manatee River): Salt Famine! These are words I could not imagine 3 years ago but is now spoken in every port & it is time to act, by God. Gerilla fighting is what is left us. But how to bait a trap when bait is the prize? Gatrell & brothers has voted & not 1 black ball against . . .

Salt Famine! My great-uncle had underlined the phrase twice and added the only exclamation mark I'd found thus far. He had also underlined steam engine, but did not explain his reference to a vote.

What did it all mean?

In my notes, I underlined the same words, then stretched and went to the restroom before I resumed reading.

20 May, 1864 (Cattle Docks at Punta Rassa): Gatrell & brothers has packed axes & tackle & smudge pots cause we will have to cut our way through the skeeters. It aint far from the bridge but a long stretch

of river up [NAME BLOTTED] which runs north off the
Caloosahatchee. There be the place to boil salt or so I
recollect. As to my Cuban wife, not one word from her
as to me spending next Christmas in Habana . . .

His Cuban wife? I didn't know which thread to pursue. Many of the entries were new to me and this was the
first mention of a wife. But I was also riveted by Capt.
Summerlin's unfolding plan. Or what I perceived to be
his intent. He, a man named Gatrell, and Gatrell's brothers wanted to manufacture salt. They were seeking a
source inland which wouldn't be spotted by the Union
Army—and they were willing to fight to do it. This all
seemed evident.

Gradually, as I burrowed through the early months of
1864, I understood the seriousness of Ben Summerlin's
plans. I also began to suspect he *might* have something
to do with Civil War graves on the Cadence property. If
true, it was one of those weird bonding coincidences that
hinted at the orderliness of family destiny and fate.

Captain Summerlin and I had something else in common: he, too, had been worried about spies getting into
his journal. More and more, he protected himself by
scribbling out words—names, usually. Names of associates and also the name of the river he had visited that
summer, a river that fed into the Caloosahatchee from
the north, which couldn't be far from Labelle. It was
here, I suspected, that he, Capt. Gatrell, and Gatrell's
brothers were setting a trap or laying bait—I wasn't yet
certain.

Was it the Telegraph River? I combed some of the illegible entries for meaning but stopped when I heard voices outside. Birdy was saying good night to Brit. A minute later, she tapped at my door.

It was one forty-five in the morning, but she'd seen my light. I expected her to have a devilish smile on her face when I answered.

No . . . my friend the deputy sheriff was scared.

9

"You won't believe what he just told me," Birdy said, pushing her way into my room. "I'm surprised you're still up, but this is important."

"Who, Brit?"

"Of course. That's why I made him leave early."

"*Early?* Did he do something stupid?"

"Brit's not the problem." Birdy looked at the bed, saw the journal, then noticed her own bare feet and legs and the baggy Red Sox T-shirt she was wearing. The shirt was on backward, which we both realized at the same instant.

"Shit," she muttered.

I said, "At least you had some quality time."

"Not as much as I wanted. Are you ready for this?"

"I'd prefer not to hear details, if you don't mind. Well . . . maybe a few."

"Lock the door and use the dead bolt," she told me, then plopped down on the bed, full of nervous energy. "Remember when Brit mentioned a crazy person but he wouldn't tell us the name?"

I was fiddling with the lock, my back to her. "He's not a gossip. Good for him."

"It's Theo."

It was so late, I had trouble processing that. "What do you mean?"

"Theo—he's not really an archaeologist."

"What?" I spun around, then rechecked the dead bolt because of what she'd just said.

"Theo Ivanhoff. He's the neighbor Brit said is *slap-ass crazy.* Those were his exact words. Do you remember?"

"Is he sure?"

"You were right about him from the start. Or maybe he *is* an archaeologist—Brit doesn't really know him— but Theo has lived in the area his whole life. Not ten minutes ago, I happened to mention the name Ivanhoff. Talk about putting the brakes on a fun evening. Christ, Smithie, now we have to figure out how to handle it if Theo shows up for our tour in the morning. Or maybe we shouldn't go. Brit offered to come along, but he's got some sort of class in Port Charlotte."

I was still a little dazed. "You mean everything Theo said was a lie?"

"That's what he's known for. Pretending to be some-one he's not."

I said, "I didn't trust him. Right off, I didn't trust him, but this is hard to believe."

"I'm still working it out myself. The feds wouldn't hire someone local to do a a local archaeological survey. I know enough about government to know that. And remember the nasty way he talked about the head archaeologist? Brit says Theo has told people he's a heart surgeon and a commercial pilot, an Army Ranger, all kinds of crazy things. That's what he does—he's an egomaniac. Not dangerous, exactly. The locals put up with him and all. Theo's . . . *functional*, you know? Plus he's a druggie, the type who experiments. Brit was worried enough to set me straight."

"Experiments?"

"I'm not sure what he meant by that either."

I checked the door again before taking a seat. "Theo knows you're a deputy sheriff. It was stupid of him to lie to us." I looked at her. "I don't think he'll show. And if he does? Well, your Aunt Bunny owns the property. He'll be trespassing."

Birdy muttered, "What's stupid is me having the hots for a freak like that," then thought for a moment. "Trouble is, he didn't actually do anything illegal. Unless . . . unless he doesn't own that camper trailer. Brit only knows him by reputation, so I didn't bring that up. But the thing about owning a chimpanzee? That's a definite possibility—dangerous animals of some type. Maybe we can nail him for that."

I was lost again. "You're talking about the snake place?"

"Of course."

"I don't get it. Does Theo live nearby? The RV park

makes more sense. I picked up on that—everyone knows him there."

The look on Birdy's face: *Whoops, I left out something important.*

Yes, she had. Theo owned the RV park *and* the Slew Vaccine company. Actually, Theo's father owned it all, but Theo had grown up working there. His father was old now and seldom left the property.

"Theo won't admit what his family does," Birdy said. "That's another weird thing about him. Like he's ashamed. Remember the nasty things he said about anyone who would go into the vaccine business? But all the locals know the truth. The only thing Theo's an expert at is getting high and taking care of the RV park—and snakes."

"There was something creepy about him from the start. A snake handler, good lord."

"I should either start trusting your instincts, Hannah, or find myself a nice, dependable score buddy. This is no way to live. Seriously, I think my hormones are out of whack."

I asked, "A score-*what*?"

Birdy looked at me and waited until I said, *"Oh.* Well . . . I've been a little antsy myself."

"Never mind. Point is, I all but threw myself at a strung-out psycho or just an egomaniac—not much difference. Part of me doesn't ever want to see him again, but I also wouldn't mind cuffing the bastard and reading him his Miranda rights. So what do we do in the morning?"

We talked for a while longer before I said, "Your aunt is paying me to do a job. I think I should be there with a camera and hope Theo shows up. The attorney wants pictures of Civil War artifacts and bones. I don't mind going by myself if you're not comfortable."

Birdy said, "Not a chance. I'll carry my Glock in my purse."

BELTON MATÁS, standing outside the rope at the dig site, morning dew and an equipment bag at his feet, called to me, "If you're looking for *Dr.* Ivanhoff, he just left. Almost like he was avoiding you, the way he ran off." He motioned toward trees that sloped toward the river. A glimpse of Theo's shoulders was what I saw, a man in a hurry, head slouched low.

I replied with a careful, "Good morning, Belton," then waited until I was close enough to speak in a normal voice. "I've got some news about Theo—if you don't already know."

Matás knew, but not in a guilty way. I could tell by the way he smiled. "Did you figure it out yourself? Or did you run into the real archaeologist? That's what I did."

"Who?"

"Dr. Leslie Babbs from Louisville. Just now, he walked back to his truck for something. Don't worry—we're going to get our tour, but he's not enthusiastic." Then, confidentially, Belton added, "He strikes me as a fussy old codger for a man not even my age. But he's no fraud. I've read his papers—Leslie Babbs knows his Civil War."

I said, "Why didn't you tell me about Theo last night? That's why you got flustered when I mentioned his award, isn't it? If my friend Birdy hadn't found out—"

"Now, now," Belton said. "Delicate situations require delicacy. I didn't know your relationship with the young man. And I wasn't a hundred percent certain he was a fraud until this morning. Ivanhoff didn't expect Dr. Babbs to arrive until tomorrow. If you'd been twenty minutes earlier, you'd have witnessed quite a scene, Hannah."

I said, "I wish I could have seen his face."

"Maybe you will. Dr. Babbs called the police." Matás moved to peer around my shoulder. Birdy, carrying a shoulder bag, a sweater knotted around her waist, was walking toward us.

"She is the police," I informed him.

He chuckled at that, but then said, "For real?"

"A deputy sheriff. And she is seriously . . . Well, I'm not going to use the term, but she's already mad at Theo. And for good reason."

"Seriously pissed off, you think?" The man lifted his face to the sun and savored the possibilities. He looked rumpled, in his jacket with elbow patches and with his slacks tucked into his boots, but spry. I got the impression he hadn't slept well but was used to tolerating the aches and pains and rough mornings that accompanied old age.

"Yes, Belton," I replied, "she is."

He grinned. "Good," he said, then used his cell to call Carmelo and remind him, "Don't forget to buy gas.

We'll have two extra passengers in the boat this afternoon."

It wasn't until he'd hung up that he asked, "Do you still want to see where we found the bottles?"

"I brought mosquito spray and a change of clothes," I answered. I'd also brought Capt. Summerlin's journal. It was sealed in a watertight bag that added weight to my pack, but I wasn't going to leave it unattended again. Not while Theo and Lucia and her witch friends were still around.

LESLIE BABBS was a nice man but distracted and lacked energy—Belton was right about that—and he wasn't comfortable bending the rules. When I asked, "Would you mind if I stood here alone for a few minutes?" he tugged at his collar and said, "Sorry, the waiver you signed requires visitors to be accompanied. And I really do want to get this Ivanhoff matter settled."

He and Belton and Birdy had turned away from an excavation where human bones nested in dirt that had been carved with the delicacy of an artist's brush. No discernible order to the scattered vertebrae, several femurs that were scorched black by fire, and at least four partial skulls and one that appeared complete. That skull, one eye socket still buried, had a bullet hole in the forehead the size of a nickel. It lay near shards of tobacco pipes and brass uniform buttons and what might have been an iron hoop protruding from the soil—but also could have been the rim of a huge boiling cauldron.

For rendering salt? I wondered. What I had read in
Capt. Summerlin's journal last night, plus new entries I'd
deciphered this morning, had created an emotional tie
with men who had lived and died during desperate times.
These were the bones of many people, not just a few. At
least one had been shot, the skulls of the others were
crushed. Their remains appeared to have been burned,
then covered in a rush under only a few feet of soil. It was
unlikely that either prayers or respect had been offered.
That's one reason I wanted a private moment to stand
there alone and contemplate. A chance to sneak photos
was another. But I minded my manners and said, "Rules
are rules," and followed Dr. Babbs and my friends toward
the road.

The archaeologist had rushed us through a tour of
two of the three dig sites and we were done for the day.
No mention of ultraviolet light. And only a few remarks
about the significance of scorched bones or finding
Union buttons issued in 1864. He was more interested in
setting the record straight on his dealings with Theo
Ivanhoff. It was Theo who had alerted state archaeologists that he'd found a Civil War burial site on property
that would soon be developed if Tallahassee didn't act
fast. State officials had contacted the feds. The feds had
sent a one-person team: Leslie Babbs, a man of slight
build and nervous mannerisms who relied on volunteers
wherever his job sent him. Theo had volunteered full-
time.

"It's because we're so damn underfunded," Babbs said
to Birdy. He had opened up to her because she was a

deputy sheriff and because she had also witnessed Theo unlocking Dr. Babbs's camper, pretending it was his own. "I knew what Ivanhoff was right away—a digger, an artifact hound. We see them all the time in my field. But he is charming. And quite smart. He caught on fast when the GPR arrived, once I showed him the basics. That's something else that concerns me."

"Ground-penetrating radar," Birdy translated. She was in cop mode. Not making notes on paper but storing information in her head until on-duty officers arrived.

"Precisely. To a layperson, the unit resembles a lawn mower. You know, a machine on tires that you push. But that's where the resemblance ends. It uses microwaves to penetrate the subsurface—radar that sees through the ground, in other words. Three-dimensional tomographic images that can be saved on a laptop. Very expensive. He had no right to do what he did."

"The GPR is missing?" Birdy sounded hopeful.

"No, but he used it while I was away. It's a calibrated system that requires tuning, so the computer keeps track. I left last Monday—an illness in the family. Since then, he's put almost twenty hours on the thing."

Birdy, walking shoulder to shoulder, said, "That's a misdemeanor at best. And only if someone saw him—unless you gave Theo permission. You didn't give him permission to use the GPR, did you, Dr. Babbs? Or your RV?"

"No," he said. But tugged at his collar. "Well . . . not written permission anyway. That's not what worries me. Theo was along last week when I made a remarkable"—

he paused, aware that Belton, yet another amateur, was listening—"well, a rather interesting discovery. This was two days before I left for Louisville. Of course Theo expected me to say 'Grab a shovel and let's start digging,' but that's not the way archaeology works."

"You wanted more images, to do some core samples," Birdy suggested. Said it in a helpful way, but was, in fact, softening the man up.

"Precisely. No one was to touch that site until I got back. But . . ." He looked from Birdy to Belton, ignoring me, the quiet tagalong. "I don't think I should say anything more until the police get here." Hands in pockets, he shook his head. "My supervisors in D.C. will want answers."

Birdy said, "He dug up the spot, didn't he?"

Dr. Babbs grunted and ducked under the rope with signs that warned *Federal Antiquities Site. Access Prohibited.* "We're so damn underfunded," he said again. "Whoever handles this case, I hope you make sure that's mentioned in the report."

What had the ground-penetrating radar discovered? That was the obvious question, which Birdy, the smart cop, postponed by asking, "You said Theo is a digger, sort of a treasure hunter. How did you know?"

Spreading his arms to indicate this weedy field and trees, the old house screened by distance, he said, "Ask yourself how he happened to dig here in the first place. He wasn't looking for Civil War materials. For one thing, there's no record of a battle. And certainly no mention of a graveyard from that period. He doesn't own the property. No, he was trespassing. But that never stops people like him."

Belton, who hadn't said much, asked, "What do *you* think he was looking for?" In reply to Babbs's chilly stare, he attempted to explain, "When you get to be my age, even obvious answers aren't obvious. Sorry if I missed something."

Dr. Babbs thawed slightly. "Theo knows next to nothing about methodology, but he has a working knowledge of excavation techniques—sizes of screening mesh, that sort of thing. And he's well versed in Florida history, I'll give him that. That told me he's a digger—a pot hunter, most likely. Right away, I was on my guard."

Birdy asked, "Are there pre-Columbian archaeologies in the area?" Her articulate question earned a nod of respect.

"I hope you're assigned to this case. You seem to know something about the discipline. But, no . . . there are no indigenous sites that I know of . . . How does that work? Who decides which officer is assigned to this case?"

"I'll talk to my sergeant, then whoever is in charge would have to request me. But back to Theo's behavior . . ."

"I didn't trust that man from the start. How many people in their late twenties volunteer full-time to do anything? I knew for sure when we were having a drink one night in my RV and out of the blue he brings up some old-time bank robber who buried a sack of money.

At first I was relieved. It seemed to explain how he'd stumbled onto a Civil War archaeology. I should have known better."

Birdy and I considered that, eyes locked, before she asked, "You think he was lying?"

"He played me for a fool." Babbs had retrieved his briefcase from under a tree and was stowing the waivers we had signed. "That's off the record, of course."

"I'm not on duty, Dr. Babbs. Anything official I write I'll ask you to make deletions or additions before I submit it. That's not procedure, but I respect the position you're in. Why are you so sure Theo was lying?"

The man appeared relieved. He asked who his department should contact to request Deputy Liberty Tupplemeyer by name. Then stored her business card away before he answered, "Because his story was so unbelievable—again, in hindsight. He claimed the bank robber—the name will come to me—that he was a direct descendant. That he—Theo, I'm saying—was a direct descendant. The clear implication was that that somehow made him the rightful heir to stolen money that was buried here"—another gesture to the field—"or on the other side of the river. Which is ridiculous, when you think about it."

"How much?"

"How much money? Wait—it gets stranger. Then Theo came right out and said he'd give me ten percent if I helped him find it. He wanted to use the GPR, in other words. Something like thirty-five thousand dollars in silver when it was stolen back during Prohibition days.

Treasure hunters, they always have some bizarre story. I didn't take him seriously."

Belton smiled, "Ten percent? He's certainly a cheap bastard."

Dr. Babbs didn't see the humor. "It made him seem harmless. With Civil War diggers, it's different. They're always after a payroll in gold that sank. Or was thrown overboard—that's the most popular story in Florida. I don't know what Theo's true intent is, but he's not going to make a member of the science academy look like a fool and get away with it."

Birdy saw that as her opening but prefaced it by saying the property owner's attorney had mentioned a bank robber from the 1930s. "I believe in being up front with the facts, Dr. Babbs."

"Call me Leslie," he said. "That's good news, actually. Knowing there's a kernel of truth might help when I have to explain this mess later."

Birdy decided it was time. "Okay, then. Now . . . *Leslie*, do you mind showing me where Theo did this unauthorized dig? If he stole something, depending on the value, we might get a felony charge."

"Just you?" The archaeologist made his meaning clear by looking from Belton to me.

Birdy said, "That's up to Hannah. I want to pursue this, but we had plans for later." She sought me for permission.

The whole time, I'd been wondering about Dr. Babbs and his credibility. I didn't doubt his credentials, but was disturbed by how easily he'd been taken in. His story didn't make sense. Trust Theo because he was hunting stolen money, not Civil War treasure? There had to be another reason. Birdy might find out.

"We'll meet for dinner later," I told her, then partnered up with Belton while Birdy and the archaeologist continued to talk.

Dr. Babbs, as we walked away, said, "Know what's sad? That young man had everything going for him. He was a decorated Army Ranger and a commercial pilot. Did you know that? But then got laid off. Post-traumatic stress syndrome, he said. But I think drugs might be an issue."

Birdy, managing to keep a straight face, replied, "Really?"

"Do a background check on him, that's what I suggest. The night we had cocktails? I might have gotten a little carried away, I admit it. But if Theo claims . . ."

I didn't hear the rest, but did hear Birdy respond, *"Really?"*

10

A MILE SOUTH OF THE OLD RAILROAD BRIDGE, where cypress and mimosa trees draped moss over the river, Belton switched places so I could see the boat's sonar screen. Carmelo, at the wheel, jabbed a finger and said, "*Fish*," while I shaded my eyes.

Cartoonish fish icons, which always make me wince, appeared in pixelated yellow around a red rectangular object. The river bottom had varied in shades from white to gray in the shallows, but here, in this shaded oxbow where depth dropped to fourteen feet, it was black.

"Hard bottom," I told Belton.

"I think it could be a sunken boat," he said, meaning whatever was below us. "Or the remains of a dock. But wouldn't that have rotted away years ago?"

"Floated away, more likely," I said, then asked something I'd been wanting to ask. "You said you did a lot of research. Was this always called Telegraph River? I can't find it on old maps." I was thinking of Capt. Summerlin's journal. In summer of 1864, he and friends had explored a north branch off the Caloosahatchee in the twenty-five-foot dory *Sodbuster.* Summerlin's concern about spies had caused him to scribble out the tributary's name. When the page was held up to a light, however, I could make out four letters—JOPO. Possibly JOPE, or even TOPE, because Summerlin's old-time penmanship placed triangular stems on some letters. I was tempted to get the journal from my backpack and show Belton but wasn't ready to risk that quite yet.

Belton replied, "That's because the river's not on maps before 1900. Not named, I mean. The telegraph service to . . . well, it's a town north of here . . . wasn't completed until the 1880s."

"Arcadia?" I suggested.

"Yes . . . No . . . Wait, I can't remember for certain. I used to have a good memory, but I lose things so quickly now." He told Carmelo to swing the boat around so we could have another look at the bottom, annoyed with himself. He used a handkerchief to wipe his face. Soon the rectangular object reappeared, along with cartoonish fish icons. "A failing memory is bad enough," he said, "but when your body falls apart, it's downright humiliating—especially when I'm with a beautiful woman." He looked at me to see how that was accepted.

I laughed. "Stop flirting and tell me why you think it's a boat."

He put his hand on my shoulder to study the sonar

but removed it when he stood. "I'm going to trust you with something—but not right now. Okay?"

"A secret?"

He motioned me away from the console and spoke into my ear. "Just between us. Carmelo doesn't know and I don't trust him as much as you think. I've got to be careful."

I said, "I think you're still flirting. If you are, it's a pretty good approach."

He smiled, a man with bright blue eyes who had been muscular and good-looking in his day. "Let's just say I hope it's a boat. Wouldn't that be fun? I wish to heavens I was a better diver—or not so damn old." He sounded wistful.

Carmelo, riveted to the screen, repeated, "Lots of fish. You want the girl to fish, Mr. Matás?"

Three times he'd asked that question over the engine noise but this time seemed to think it was a fresh idea now that we were idling in water that was black as oil but clear when I looked straight down if the sunlight hit it just right.

"No, thanks," I told Carmelo, then reconsidered. I had never met a simpleminded person who owned an expensive red Bass Cat skiff outfitted with dual electric trolling motors that could pull the boat along as fast as some gas engines. It crossed my mind that a captain didn't have to be smart as long as he produced results. I didn't want to believe that. If I was right, Carmelo was either acting or the boat did not belong to him. As a test, I asked, "What kind of fish are we talking about?"

"Big-assed." Carmelo laughed. "See?" He pointed to the fish icons that stacked and rematerialized like targets in a video game.

Had our guide said *big-assed* or *big bass*? I gave him the benefit of the doubt. "Bass are fun on top of water plugs. Not that I've caught many. Is it best to anchor? Or do you use the trolling motors and cast into eddies?"

"Yes," Carmelo replied.

Belton chuckled at that. "We'll go ashore same place as yesterday." He pointed. On the east bank, two jagged pilings, black as dinosaur teeth, showed where there had been a pier. Presumably, it had serviced the homestead I'd seen in photos. The pilings were only a few boat lengths upriver from the sunken object.

I remarked, "If a boat sunk at the dock, it could have drifted down. You might be right. But, Belton, this water's not that deep. You don't need tanks to find out, just a mask and fins. Doesn't Carmelo free-dive?"

Carmelo, who had a tough-guy face to begin with, became positively fierce. "Nope. Ain't gonna swim. Don't tell me again."

I said, "I wasn't ordering you, it was a question. Are there gators around?" I hadn't seen any, but there had to be a reason.

Belton, getting impatient, said to Carmelo, "I'll take the wheel. Why don't you untangle some of those ropes so we can tie up?"

Carmelo did, but I heard him mutter, "Girl . . . stick your hand in that water, you find out."

. . .

AFTER EXPLORING the bricks and boards and fences of
a homesteader's vanished dream, I did it—stuck my hand
in the river. I am too comfortable outdoors to be spooked
by the power of suggestion, but it doesn't hurt to be
careful. First, I stirred the water with a stick. It was black
as a winter night, clear as gel.

I looked around. No alligators . . . no snakes. Bull
sharks liked to swim up rivers, but they had those car-
toon fish to eat if they were after food. Same with pira-
nhas, if some deranged person had smuggled them
in—Theo came to mind. I pushed my sleeve up and made
some false attempts, then decided, *If someone's watching,
they'll think you've lost your mind. Just do it.*

I did. Plunged my arm deep, but just for a moment.
Then checked the path leading to the fallen homestead. I
had left Belton there with Carmelo, Carmelo knee-deep
in muck searching for bottles in a cistern that did indeed resemble a crypt. Most of the cistern's roof had
fallen in, the whitewash had faded. But a graceful brick
arch remained to disprove any thoughts of sloppy work
or ignorance.

A competent bricklayer had left his mark on this lonely
place.

That meshed with something I'd read in the journal.
The entry had motivated me to return to the boat and
refresh my memory as well as to test the water. But I
couldn't open my backpack until I was alone, so I had

roamed the property enjoying a polite interval of time. Holding Belton's elbow, I had steadied him while we paced the distance from the chimney to the first fencerow. From the way the earth undulated, he guessed this quarter-acre patch had once been a garden. I asked, "What about salt pans?" Threw it out there in a breezy way to see how this amateur expert reacted.

All he said was, "Salt was hard to come by in those days. But you can't make salt from a freshwater river."

Was he right? That was something else I wanted to check privately. My biologist friend and sometimes lover had several types of salinity meters in his lab. But my lips would serve almost as well, as would the knowledge that saltwater is heavier than fresh so it sinks to the bottom.

Again, Capt. Summerlin's journal had fired my curiosity.

As I moved around the boat, I heard Carmelo yell out a complaint or celebrate a discovery, his voice garbled by distance. Closer, somewhere inland, I heard branches cracking—the clumsy weight of an armadillo or feral hog, I assumed. I pushed my sleeves higher, leaned off the boat, and breached the surface with both hands. Water was cool, a slick, weightless feel, then I tasted it— fresh, but a hint of brine. That was encouraging.

I decided to find out if it was saltier on the bottom.

With my help, Carmelo had tied the boat's bow to a tree after dropping a stern anchor. I hauled the anchor, sloshed the flukes clean, then opened my backpack in the hopes of finding something useful. Along with the journal, I had things I carry on my own boat in case I break down. There were extra clothes, bug spray, a sewing kit, flares and sunscreen, but nothing that could be used to collect water from the river's deepest spot.

Finally I chose an empty Coors bottle from the Igloo and used fishing line to clove-hitch it to the yoke of the anchor. I wanted the bottle to sink fast. Air pressure, I hoped, would prevent it from filling until it got to the bottom.

When the bottle was secure, I pushed the boat away from the tree and waited for the line to pull taut. The drop-off was many yards astern. Too far to heave a ten-pound anchor. I realized I'd have to balance myself on the transom and use the engine as a knee brace to add distance when I tossed the thing. That was risky. So, before I went to work, I placed my phone on the console, along with my backpack and the journal, which I'd removed from its watertight bag—and couldn't help reading a few passages before getting my hands wet.

It was a wise precaution. My first throw, I stepped on the anchor line. The next try, I checked my feet, got a good pendulum motion going, then heaved the anchor hard. Too hard. The engine, instead of supporting my weight, gave way, spinning to the left, and I went overboard. It is possible I hollered *"Damn!"* just before I hit the water.

But no harm done. I was wearing jeans, a long-sleeved blouse, and Nikes, not boat shoes, because I knew we'd be hiking. Fishing guides are used to soggy clothing. I'd also brought a towel. So I was smiling at my clumsiness when I surfaced. I combed hair out of my face and decided to enjoy the situation. It had been hot in the stillness of the homestead's wreckage and the water was cool. So I sculled toward the middle of the river, seeing mimosa trees, dragonflies, the reflection of a passing egret from a duck's perspective. Several hard green fruit that resembled apples, too, afloat like golf balls, and a flotilla of seedpods, long and brown. They parted at my approach. I continued on, only my eyes and nose, periscope-like, breaching the surface.

Thankfully, my ears weren't submerged—which is why the sound of breaking branches caught my attention again. I listened briefly, gauging the size and weight, and decided I'd been wrong about the armadillo or some other small animal. Something big was pushing its way through the brush . . . not fast, but definitely headed my way.

I swung my legs around and sculled toward the boat, all senses alert. If it was a feral hog, normally no problem. I had once been confronted by a big boar in attack mode, however, and some memories are forever fresh. My real fear was that a large gator had gone inland for some sun and was now plowing its way back to the river for an afternoon meal.

I sculled faster. The temptation was to stretch out and swim hard. In high school—not a pleasant period in my life—my happiest moments were playing clarinet in the band and being on the varsity swim team. Breaststroke was my specialty, but I can flat-out fly doing freestyle, too. Trouble was, if I swam, whatever was approaching might enter the water unseen. I found the prospect unsettling. Better to know what was coming and deal with it.

And that's exactly what I had to do. Now bushes were moving along the path that led to the old homestead, the heavy snap of branches still clumsy but moving faster and with purpose. Finally I understood: the splash of me hitting the water had traveled through the trees. Something had heard me and was on its way to investigate. I might make it to the boat first, but whatever it was would be right there waiting.

To hell with caution. I swam—long, strong strokes— my clothes a dragging weight, my shoes useless as fins. Then my hands were on the boat's transom, but my foot somehow snagged the anchor line. I fell back in. Bubbles boiled around my eyes. I was terrified of what might grab me from beneath—the water so black and clear. I resurfaced with a yelp and lunged for the boat again. This time I made it, floundered up over the transom and skidded like a wounded seal.

I was winded but immediately looked up—and there was Belton Matás. He was grinning but had a concerned look on his face. "You should have told me you were going in for a swim. Isn't there something called the buddy system?" He removed his glasses and squinted. "Are you all right?"

There was no recovering my poise. That had vanished when fear took control. "Oh, Belton, some expert I am. I fell in. Then I thought you were a . . . I don't know what I thought. My lord, I almost never scream like that." I sat up and pulled my blouse away from my chest—still prim and proper despite everything else.

The man said, "I didn't hear a scream—I assumed you were having fun. In fact, I was going to ask . . . Well, never mind."

"Fun?"

"Yes, you made a sort of laughing sound. That's what I heard anyway."

"Well . . . good . . . Ask me what?"

"Just an idea I had because you were already in the water. And swim beautifully. Are you hurt?"

I got up and took a peek downward to confirm my wheat-colored blouse wasn't see-through. I still had my shoes, too. "I'm used to bruises from falling over my feet. I *was* enjoying myself until I heard you coming through the bushes . . . And after what Carmelo said about the water—"

"Carmelo? He can't swim, doubt if he even showers. Watch your balance . . ." Belton stepped aboard and reached for the console to steady himself. I realized he would see the journal sticking out from beneath the towel.

He did but said, "Do you want this?" meaning the towel, which he handed me, his eyes lingering momentarily on the leather-bound volume. It could have been one of those awkward moments but wasn't. The gentleman from Richmond, Virginia, behaved like a gentleman.

I said, "What did you want to ask me?"

"Well, at the time it seemed like a good idea. Wait . . ."

He signaled for my attention with an index finger. Turned, opened a forward hatch, then faced me, holding a mesh dive bag that looked new. Inside were a mask and snorkel, still in plastic, and cheap adjustable swim fins. "I bought these yesterday—no idea Carmelo is scared of the water. Then, when I saw what a good swimmer you are, well . . ." A humorous shrug.

I said, "You want me to see what's down there, don't you?"

"No. Well, unless you really *want* to."

I had to think about it. Normally, I would have been eager. From the journal entries I'd read that morning, I knew that Ben Summerlin might have traveled this very river. If true, there was a chance he had scuttled his dory somewhere along its length. Which meant there was a *remote* possibility that Belton had found my great-great-uncle's boat—astronomical odds, but why not take a look?

My bout of wild panic, that's why. But I was feeling better, more sheepish than suffering any real fear of the river. Something else: I had an ulterior motive. The beer bottle . . . it was still clove-hitched to the anchor. To explain honestly, I would have to admit concealing information from a man who had been open and kind to me. Better to nab the bottle while underwater and broach the subject of the journal later.

Using the towel, I scrubbed at my hair. "I'd like to see what's down there myself—if you're willing to watch for alligators. And if the mask fits. I can check without going in."

I didn't expect the look of gratitude on the man's face. "I'll get Carmelo. It'll be safer with a younger set of eyes. You are a valuable young lady, Hannah."

He placed the mask and snorkel within reach and moved quickly, for a man his age, up the path toward the homestead.

WHILE I WAITED, I tested the mask, but only after retrieving the beer bottle and touching a finger to the water, then my lips.

Very salty.

My concerns vanished. Suddenly, the exact wording of an entry Capt. Summerlin had made in the summer of 1864 was important enough to sneak another look. I listened for noise, then opened both the journal and my notebook, hurrying so I could cross-reference a few entries before Belton and Carmelo returned.

9 June, 1864 (aboard Sodbuster): The Blues is camped at Ft. Myers & Labelle which aint much of a fort but they do have a supply shed & a brace of 4" canon that can shoot acrosst bank to bank. What they aint got is a shoal draft dory, nor a knowledge of the creek that branches north of Labelle & [NEXT FIVE LINES BLOTTED].

Hmm . . . the entry referenced the right boat and possibly the right river, but it was not the passage I was after. I continued reading.

12 July, 1864 (Old Tampa): Deserters & runaways of
the roughest sort have slipped into Florida like filth
from a honey bucket. The railroad yard smelt like shit
too & aint no place for a ships master but it is wear
sutlers deal Yankee silver for cattle. The Frenchman I
was to met did not show & I fear it aint true he owns a
locomotive nor even the boiler what sunk in the [NAME
BLOTTED]. I got more faith in the Cubans I will meet
come morn if this weather breaks . . .

Wrong entry again. But I read it all because my great-
uncle's sudden interest in trains and boilers seemed key
to a bigger story. The same was true of an entry made in
the spring of that year.

1 September, 1864 (Key West, Hawks Channel):
Loaded aboard is 36 mixed longhorn @ $6 silver per
head but not one hogshead of beef or mullet cause of
this situation. The victuallers in Habana will be sore
disappointed but the beef will turn a pretty profit &
guarantee the money required. On the Sunday before
Christmas we are promised to deliver 100 silver dollars
which aint easy considering the cost of what follows in
expenses . . .

Ben Summerlin had a plan. His plan included a train
or a boiler, or both, and a river that fed into the Caloosahatchee from the north. He had sailed to Cuba to fi-
nance the project.

That made sense. To make salt for thousands of

people, a boiler the size of a train's might be required. But where was the reference that tied things together? Finally I found it by backtracking, a fragment from an illegible entry made earlier in 1864 I had failed to note in my time line.

27 May (Punta Rassa): . . . and what I tolt Gatrell & brothers they [NEXT FOUR LINES SMEARED] . . . that the bridge aint to far. A salt spring is there neath the surface owned by a Spaniard who is expert at [SMEARED OR BLOTTED] a master of trowel & square so this man is likely [ILLEGIBLE].

There! My subconscious had put it together, but here was written proof. The *Spaniard* was the Brazilian who had planted timber before selling the property to Charles Cadence. Proof that a master bricklayer had lived at this spot was the cistern I had seen only minutes ago. And I had just tasted the *salt spring . . . neath the surface* with my lips.

Additional proof: remains of a railroad bridge were only a mile from where I sat. I wasn't certain the bridge had existed in the 1860s, but it might have. That was good enough for me. Ben Summerlin had guarded this river's name, but, even if he hadn't, the name had changed since Civil War days.

It all fit.

I felt sure of it. And, because I was convinced, I knew something else: whatever had sunk here wasn't my great-uncle's lost dory. Journal entries from late 1864 weren't as badly damaged, so I knew from skipping ahead that he'd scuttled the dory while being chased by Union soldiers. Maybe the soldiers had discovered him making salt. Or maybe he had used salt as a ruse to spring a trap. The journal had yet to reveal the whole story, but Ben Summerlin was no fool. He wouldn't have fled *upriver*—there was no escape in the cypress swamps and palmettos to the north. And he wouldn't have scuttled his boat so close to another man's dock.

Whatever the sonar unit had found on the bottom was too near the old homestead to be my great-uncle's boat. In a way, I was disappointed. On the other hand, *Sodbuster* was somewhere on this river, still waiting to be found.

"We're coming, Hannah dear!"

Belton's voice reached me from the undergrowth. I closed the journal and slipped both books into my bag. I felt a twinge of guilt for being sneaky but then decided when the timing was right I would lay out the whole story, journal, notes, and all, for Belton to see. Who better to help than a retired Civil War expert with time on his hands and who was trustworthy?

But not Carmelo. There was something wrong about the man that had nothing to do with his weak intellect—or his simpleton act. I would have to feel out Belton's loyalty before I moved ahead.

When the two men appeared on the bank, I had the mask pressed to my face, but it fell away—no suction to hold it in place.

"How's it fit?"

I said, "It'll be okay, I think."

That was a kindness. If a mask doesn't cling to your face, it will leak. I knew it but was unconcerned. Only two or three shallow dives would be needed for me to find out what was on the bottom. So I wouldn't bother with the cheap strap-on fins either. But I would use the snorkel.

No . . . No, I wouldn't. The tube leaked, which I discovered while breaststroking toward the deepest part of the river, an oxbow shaded by mimosas. So I swam back and tossed the thing into the boat. Unfortunately, Carmelo was busy netting seedpods, for some reason, and the snorkel hit him squarely in the forehead.

Belton laughed.

Carmelo did not. His tough-guy face turned fierce. "You gonna get burnt, girl," he said as if he wanted only me to hear. "You'll see."

11

It took several dives to locate the right spot, but the first confirmed I was diving into a salt spring. Only a body length underwater, there was an abrupt temperature change. It was like swimming into a refrigerated vault—a sealed vault, because visibility changed from fair to poor.

A leaking mask added to my discomfort. As I neared the bottom, pressure increased, temperature dropped, and water flooded in. Salinity was so strong, it hurt my eyes. Is that what Carmelo had meant by *You're gonna get burnt, girl*?

Unlikely. A man who can't swim is a poor adviser when it comes to thermoclines.

I surfaced, stripped the mask off, and fiddled with the straps while Belton called, "What did you see?"

"Use your hands and steer me toward the wreck," I answered. "It gets murky near the bottom."

He directed me away from the dock and farther downriver. "If that doesn't work, we'll use the fish finder and drop a buoy or something."

I said, "You watch for gators. Carmelo, I want you to watch, too. This shouldn't take long."

Yes, it should have been easy, but, three tries later, all I'd found was a bottle encrusted with a white coating— salt.

"Save it," Belton called, "or swim it to me."

I jammed the bottle in my pocket and said, "I'm not coming back until I find the darn thing."

That was nearly true.

I took several deep breaths and knifed downward. So far, I had done quick bounce dives. This time, when I got to the bottom, I leveled out and pulled myself downriver, feeling my way through the murk. Mussel shells, waterlogged seedpods, everywhere . . . Then my shoulder banged into something that had an elastic give to it like a rope. It startled me. I couldn't help but grunt in surprise.

Automatically, I started up. If I hadn't been taught to extend my hand when surfacing, my head would have collided with something that, inexplicably, wouldn't allow me to surface. It was a black mass that raced toward my mask moments after my fingers made contact. I exhaled another grunt, accompanied by bubbles, but stayed calm. I reminded myself I was in less than ten feet of water. Find a way around the object, I would be on the surface within moments.

It wasn't that easy. I used both hands to push myself clear, but the black mass stayed with me. It seemed to be long and tubular when my face banged into what felt like a metal wall. I turned, tried the opposite side, and banged into another wall. Definitely metal. When I spun and hit what felt like a steel bar, I became disoriented.

A drainage culvert, I thought. *Someone dumped a drain pipe.*

But how in the world had I managed to thread my way into a pipe? And why was it suspended several feet off the bottom?

They used an anchor, I reasoned. *That's why it won't budge.*

Impossible. Drain culverts don't float. Even thinking such an absurdity proved that fear had stunted my ability to reason. Something that didn't require analysis was obvious: I would drown if I didn't find a way out. The metal bar was the only constant in a blind world that was suffocating me. I grabbed it and felt the structure move. That provided another absurd hope—maybe I could push it to the surface, then escape.

No. My head banged against a ceiling while the object strained against its tether, the structure buoyant enough to pivot. I kicked and pulled with my free hand, but the thing refused to ascend more than a few inches. My god . . . was I going to die like this? I was trapped from above—yet my lower body remained unobstructed.

A final option came into my mind: *If you can't go forward, reverse your course.*

The idea was reasonable, even though I was beyond reason. My heart pounded, burning oxygen, and I was nearly out of air. With exaggerated calm, I did it—pushed toward the bottom, then scrabbled backward until I felt the rope, or whatever it was, graze my leg.

So far, so good. I clamped my fingers around the thing—yes, a slimy length of rope. I followed it upward and soon my eyes fixated on an onyx glow that blessedly, blessedly, I knew was sunlight.

I had escaped. But escaped what?

Fortified by my new freedom, I indulged myself by confirming what the rope was attached to; actually paused to note a few details. Only then did I rocket to the surface and inhale big, balmy, wonderful gulps of October air.

Belton had started the engine—how had I not heard a 225-horsepower outboard fire up? It didn't matter. I was alive. And only midway through another lazy, uneventful day in Florida. I felt like laughing but didn't. It was because of the gentlemen rushing to my rescue. Belton's face was white with a fixed look of terror until he spotted me. Then he visibly sagged and let Carmelo take the wheel.

I shouted, "Is Belton okay?"

Carmelo, standing with his hard, stunted eyes fixed on me, tapped the throttle forward and didn't respond.

I watched for a moment, then yelled, "Slow down," because the boat was already so close, I would soon disappear under the bow. Run me over, I'd be lucky to escape the skeg or spinning propeller.

Carmelo didn't seem to hear. I shouted again: "Put the engine in neutral!" That's when a horrible thought entered my head: Carmelo had done something to Belton. Now he was coming for me. He wanted to hurt me, perhaps kill me, for no other reason than I had whapped him in the face with a plastic snorkel.

But I was wrong—half wrong, at least—because Belton rematerialized at the wheel and switched the engine off while the stern swung so I could climb aboard. His coloring was still bad, but he showed some life by scolding me. "Young lady, you stayed under way too damn long. My heart can't take that sort of thing."

With a weak smile, he tried to make light of the comment, but what he had said was true and I knew it. That changed everything. I wanted to confront Carmelo and demand an explanation, but I couldn't risk more upset. So I, too, made light of what had happened. I replied, "I must have lost track of time. But I know what's down there now." I tossed the mask into the boat and got my rump on the transom.

From the way Belton rambled on about how worried he'd been, I feared he actually had suffered a stroke, but then he regained his composure. "Carmelo—help the lady up and into a dry towel. I think a cup of that red wine is in order. Hannah, then and only then can you reveal the mystery to the old fool who should have never let you dive to begin with. My god, girl, I stopped keeping track at ninety seconds."

Only ninety? I felt like I'd been trapped underwater for five minutes—and a full minute is a long dive for me. But I only laughed and waited until I was aboard to say, "Don't get your hopes up, Belton. It's not a boat from the Civil War."

I expected a theatrical groan of disappointment. Instead, for an instant, his old blue eyes glittered with the focus of a younger man. It was those eyes that bore into me when he responded, "Really? That's too bad. Then I suppose it's one of these hopped-up bass boats. Or a motorboat. Probably stolen, so we'll make a pile when we tell the insurance company." A joke, but something cold at the source of it.

"Not even close," I said.

His expression asked, *Are you sure?*

I nodded. "What's down there is—"

Belton interrupted, "Not until you're seated with a towel. I can wait for the big news."

His indifference was a lie, I sensed that. He'd already told me he didn't trust Carmelo, but this was different. Something had happened, an incident or reckoning that had taken place recently. So I made a few glib remarks while I dried my hair and sought Belton's eyes for an explanation. Within seconds, though, those youthful eyes faded into the face of an eighty-year-old man who had suffered a fright.

He asked, "Didn't you say you brought a change of clothes? You can't stay in those wet things. Carmelo"—Belton, from his chair, was giving orders again—"we will stand with eyes to the front while Hannah changes. And if you so much as peek, I will have you arrested and thrown into prison for the rest of your unnatural life." An old man's laughter should have dulled the sharpness of his words but it didn't.

If it was an act, Carmelo accepted it. Or pretended to. He handed me an inch of wine in a plastic cup and said, "Right away, Mr. Matás," but started the boat as if he'd misunderstood.

Now I didn't know what to do. What I had found anchored to the bottom wasn't shocking, but it was unusual. Was there a reason he didn't want Carmelo to know?

Belton's behavior became more confusing when he made the decision for me. "Shut off that damn engine. Maybe Hannah wants to take another look before she tells me. Or"—he remembered his recent offer—"would you rather change into dry clothes and forget it?"

I decided to share a half-truth. "It was a big chunk of pipe," I said. "That's what it looked like. But it must have flotation because it's anchored about six feet off the bottom or maybe snagged on something. I banged into it as I was surfacing."

Carmelo busied himself getting a beer from the cooler, but Belton was concerned. "Did you hit your head? Let me see."

I was thinking about what I'd actually found: a canoe—an aluminum canoe—old with dents. "No, it couldn't have snagged," I amended. "It's floating parallel to the bottom, so there has to be at least two anchors. Which means someone sunk it intentionally."

"A chunk of drainage pipe? That makes no sense

whatsoever." Finally Belton looked at me long enough to understand what I was doing. "On the other hand . . . I guess it could be some kind of fish trap or turtle trap, possibly. Damn bad luck, it not being a boat."

I said, "Fish collect around structure, don't they, Carmelo?"

Our guide was smart enough to know drainage culverts don't float. Even so, he replied, "Lots of junk in this river."

I looked toward the spot where seedpods and twigs were gathering. "One thing's for sure, it's not worth going back in the water."

Belton picked up on that, too, and changed the subject. "What about that bottle you found? It looked like it was covered with coral. But not in fresh water, I wouldn't think."

The bottle was gone, but I patted my pockets anyway. I didn't mention the salt spring either. All I said was, "Sorry." That's how uneasy I felt.

"Then the two of us should drown our sorrows in wine." He touched a plastic cup to mine. "One of these days I'll make a major archaeological discovery—but not here, I'm afraid. And not today."

"You don't want to come back here no more, Mr. Matás?" Carmelo was testing for something else. I sensed that, too.

The older man shook his head. "We didn't find any more unbroken bottles either. The whole darn day is a bust—but thank god Hannah wasn't hurt. All for a lousy piece of junked pipe."

We made small talk after that, but I kept an eye on Carmelo, who had gathered a bagful of mimosa seeds. I wasn't going to ask why. But when he felt me watching, he leaned over the side and pointed at one of the apple-sized fruits. "Them things is bad. 'Bout bad as it gets. But these things here"—he held up a mimosa pod— "they good. Not to eat. But they still good."

Belton had already asked about the seeds, apparently. "He starts seedlings and sells them. I guess the trees here are unusual. Expensive, if you're a landscaper."

That's not what Carmelo meant. "No, them little apples is poison. And them apple trees, you touch them, they burn you bad." He checked with me to see if I understood.

Suddenly, I did. Behind us were two waxy-leafed trees mixed in with towering mimosas. I had noticed them peripherally but hadn't made the connection with the apple-sized fruit. I asked, "Is that why you wouldn't get in the water?"

"Not at this place, girl. It burn the hell out of some people. Burnt the hell out of me once."

Belton was lost. "What's he talking about?"

I said, "I owe Carmelo an apology. When he warned me about getting burned, I took it as a threat."

"Of course you did. He shouldn't have spoken in that tone. I told him so when we were looking for bottles, didn't I, Carmelo?"

Carmelo shrugged and glowered, which seemed to explain the tension between the men. Or did it? I attempted to clear the air anyway. "He was doing me a favor,

Belton." I pointed behind us. "There're only a couple, but see those trees with the low-sprawling limbs? I think they're manchineels. I should have realized."

"What kind?"

"It's a Spanish name that means *little apple*—or something similar. But they're not really apples. Manchineel trees are common in the tropics. Since you're from Richmond, I wouldn't expect you to know." As I spoke, it crossed my mind that Charles Cadence had also moved south from Virginia.

"Burn the damn hell out of you," Carmelo said, pleased he'd finally gotten his point across.

Belton wondered, "Is that true?"

"The fruit's poisonous and so is the bark. If you stand under one in the rain, it'll blister the skin off you. I've been told that anyway. And . . . Well, here's an example: Indians dipped their arrows in the sap and that's supposedly what killed Ponce de León."

"The Spanish explorer?"

"That's what I've read. He died in Cuba, but he was wounded somewhere near Sanibel. It takes the poison a while to work, I guess." After considering a moment, I added, "It's the beginning of the dry season, but the sap might float on the surface after a lot of rain. Maybe that's why I was okay."

Carmelo said, "Don't touch them apples either," and plopped down behind the wheel, a bag of seedpods at his elbow.

About the waxy-leafed trees, I said, "I guess we ignore the things we don't expect. Usually, they grow closer to a beach. And I've never seen manchineels that big—they've got to be a hundred years old. But those apples should have warned me." Now I was thinking of the Brazilian who had planted exotic trees before the Civil War and the schoolteacher who had written about blistered skin. The mimosa trees were different here: tall, lean, with lichen-splotched trunks, their seedpods longer and thinner than the mimosas in my mother's yard.

I spoke to Carmelo. "Can I see one of those?" He had lost interest and was focused on the sonar again. When I reached for his sack of seeds, though, he came to life and blocked my hand.

"Mine," he said. He spoke like a simpleton, but his eyes were sharp and sure and seemed to taunt.

The look on Belton's face told me, *Let him have his way.* So I did, no problem. There was a seedpod on the deck I could cover with my foot, then pocket later. Belton acknowledged that option with a nod.

During the return trip, we discussed harmless things—an unspoken agreement to wait until we were alone to talk. It proved to me that Belton's distrust of Carmelo ran deeper than a misunderstanding.

WALKING FROM the flimsy docks and fish-cleaning table toward the RV park, I nodded hello at the tiny blondes who didn't look like twins but did look stoned. Belton waited until they were past to ask what I'd found underwater.

I said, "Maybe it was silly keeping it from Carmelo,"

then, without including how frightened I'd been, told him about the canoe.

He was disappointed. "Was there a motor on it?" That sounded important for some reason.

"I only saw one end and didn't get a very good look. You were hoping it was a bass boat, weren't you?"

His mind was focused on what he'd just heard. "An aluminum canoe with obvious dents. Like someone used an axe to punch holes?"

"I'm not sure, but whoever did it went to a lot of trouble. If they'd used just one anchor, the bow or stern would stick out of the water."

"Then it was stolen. They'd probably knock holes. You just didn't see them."

"I don't know what canoes have for flotation, but it's generally riveted into the forward and aft bulkheads. In fact, whoever did it had to *get in* the water and force it under before they tied off. Weird—why would thieves care enough to bother? They'd either keep it or sell it or cut the thing loose when they were done."

Belton said, "It certainly wasn't to collect insurance."

I shook my head while thinking I should have mustered the nerve to do another dive.

"A damn canoe," he muttered. "But on the fish finder the thing looked a lot bigger to me. Rectangular, sort of, you know?"

I said, "The water is murky once you get down. There could be something else on the bottom. Maybe the canoe is next to another boat."

Thinking aloud, Belton said, "A rental boat—a canoe with a motor. They rent canoes everywhere." He glanced back to where a kayak and a square-stern canoe lay upside down on the bank. Nearby were two small aluminum boats with kicker motors. Also rentals.

I said, "The odd-looking one is called a Gheenoe. If you hoped to find a boat from the Civil War, why is a motor so important?"

The old man's focus had shifted to the miniature blondes. They were on a dock, walking single file, while Carmelo, on the next dock, hosed his boat. He appeared to be in a hurry.

Belton said, "That man's not as stupid as he pretends."

"No, he's not. I sensed you two had a falling-out. I hope it wasn't because of me. I didn't mean to hit him in the face with that snorkel. And it was just dumb of me not to notice those manchineel trees."

He replied, "We should call the police," which startled me until I realized he was referring to the sunken canoe.

"I was going to tell Birdy about it first. But I'll do whatever you want."

"It would be nice to know more before we bother the police. Do you think there could have been a . . . well, something inside the canoe?"

I said, "Like a registration, you mean? I didn't check for hatches."

"No, you said it was floating upside down. Something could be jammed under there. Stuck, if it was buoyant."

I didn't like the sound of that. The image of a dead body came into my mind, floating in darkness, while I battled to find my way out.

Belton put it more delicately. "A cooler with identification, possibly, or a bag. If credit cards are missing, that would mean something. Unless you searched from one end to the other—you were certainly down there long enough—I hate to scramble the police for something that has a benign explanation."

I said, "I should have done a couple more dives. Or thrown an anchor, we could have snagged the thing and pulled it up to get registration numbers." I hesitated before adding, "I'll go back, if you want—but what about him?" Carmelo had pushed his boat away, ignoring the two tiny women who watched him start the engine.

Belton understood my meaning. "Your intuition is uncanny, my dear. What to do indeed."

"I knew there was a problem between you two."

"Oh, there is. But he doesn't know yet. This morning, I saw him talking to Theo. This was before Theo's big scene with Dr. Babbs—but *after* I told him to stay away from the guy."

I said, "Told Carmelo to stay away from Theo."

"That's right—him and anyone else who might take advantage of what I found in that cistern. I suspected those two have some kind of private deal going. Now I know. I was taking my morning walk and there they were, sitting like kings, on his bass boat. That guilty look people get sometimes? I pretended like I didn't see, just kept walking. Don't forget, I exchanged several e-mails with Theo before coming here."

"You surprised them?"

"Not intentionally. Let's call it a stroke of good luck."

I agreed with Belton's instincts but not his reasoning. "I'm not taking sides, but I don't see anything wrong with people talking to whoever they want. And, without Carmelo, you wouldn't have found the cistern, let alone those bottles. On the other hand, I see your point—there is *something* about Theo that—"

"I lied to you about the cistern," Belton said, then softened it with a sigh. "Well, I didn't exactly lie. Carmelo was the one who was lying. He didn't know the place existed until I showed him satellite photos. The deep spot on the river? Yes, he knew. But not the old homestead. Even then I had to help him with the GPS. He made up that story about deer hunting when he realized I might have found something valuable. His way of staking a claim, I suppose."

"But he didn't make up the story about the manchineel trees," I said.

"About being burned? He might have. He's a lot smarter than he lets on—and he does know that river. He tried to scare you, Hannah. That's what I think. He used those little apples as an excuse. A double entendre, hidden meaning. See? The man's shrewd."

"Because he didn't want me to go into the water? Then why take us there in the first place?"

"Carmelo thinks I'm a naïve old man, which is to my

advantage. Being underestimated is always an advantage, so I'm happy to keep *him* happy. That's why I passed along his deer-hunting story."

We were on a path that would soon exit into the clearing where RVs and campers were parked. I stopped. "You're paying him? A guide should keep his clients happy, not the other way around. What's this *really* all about?"

Belton urged patience with a gesture. "For now, I need Carmelo's knowledge and his boat. Unless"—he paused to think—"well . . . unless you're willing to drive me around in one of those little rental outboards. I have Carmelo booked for two more days, but I'd rather pay you."

It was one of those bright-idea moments that caused the man to smile but only made me suspicious. I said, "There's something you're not telling me. In fact, there's a lot you're not telling me."

"I admitted I have a secret—you don't remember?"

"Of course I do. And I'm not taking you back there unless I know the whole story. That's what you want, isn't it? For me to dive that spot again."

"Not if it puts you at risk. Can we discuss it later? Tonight, I'll buy you dinner and a good bottle of wine, but right now, dear, I need a shower and a nap."

Belton Matás had a wide amiable face that was disarming and he knew it—as did I. He was also an old man in poor health who was exhausted. I didn't want to push too hard, but I had come close to drowning after all.

"Save the whole story for later," I said. "I'm fine with that. For now, a summary will do."

"You are one stubborn woman."

I replied, "Would you rather spend tomorrow with Carmelo? Or in a boat with me?"

The man had a sense of humor and surrendered with a sigh. "Okay, here are the bare basics: Theo and another person were hunting for the same thing. Theo's still after it. That's why we exchanged e-mails. Carmelo doesn't own that boat, it's Theo's—or he at least made the down payment. Happily, they both think I'm a fool."

I waited, thinking he would say more. He didn't. "That's it? You're talking about the money stolen by the bank robber, John Ashley. Thirty-five thousand in silver."

Belton shook his head. "No, you're wrong. Remember Dr. Babbs's story about a Civil War payload? That's part of my secret. The story's not a myth. I have copies of documents; an officer's letters, in my office. A Union paymaster, 1864. He was sent to purchase cattle and pay troops at Fort Myers. When he was ambushed, he dumped the gold rather than let the Confederates take it—actually, what they called the Cow Cavalry. Cowboys, not Confederate soldiers."

Cow hunters, I thought while Belton continued, "They surprised him with a couple of small cannon, and his boat was sinking, but he survived. In a later letter, he described what he called a brick sepulcher near the spot— a cistern, you call it. He was impressed by the workmanship. The next day, troops were sent to recover the gold and were ambushed—a battle that didn't make it into the history books."

"Small cannons," I repeated, said it in a way that told Belton it meant something to me. The leather-bound journal; he had to be wondering what I knew, but he didn't press.

"I'd rather explain the rest over dinner."

"Who's the other person? You said Theo and someone else are after the gold, so why—"

"Hannah, dear, *please*. I'm dead on my feet—and I if I don't take my meds on time, well . . ."

The last part was embarrassing for him to admit, which touched my heart.

I said, "I'll walk you to your camper," and gave him a little pat. On rough sections of sand, I took his elbow to steady him, a proud man—but not an honest one. Not yet.

Civil War gold wasn't transported on boats powered by outboard motors.

12

BIRDY AND I HAD TEXTED BACK AND FORTH that afternoon, which is why I was surprised she was in uniform when she tapped on my door at the River's Edge Motel. It was around five, two hours before sunset, but I had been too busy with calls to a local librarian and a friend named Tomlinson, as well as my research to notice the time.

"There's a question of jurisdiction," she said. "Wouldn't you know? The property lies in the corner of three counties. Like crosshairs, when you look at a map. So I wore my uni to impress a sheriff I'd never met and a detective I hope I never meet again. What a pain in the ass. She doesn't like working with women. Go figure."

I said, "You're talking about the archaeological site and Theo?"

"That, too. But there's a bigger case I didn't know

about. Finding human bones is always a big deal, but, turns out, three people have disappeared in that area in the last five years and none of the cases has been closed. When Leslie called and mentioned bones, cops from every department showed up." In reply to my blank look, she added, "Leslie . . . as in *Dr. Babbs*?"

The first thing that came into my head: *That's why Belton's here. He is searching for someone.*

My friend, going into the kitchenette, noticed my expression. "What's wrong?"

"I'm not sure. Who's missing? I remember reading something in the news, but it's been a while. Are you saying those bones might not be from the Civil War?"

"That's because people go missing every day, so they drop the story unless it's a child or we find a body. These were adults, two males and a thirty-year-old woman, all unrelated cases. The woman was a beauty queen, from her pictures and bio. Hate to say it but that's enough to keep a case alive. No one really gives a damn about the men." She opened the fridge and looked inside. "Good god, you made iced tea. On plane flights, I bet you pack a thermos in your carry-on."

"Sweet tea," I said. "Good tea is hard to find when you travel. What do you mean 'disappeared in the same area'?"

Birdy said, "I know, I'm addicted," and poured a glass over ice. She drank it half down, poured more, then sat at the desk where there was a motel binder containing a list of restaurants and other tourist stuff. "One man and the woman, their cars were found abandoned within a few miles of the old Cadence house. I don't know any details about the second guy. Usually, men are dead-beat dads or on the run. But the woman was the morning weather girl at an Orlando station, a cheerleader in college—Tallahassee, I think. I remember reading about her. That was before I moved down—about four years ago."

I said, "She was never found? I followed the story for a while, but they stopped writing about it so I figured she was okay. It seems like more than four years. You didn't answer my question about the bones."

"Nope. Five years next September. At the dig sites, no, there's nothing that appears to be modern era, but they still have to check." Birdy sipped her tea while her eyes took in the journal, my notebooks, then found the mimosa seedpod on the night table. "You've been working all afternoon." She studied me. "And you look upset."

I said, "It was something I just read. I doubt if Theo's smoke treatment killed any scorpions, but it dried more pages free in the journal. That Civil War was so . . . damn ugly, the way people from the same country treated each other. Reading about it in history books is one thing. But when a man you're related to writes about it through his own eyes . . . well, all that ugliness becomes real."

I saw a flicker of a smile. "You said *damn*."

I hadn't yet processed the entries I'd just read and wasn't ready to discuss them. "Was there any mention of them renting a canoe? I'm talking about the missing people. Or owning one?" Birdy gave me a confused look, so I added, "We found a sunken canoe this afternoon. It was underwater but anchored. Someone went to a lot of trouble so it wouldn't be found."

"*Really.* No, but I didn't ask. The weather girl was on her way to Labelle to attend a rodeo, so you can scratch the canoe theory. She'd left Orlando after midnight but didn't show up."

I said, "I've been to a few rodeos and certainly didn't see any TV stars walking around. I wonder why she went."

"Weather girls aren't considered stars, I don't think. In Labelle, though, well . . . maybe she was making an appearance." Birdy looked through the window, the houseboat beyond. "Or could be she liked cowboys. Yesterday, I couldn't have related"—Birdy vamped a look—"but now I do."

"All the way from Orlando for a rodeo. Where'd they find her car?"

"Both cars were found in the woods—different places, and years apart, but similar—within four or five miles of the Cadence place. There's no evidential connection, but that hasn't stopped the rumors. I've got names of two cops who might talk to you off the record. What they told me is, the place is poison. The Cadence house." She smiled. "You'll have all the proof you need the house is stigmatized."

Poison. Birdy had used that word in an earlier text, which I'd found interesting because, at the time, I was doing an Internet search on manchineel and mimosa trees—there are dozens of varieties of mimosas. Matching the seedpod to a photograph hadn't been easy, nor conclusive.

More information had come from my friend Tomlinson, who seemed to know a lot about "experimental drugs"—possibly because he lives aboard a sailboat and travels. In Brazil there is a species of giant mimosa that locals used in traditional medicine. Sometimes used the roots, often the seedpods. Tomlinson claimed that powder made from the seeds had recreational uses as well. But agreed the photos I had texted didn't confirm that the Telegraph River mimosas were from Brazil.

I was sitting on the bed, my feet on the floor, and opened the second notebook. It contained notes from my interview with the librarian and abbreviated versions of the stories Brit had told us. I handed the notebook to Birdy, along with a pen. "Write down the names of the deputies, if you have them handy. I've got some other things to tell you, but you go first. What about the spot Theo dug up?"

She talked while she swiped at her iPhone. "He wasn't authorized. That much, Leslie will swear to, but that's not enough. I had my hopes up because the GPR produced several three-dimensional images that looked like coins scattered over more coins about four feet deep. That's the spot where Theo dug. Metal, plus what appeared to be more human bones. No doubt about the metal, but, when we got there, Theo had already filled the hole in."

"Today, you mean?"

"Early this morning. Leslie was pissed." She paused to write the names and numbers, then handed the notebook back to me. "He wanted to wait until the other cops arrived, but I talked him into going ahead. We took turns with the shovels until we got close, *then* we waited. After that, with a dozen uniforms and detectives watching, we used trowels and brushes, which took damn-near forever. They weren't impressed by what we found. I don't blame them."

I checked the names she'd written down. Both were unfamiliar. "I bet I know why—Theo stole all the valuable stuff. The coins—of course he took those. Could Dr. Babbs tell from his radar unit if they were gold or silver? I know a man—a former lieutenant governor, in fact—he has a metal detector that supposedly can tell the difference."

"Not so fast. There's no evidence that Theo took a damn thing. That's the problem, which was no surprise when we saw what was there. No coins, just stacks of crumbling cans and jar lids. You know, metal that looked like coins in the photos. That's probably why Theo filled in the hole. Oh, and a pocket watch. That was interesting, at least. And the bones might be cattle bones."

I said, "All that work for a garbage dump? Dr. Babbs told us he'd made a remarkable discovery."

"You've got a lot to learn about archaeology. Garbage collectors from the future, that's what field scientists are. Leslie was happy as a kid on Christmas morning. Apparently, canned food was a big deal during the Civil War. The Borden Company, same one as today. Food in cans was issued later in the war, mostly, and mostly to Union soldiers. To an archaeologist, that's a great find. How did Union supplies end up in the middle of nowhere Florida? Pocket watches were a new thing, too. Every cop there was, like, *What a waste of time,* but not Dr. Leslie. He's a kook—a lot of them are—but cute in his way."

I said, "No more tequila for you if you think Leslie Babbs is an attractive man. Were the cans and things too fragile to touch? I'm wondering why they were found in one pile. People weren't fussy about littering in those days. What I'm getting at is, why did they bury it all in one place?"

"Of course he didn't touch anything. I helped him rig a scaffolding so he could use a handheld macro lens and a laptop to snap stills. All he had to work with was the surface layer, but he got some decent shots—the name Borden Meat Biscuits was stamped into a couple of lids. That was pretty cool. Contextually, Theo had done very little damage. I don't know why unless it's because he got interrupted—or it didn't cross his mind there might be something *under* all that rust and tin."

I said, "That's it? Theo's not going to be arrested?"

"For what? No eyewitnesses, no proof. You and I saw him inside Leslie's camper, but you heard Leslie's version this morning. He said he doesn't remember giving Theo permission. There's a reason he doesn't want to press the issue, I think." Birdy stood, walked to the nightstand, and picked up the seedpod, not particularly interested but before I could stop her.

"What's this?"

"I'm not sure yet. Now that you've touched it, go wash your hands."

She dropped the thing as if it were hot. "Why?"

"I just told you—I'm not sure what it is. But, if I'm right, it might explain why so many bad things have happened at the Cadence house."

"My god, you could have warned me." She went to the sink, hands up, palms turned inward, like a surgeon awaiting gloves. As she washed, she asked, "Those are poison, you mean? What's that have to do with the Cadence house?"

I said, "You'll be the first to know when I find out. You were talking about Dr. Babbs. That he didn't want to press some issue, but you didn't say why."

"Oh. Leslie and Theo got drunk together one night and something happened. I'm not sure what. It was in Leslie's camper . . . Weren't you there this morning when he told me?"

"You don't have to scrub the skin off," I said. "I tried to eavesdrop but missed that part."

Birdy shut off the water and found a towel. "Oh . . . Leslie said he got a little carried away—he didn't say carried away doing what—but told me not to believe Theo no matter what Theo claimed. That means it was either illegal or immoral. So I'm thinking drugs—Theo's a druggie, remember. He *experiments*, whatever the hell that means. Or Theo brought Lucia and her friends to the camper and Leslie had some wild fun with them—or maybe Theo. Or maybe all of the above."

The idea didn't shock me, but I must have appeared

shocked because Birdy laughed when I said, "Group sex with those women? *Dr. Babbs?*"

"Don't underestimate nervous little men with doctorates. I had this professor at BU"—Birdy turned with the towel in her hands—"well, let's just say skill is more important than the toolbox."

When she didn't elaborate, I said, "You always do that."

"What?"

"You know. I can't help liking those kind of stories—everyone does. Which is why you dangle them out there, then leave me hanging."

Birdy, still laughing, said, *"Dangle,"* and walked past me to the window. Stood there, the late sun flooding in, and thought while she folded the towel. "You know, the spot Theo dug up is only about fifty yards south of the Cadence house. That might explain why he was spying on us last night."

"I knew it was Theo. What did the deputies say about him?"

"I asked about his family, too. They were carnival people—exotic animals and sideshows. His parents moved from somewhere near Fort Myers and got into the antivenom business. Snakes, they already owned a bunch and knew how to handle them. This was a long time ago. No one was sure when but Theo's mother supposedly died of a snakebite. But the woman I mentioned, this prick of a detective, she said that was just a rumor."

I said, "It would explain why Theo's so bitter about the vaccine business."

"Maybe. Or maybe he was acting. People like him, they're chameleons. That's probably why he has a fairly clean record. He was arrested only once for possession, but the county cops have been called out on several complaints. Mostly complaints about animals running loose."

I said, "Don't tell me."

"Chimps or monkeys. I asked the same thing but no one was sure. They definitely had a lion for a while and a trained bear—carnival animals left over. Complaints about Theo, though, there was one for conning some guy, but the rest were nine-one-one calls from women. Usually Peeping Tom stuff, and one almost-assault, but she backed down and refused to press charges." Birdy's eyes found me over the rim of her tea glass. "Sexual assault—as in attempted rape."

I said, "That son of a bitch."

"Yeah."

"I'm not spending a night in that house with Theo around. Not alone anyway."

Birdy said, "You don't need to. I talked to Bunny on the way here. She agrees it's not worth it."

"Your aunt said that? I left a message for her an hour ago. There's something I want to discuss."

Had Birdy asked me, I would have shared my theory about her aunt's astrologer being a gossip—or possibly even knowing Lucia and the witches. But Birdy didn't ask. Instead, she told me why we were all but done with the job I'd been hired to do. "With what I found out today, and what you already have, it should be enough. The only problem is, Bunny's attorney wants photos of the grave sites. Human bones are good for dramatic effect, I guess. I didn't see you take any this morning. Or did you?"

"I never got the chance. Dr. Babbs wouldn't give me a moment alone."

"Then do it tomorrow. Schedule your interview with the two cops and we're free to have fun tomorrow night—if they'll talk."

I said, "Nope. I'll do it now. I can be at the house in forty minutes and be done before sunset—if no one's around. The interviews I can do by phone. Belton wants me to stop by tonight anyway. I like him; a nice old guy in his way, but he's holding something back." I got up and began collecting things. "You're coming, aren't you?"

No . . . Birdy had something else in mind but took her time getting to it. "I didn't plan on checking out of the motel until Monday morning."

"What's the difference?"

"Well, what I'm thinking is, the cops said that Saturday and Sunday before Halloween are the two busiest nights of the year at the Cadence house. Teenagers go there to park and dare each other to jump the fence."

I had my carry-on bag open on the bed but stopped what I was doing. "You're saying I should be there with my camera tonight because it's Saturday?"

"No, I'm saying *we* could hide inside and get video— or scare the hell out of them. Live video would make Bunny's attorney very happy." She laughed, picturing how much fun it would be.

I didn't mind altering my plans with Belton, but there was an obvious problem. "You have to be at work at six in the morning and I planned on going to church. We wouldn't get back here until late tonight."

"I'm talking about tomorrow after I get off. Sunday will be just as busy and I work four to midnight on Mondays. We can stay as late as we need to and sleep in."

Her eagerness was the tip-off. Suddenly, I knew what this was about. I said, "Brit's attending brushfire school in Port Charlotte. That's where you're going tonight, isn't it? It's more than an hour away and you're not coming back. Tomorrow night is a trade-off so I won't be mad."

The expression on Birdy's face was partly genuine, partly mock surprise. "Psychic, that's what you are. You and Lucia should compare notes."

I said, "No, I had coffee with Joey before you got up this morning. By sunrise, I'd learned more than I wanted about how to set a woods on fire—controlled burns, state regulations—all sorts of things. That man's as talkative as you when he's full of caffeine. Well . . . actually, he's shy and that's how he covers it. Talking. Some people do."

Birdy went to the window, a wicked smirk on her face. "Before sunrise, huh? So tell me, Hannah, how'd *you* sleep last night?"

13

15 October, 1864 (aboard Sodbuster) [LOCATION AND FIRST FOUR LINES BLOTTED]: . . . the Spaniard is a member of the Craft & what them 3 gerillas did to his wife and t'other woman now bind us by Sacred Obligation. The use of a cable & a tongue cutting might be due we will see. Glass rising and damn cold. Good NE wind for long reaches, a Lords blessing . . .

17 October, 1864 [no location]: Unknown raiders has sent them three Yankees to hell & now has the 4" guns from Labelle altho it aint much of a fort being only tents & a sutlers shed. But no help to a woman who kant talk for screaming prayers to a God who aint traveled this far inland. Sheepherders madness, the Spaniard calls it. This being a sickness that afflicts women in lonely country. But the Spaniard knows

good as us that a bullet is his woman's only cure. They
was 5 Yankees she says now. Not 3.

On this windy Saturday before Halloween, the Cadence
house looked forlorn and restless when I arrived at a little
after six. It was not as busy as predicted, but I'd seen two
big-tired trucks, one loaded with teenagers, on the access
road when I turned in.

I was glad they were gone. The sky had descended on
gray streaming clouds, but there was still plenty of light
for photos. That gave me time, so I allowed myself to
reread my recent discoveries in the journal.

I don't know why I felt compelled to do so. My great-
uncle's callousness was as upsetting as the tragedy that
had befallen a woman who was nameless and faceless to
me. She hadn't lived here in the old house, but I had
walked the ruins of her property and life earlier that
morning. I felt sure it was the homestead a mile downriver.

The "Spaniard"—a Brazilian timber grower—had
been a master brick mason, as the cistern proved.

Sheepherder's madness, he had said of his wife. The
man sounded slightly mad himself, although I could
force myself to understand. My well-educated friend
Birdy had remarked on the difficulties that women
faced when isolated by wilderness. But neither of us had
projected the danger of living in a spot that might attract roaming bands of soldiers who were far removed
from home and their own conscience. Little food, no
salt, but time enough to get drunk—someone had stood

by that cistern and emptied bottles of strong ale from
Massachusetts.

A woman who could only scream prayers, not speak,
had endured more than I wanted to think about but
couldn't help imagining.

Five men. Not three, she had said.

Brutes. The word was not strong enough.

Predators—it ignored the pile-on savagery of pack behavior.

Inhuman . . .

The word worked, but wasn't quite right. Sadly, it described the behavior of more than the woman's attackers.
Captain Summerlin could be included after the threats
he had penned. Hang the men with a cable, cut out their
tongues. I could only project from his cryptic wording.
To then reference a *Sacred Obligation* had the taint of
blasphemy. But who was I to say what was conscionable
and what was not during such a war? A man of my own
blood had lived it. He had seen and done things his
own way.

20th October, 1864 (Ft. Thompson, Labelle): The
Federals sent Gen. Woodbury from Key West with a
fresh troop in new uniform & kit to Ft. Myers & shoot
our cattle where they stand. Goddamnt let them come.
No one expected these sorts & it has turnt the
stomach of even them that backs the North. For the
price of a bushel of salt we expect the pleasure of
settling this matter. Says Bro. Gatrell: lure the enemy
so close it's up to God to decide who lives or dies. I

says Amen. 4" canon loaded with nails & pig shit will
make quite a party for them who wants to dance. For
them who runs, the fat pine is strung at every fence
row. The Gerillas has been loosed & hells flames is
ready . . .

Gerillas. Captain Summerlin had meant *guerrillas,* of
course, a man who had seen much of the world but seldom the inside of a schoolhouse. There was no confusion, however, regarding his remarks about *fat pine* and
hells flames.

I knew exactly what he meant. My mother's old house
is built of heart-of-pine—*fat pine,* or *lighter wood,* as it is
known. Lumber so crystalized with turpentine, you can't
drive a nail through it even after a hundred years of cur-
ing. But a single match can cause a wall—or a fencerow—
to explode into flames.

The knowledge produced in me an irrational shame
for events that had occurred generations ago. Why hadn't
Capt. Summerlin blotted out his threats? Even with his
coded mix of apostrophes and numbers, they were read-
able to someone willing to invest the effort. I had proven
that. The man had protected himself in earlier entries but
now laid the truth bare.

Why?

The question led to a truth I felt, not thought: this
entry was Capt. Summerlin's declaration of war. He had
finally chosen a side, yet his convictions were neither blue
nor gray. Revenge was the motivator but his true alle-
giance was to Florida. Vanquishing invaders was his goal.

He and friends had baited a trap with salt—bushels of salt, of all things!—and those who entered were to be fired upon by cannon. For those who escaped, there was no escape. I had helped Belton Matás pace the distance from the cistern to a fencerow. Fifty long strides, for a man sprinting for his life. No evidence of fire remained, but I suspected it had once been a barrier of flames.

The scorched bricks we'd found came into my mind. The scorched bones I had seen behind the Cadence house materialized behind my eyes.

The leather-bound journal was on my lap. Once again, I attempted to open the next few pages. Used my finger-nails, then a fingernail file from my purse. As I knew from experience, this had to be done gently, couldn't be forced, so I had to govern my eagerness to confirm what I knew in my heart: Ben Summerlin and friends were the *unknown raiders* who had killed three Union soldiers near Labelle. Weeks later, they had laid a trap of cannon and flames on an unnamed river—*this* river. Lift my eyes, I could see the tree canopy that shaded water flowing a quarter mile away. My great-uncle had been among the *gerillas* set loose, a band of cow hunters turned man hunters. They had orchestrated the killings of an enemy who had perished under fire and in flames. Then he and his friends had allowed the dead to burn while digging shallow graves. What else explained scorched bones?

It was a time of war. Loathsome crimes had been committed. But I also had to wonder if greed had played a role. Belton had told me of the Union paymaster who, in 1864, had been sent to purchase cattle and pay troops at Fort Myers, but his boat had been ambushed by four-inch cannon. Rather than let the Confederates take the gold, he had jettisoned the money. No . . . Belton had clarified that point—the *Cow Cavalry* had ambushed the paymaster, not Confederate soldiers.

It was impossible to believe all these elements were coincidental.

Greed—it sullied whatever justice had been done. But who was I to say? I hadn't suffered that poor woman's pain and I was looking back from the distant, distant land of almost two centuries. Any attempt at moral judgment only proved my own callowness. My family disloyalty, too. Yet the shallow graves I had viewed that morning still nagged at my conscience. The graves were haphazard . . . indifferent . . . chaotic—but there was something else that troubled me. I couldn't quite put my finger on it. The answer, I hoped, was hidden between these damn stubborn pages that I continued to pry into and cajole.

Finally . . . finally the paper began to separate from the glob to which it had been adjoined for decades. I put an eye to the open space and was disappointed to see the first lines of the next page had been scribbled black. When I attempted to see more, the snap of flaking paper forced me to stop.

I took a break to calm my fingers. It was six-fifteen. The sun would set in an hour. Still time for photos, but the harsh late-afternoon light was draining westward. I checked phone messages, took another look at the house. Windows above the balcony had dimmed to black domino eyes; the music room and cupola were isolated chambers joined by a pitched roof. The house bore the weight of wood and years in silence, indifferent as a rock, but the structure was animated by wind-churning trees and cawing crows and . . . something else.

I used a tissue on the windshield to confirm what might have been imagined. Smoke . . . Smoke leaked from the chimney as indiscernible as mist. Last night's fire would have gone cold by dawn. Why was there smoke?

I lowered the windows and sniffed—woodsmoke. But that proved nothing. Ranchers in central Florida do controlled burns off and on all winter long. Somewhere someone—Joey Egret, possibly—had set a fire to clear brush that might fuel a major forest fire come spring. No doubt, however, the fire inside the house still smoldered. The chimney proved it.

I had the keys to the padlock, planned to enter the house anyway. I wanted wood samples from the floors and walls—especially wood from near the fireplace. Eighty years earlier, a teacher had written of blistered skin and the aberrant behavior of good children. Last night, in a flashlight's beam, the joists had glittered with sap. Pine sap, I had assumed. Now, however, after researching manchineel and mimosa trees, I suspected it wasn't true.

My reasons for seeking a rational solution were selfish, but in a yearning, hopeful sense. I am a believer in good and evil. I *choose* to believe that a divine purpose cushions whatever tragedy befalls us and that order is of the highest design. There is no room in my faith for haunted houses or supernatural devilry. If there was a solid explanation, I wanted to know it. My faith is shaken often enough by reality.

That's why I wanted those wood samples. First, though, I went back to work on the journal, hoping to read at least one more page. The result was disappointing: days or weeks after fighting had occurred here in 1864, Ben Summerlin had used ink to obliterate what he had written—two full pages. Then he had sealed those pages with daubs of tar.

His last entry about the incident was penned two months later and among the first I had read as a teenager, sitting in the attic of my mother's house. Frustrated, I now skipped ahead and read the passage one more time:

December, 1864 (Punta Rassa Cattle Dock): Gossip tween Tampa & Key West says I kilt Sodbuster & God knows who else in the switchbacks of some damnt river when drunk. This aint true. It werent cause I was drunk I left behind a box of silver Liberties & the purtiest little dory this coast ever seen. What happened is Union Blues took me by ambuscade at night & I out run them. Figured they was bandits. A cable length from the Crossing I opened the seacocks & did not wait to watch Sodbuster sink. 100 silver dollars gawn & the purtiest little dory. I have never been so drunk as to abuse a vessel purty as Sodbuster. Better she is on the bottom than with bandits is what I thot. Same with them

silver Liberties. So to hell with them that gossips of
murder & drunkenness & thievery. I got a ranch in
Cuba what needs tending. Florida is a might warm for
me now . . .

When I was a girl, Capt. Summerlin's language and
allusions to danger and treasure had struck me as roman-
tic in a *Pirates of the Caribbean* way. But they also left
unanswered questions that were never addressed in later
entries—an oversight, I had believed.

Not now. The man had been in fear for his freedom.
Trivializing the matter, then dismissing the subject, had
been his way of closing a door. By referencing Havana, he
was also addressing the subject of murder. A hard-nosed
sea captain cared nothing about rumors. But he knew the
law. That's why he had blotted out the facts and sealed
them with tar before sailing south.

Tar . . . I closed the journal, pleased I had guessed
right about exposing it to the heat of a fireplace—until I
remembered that Theo had seen some of these entries.
But after reflecting for a moment, I felt better about that,
too. Captain Summerlin had been so vague about his
dory's location—a *cable length from the Crossing*—that
Theo's chances of finding it were less than my own. Besides, he was after the paymaster's gold or John Ashley's
fortune, not a measly one hundred silver dollars.

I did feel a frustrating sense of loss, however, about
the blotted passages. An expert might know how to retrieve my great-uncle's lost history, but it would have to
wait. Daylight and the photographs I wanted could not.

I stepped out of my SUV, opened the trunk, and got the camera ready.

WHY WAS *a woman dressed like me, with hair as black as mine, inside the music room off the balcony?*

I wasn't imagining the ghost of Mrs. Irene Cadence—because I didn't see the woman. Not at first.

The camera did.

The biologist had loaned me an expensive 35mm with a tripod and a wireless shutter attachment after I'd mentioned how much I admire the Everglades work of Clyde Butcher: black-and-white landscapes of cypress and saw grass that captured subtleties of color better than any color shots I have ever seen.

"In the hands of the right photographer," the biologist had explained, "a fine lens reveals details the human eye can't see."

What a lovely notion, I had thought at the time.

The observation didn't seem so fanciful now.

The biologist had loaned me a fine lens, too—a Canon 24mm with incredible light-gathering capabilities. It also had an incredible price tag—I'd checked—so I was extra careful as I set everything up and took a few practice shots outside the gate.

The house became my subject. Harsh sunlight flared off the windows. It put an icy edge on falling leaves. I snapped a few images on full auto, then experimented with slower shutter speeds. To avoid camera shake, I used the *Remote* button and kept my distance. After a half dozen or so, I checked my work on the LCD view screen.

Nice shots. The wide lens allowed the house to be itself, old and rambling, aloof to trees that had shaded it for a hundred years. Brash sunlight was transformed into saffron and bronze. The porch off the sitting room was a cavern of shadows. Above it, the balcony was bright as a New Orleans stage but solemn for its emptiness.

Or so I thought until I saw what the lens had seen.

Three frames in, there she was: a blurred image through the upstairs window. A blouse of lipstick red, a face as translucent as moonlight. But tiny because of the wide-angle lens. My head swiveled between the LCD screen and the house while I checked two more frames. In the next shot, only a smear of her shoulder appeared . . . then the women's face in profile, but no more detailed than an antique cameo. She wasn't overweight like the witches, nor was she silver-haired like Lucia. This woman was young, lithe, full-breasted.

The woman on the balcony . . .

The ghost story about Irene Cadence came into my mind, a lady of great beauty with raven-black hair. It couldn't be her, though. Ridiculous, even to linger on the possibility. But, if not . . . who had the lens discovered?

I looked up from the gate, studied the window, then yelled, "Hello? Are you there?"

Not now, she wasn't. I opened the gate, took a few steps but lost my courage. So I returned to the camera—which is when I realized that *I* was wearing a blouse of copper red. Not as bright but similar. And I, too, had black hair, although it was pulled back in a ponytail. The explanation was obvious: I had photographed my own reflection.

Of course!

I was convinced. But the feeling didn't last. The woman in the photo couldn't be me. I was at ground level. She was upstairs behind the French doors that connected the balcony to the music room. It was an impossible angle. Or was it? I turned and looked. My SUV, with its big mirrors, was behind me. If the sun had hit a mirror just right, and if I was standing just so, and if the light had ricocheted upward . . .

The solution was too complicated. What I needed was a closer look at the photos.

The camera's electronics were high-tech. It took a while to figure out how to zoom in on the LCD screen. A toggle switch, click by click, magnified the image, but was no help. The woman's image was soon so pixelated, she vanished in a shattering of red and moonglow skin. That caused me to wonder if my imagination had reconfigured oak leaves and light into a female form. Another look at the images proved it had not.

Well . . . there was an easy way to settle the matter. I would go inside the house. First, though, rather than leave the camera unattended I returned to my SUV and opened the back. When I did, a startling option presented itself. Piled against the seat were a blanket and a few towels. Beneath them, I had hidden the pistol that

Birdy had wanted to see. There was a loaded magazine, too.

Put the gun in the camera bag? I thought about it for a moment, but only a moment.

No . . . I didn't need a gun to confront a woman even if she was a ghost. I had my cell phone. If the woman didn't make her presence known when I entered, I would press the issue—but only *after* getting the pictures I needed.

I was losing my light. It is a phrase that photographers use.

THEO HAD BEEN inside the house . . . and maybe still was. The lingering odor of marijuana and freshly burned resin hung at nose level when I entered. A broken cookie on the floor told me Lucia and the witches had been here, too.

I stopped in my tracks and listened. Theo, the non-stop talker, couldn't bear silence. But that's what I heard, silence: the slap of wind against roof, the creak of old wood. A full minute I stood there.

The fire, although smoldering, was nearly out, but that was no guarantee the house was empty. The realization spooked me. If there was a woman upstairs, ghost or not, she was welcome to leave or stay. That was up to her. I wasn't going to risk confronting a man who had dodged a rape charge. Another concern was that, after only a few minutes inside, smoke that hazed the windows had already moved into my bloodstream. I could feel it. The chemical it contained sparked a glowing clarity that soon teetered between giddiness and despondence.

Maybe I spoke my thoughts aloud. *I've got to get out of here.*

I did. I retraced my steps, padlocked the door, and was dialing 911 when I remembered why I'd come. Pictures . . . I needed pictures. Photographing the archaeological dig site required me to break federal law. I couldn't call the police. Not yet.

Damn it.

It made me angry to be in such a position—caught between the law and my fear of a man I had disliked at first sniff. Which is why, when I opened the back of my SUV, I made a decision that was unlike me. I pulled the blanket back and removed the pistol from its clever carrying case. And it *was* clever: a leather box the size of *Webster's Third*. It looked like a book, too, NEGOTIATORS embossed in gold on the cover. I had no idea what the title meant—another ruse, I assumed.

My Uncle Jake, in life, had been wise and sweet and bighearted as a retriever. But, in death, by leaving me this gun, he'd become a man of mystery. The gun was silver steel, smooth as glass in my hand, and a mystery in itself. Even finding it on the Internet had been a chore. Thirty-some years ago, a master gunsmith had produced a concealment weapon for a government agency. The name of the agency was still classified, although it was known that fewer than two hundred of the special weapons had been produced. The pistol was a shortened Smith

& Wesson with a hooked trigger guard, a sleek fluted barrel, plus other tweaks for fast and lethal shooting. My gun expert friend, Birdy, had pronounced it "Beautiful; perfectly balanced."

Odd . . . Until this instant, I had thought the pistol ugly, even brutal, in appearance. There was a reason. I had used it to shoot a killer. The thump of bullet taking flesh, the man's screams, still troubled me during moments when I lacked confidence or doubted my own virtue. Even touching the barrel could spark a response similar to what I'd felt that day: body shakes, labored breathing. It was humiliating what fear had done to me. And that was the problem. I felt no guilt about shooting the man. Quite the opposite. Bunny Tupplemeyer had guessed correctly about me first aiming at his genitals but losing my nerve. What haunted me was the memory of how helpless I had felt . . . and the knowledge that the frightened girl inside me could not be trusted to overcome life's inevitable dark surprises.

The gun reminded me of the truth. That's why I avoided the very sight of it. Perhaps I was feeling the effects of the smoke and whatever drug it contained because the truth was vividly clear now. And the truth was this: fear was my enemy, not the gun. Fear—and weakness—both separated me from the woman I pretend to be. Why hadn't I realized this before?

Suddenly, the decision was easy. I was alone in a lonely place. Theo Ivanhoff was somewhere nearby. I had a right to defend myself . . . And yes, by god, I would.

A magazine loaded with seven bullets was also in the

box. Federal Power-Shoks. Birdy had said they were the best man-stoppers made and had given me a box. I inserted the magazine with care, then held the pistol away to catch the sunlight. On the handgrips, in red, an archaic Scottish word was stamped: DEVEL. That had taken some time to research, too. The word meant *to smite* or *knock asunder*. It could be pronounced *DEAH-vil*, but I preferred *dah-VEL*, which was acceptable according to the *Oxford English Dictionary*.

As I studied the pistol, I realized I should have also taken it to the gun range and practiced. Birdy had invited me often enough. Three times I'd joined her, wearing safety glasses and earplugs. We had taken turns firing her Glock, which was lighter and, in appearance, as utilitarian as a cookie punch. There's nothing elegant about plastic. But the Glock held eighteen bullets, not seven like mine. And it was foolproof enough that I had outscored Birdy on our first trip to the range—a mistake on my part because it put her in such a foul mood. After that, missing the center ring had taken more effort than hitting it. But I'd managed.

The fact was, my Uncle Jake hadn't just taught me to shoot, he had made me practice until my hands and eyes automatically knew what to do. Hundreds of rounds through a little .22 caliber revolver, then hundreds more with a variety of guns. Same with using a fly rod and an axe—an approach that worked equally well with the clarinet. Jake had been very proud when I was named first chair as a junior.

"Women learn faster than men because they *have* to,"

he had said. Which, to a girl of twelve, had seemed a frivolous compliment, but now, standing outside the gate to the Cadence mansion, assumed an unsettling new meaning.

I did a quick review of the pistol's mechanics: on the left, beneath my thumb, was a de-cocking lever. The weapon had no safety or other frills. The front sight was iridescent red. Shuck the slide, point, and pull. Simple enough. Unless that red sight was centered on an attacker's chest—or his genitals, as I knew too well.

Enough! Let it go.

I did.

I stowed the pistol in my camera bag and said aloud, "You're a fool if you try." A warning that was also a plea, both of them directed at Theo as if he were listening.

Had Birdy's words about fortune-tellers and electronics come to mind, I might have realized *Maybe he is.*

14

I WAS DONE WITH PHOTOS, PUTTING GEAR AWAY, when I heard a shriek that had an animal quality. Not human—or so I believed. I figured a hawk had snatched something warm and furry that, in its death throes, was alerting its kindred to hide. Rabbits can rival operatic sopranos in volume. I had heard them often enough with Jake, who liked hunting in the Everglades.

I looked up, thinking I might find the hawk. No . . . only vultures adrift on a molten sunset. The lighting feathered trees with lace while the sky descended, joining clouds with mist and smoke from distant fires. Daytime vanished in a gray haze. My eyes were still in photographer mode. Had I looked an instant later, I would have missed the abrupt transition from daylight to dusk. I also wouldn't have seen dust from a vehicle that was leaving or approaching the house. Driving fast, too, on the gravel road.

That gave me a start because I was standing between two fresh dig sites where signs warned *Federal Antiquities Site. Access Prohibited.*

I grabbed my bag, bundled the tripod under my arm, and ducked beneath the rope in a hurry. When I'd put some distance between myself and an arrest citation, I stopped to reorganize. As I did, it dawned on me to hide the camera's memory card. If police had arrived, I didn't want to provide them with easy proof I had been trespassing. I also didn't want to lose the hour's work I'd just finished. Work I had enjoyed, true, but still intense and draining because of the subject matter.

I had been photographing mass graves.

I ejected the memory card with care. It contained more than two hundred images of the dig site we'd seen earlier, plus another site that Dr. Babbs had claimed he was too busy to visit. By carefully placing the tripod inside the excavations, I'd been able to shoot close-ups without risk of damaging artifacts that lay exposed or just beneath the surface.

I felt good about that. Further penance was the opportunity to whisper a prayer for those whose lives had ended here in violence. No fewer than ten human skulls lay exposed, maybe more. Most had been shattered and burned, so it was difficult to be sure. Three had been pierced by bullet holes.

According to Capt. Summerlin's journal, five men had

been guilty of attacking the Brazilian's wife. But twice that number of bodies had been tumbled into these holes. Members of the Cow Cavalry would not have treated their own with such disrespect, so I knew these were the remains of their enemy.

The bones told a story: what had started as a quest for revenge had turned into a bloodbath. The question nagging at me was answered when I understood that. Yes, the shallow graves were haphazard and chaotic. Yes, they contained the remains of Union soldiers. But, in fact, these were not Civil War graves. What the archaeologist was actually excavating was *a crime scene*—victims whom killers had tried to cover in haste.

I had dozens of photos of other artifacts that, to me, proved the theory was valid: two rusty cannon with four-inch bores, two bayonets with Union markings, a gold pocket watch with a Masonic emblem on it. Soldiers would have taken these valuable spoils of war. Only murderers would have buried them.

A second prayer was offered on behalf of Capt. Ben Summerlin, a solid man who had given in to his darkest instincts—*if* I was right. And feared I was. Once again, understanding such brutality failed me. What had driven my great-uncle to cross the line?

The Gerillas has been loosed & hells flames is ready. His words, written a century and a half earlier, hinted at an explanation. Guerrilla warfare was unconventional. Jungle tactics had no rules or moral boundaries. Survival demanded that the beast within a man be unleashed.

Once victory was secured, the beast could be returned to its cage. But only then.

The beast within. Better than any other, the term fit. It could be blamed for every savagery and sin I could think of—a disturbing concept to linger on, so I shoved it aside.

It was a little after seven. I ejected the memory card, which I slipped into a change pocket. I was going through the camera bag, looking for a card to substitute, when I heard a second shriek—but this was no rabbit. It was a response to terror. And unmistakably female.

Instantly, my brain associated the sound with dust rising from the gravel road. What if Birdy, in her BMW, had returned and surprised the occupants of another car? Theo and Lucia, possibly. That's what I feared.

I dropped the tripod but hung on to the camera bag and ran toward the trees, the old house hidden just beyond. A sustained scream caused me to slow, but only long enough to dial 911.

The dispatcher who answered was dubious. After I had repeated my name, repeated the address, and twice explained why I was breathing so heavily, she said, "This is the third call we've gotten, ma'am, and the officers didn't find anything earlier. Are you sure it's not just kids having fun?"

I asked, "Are you talking about the old Cadence house?"

"This time of year, we get two or three calls a night. High school kids like to go there and scare each other. Did you actually see something?"

I was on a weedy footpath that led through the trees. "I told you, a woman was screaming. I'm not making this up."

"Are you in the house?"

"No, but—"

"Do you *see* anyone inside?"

"I'm not close enough. Look, the woman I heard wasn't having fun."

"Then how do you know she's inside? Unless this is an emergency, ma'am, Saturday nights we're spread pretty thin. Where are you *exactly*?"

I was exiting the path from the southwest, the house's tin roof and cupola silver in sunset's last light. There were no cars outside the gate except for my SUV. No one on the balcony either. The front door was still chained, no sign of light or movement inside. I said, "I wasn't imagining things. Someone is inside that house and she's in trouble."

"Do you still hear her?"

"Well . . . no."

"Let's give it a few seconds. I'm not doubting your word, ma'am. You said your name is Hannah Smith?"

I continued toward my car and opened the door, phone to my ear. While I waited, I hid the memory card in the glove box. Soon she asked, "Still nothing? Then it was probably kids in a passing car. That's usually what it turns out to be. Are you in any *personal* danger, Miz Smith?"

I said, "Could you please send a deputy just to check it out? I'll stick around. And you have my number."

"As soon as one's available, I'll get a car there," the dispatcher assured me.

Of course the moment I hung up, I heard another scream from somewhere beyond the balcony. I looked at the phone, then shoved it in my pocket and ran toward the house. The screaming did not stop until I had managed to open the padlock.

It seemed to take forever, the way my hands refused to cooperate.

IN THE PARLOR, with its chandelier, the fire was out, but the room was still smoky when I entered. Not thick, but enough to swirl aside when I crossed to the stairs and called, "Who's up there?"

No response.

I shifted the bag on my shoulder and tried again. "If you're in trouble, I'll help. Say something."

This time I heard a click and muffled thump as if someone had closed a door.

I fanned the air to get a clean breath, unsure what to do. A woman didn't make the sounds I had heard unless she was at her wits' end. I couldn't go off and leave her. But I also didn't want to climb those stairs.

It wasn't dark, but windows were dimming, so I opened the bag and chose my little flashlight, not the pistol. Smoke tunneled the beam when I switched it on. In a way, what I saw was comforting. Someone had been very busy here during the last hour. The broken banister had been moved and the stairs were draped with toilet paper. White streamers hung from the landing and chandelier. Oh . . . and a crushed Budweiser can was balanced between the horns of a hat rack. Several scorpions smashed flat on the floor, too.

Theo and Lucia hadn't done this. The dispatcher had been right about teenagers. They had broken in and had fun decorating as if for a prom. I hadn't heard their vehicles coming or going, had seen just the dusty signature of a car that hadn't stopped . . . or had stopped just long enough to gather a few artistic vandals.

At least one young woman, though, had been left behind.

I tilted my head toward the upstairs. "I know you're up there. I already called the police, so you might as well come down and explain."

Mentioning police did it. A door banged open amid wild laughter. Footsteps galloped overhead while a girl's voice warned, "Krissie, we're gonna leave your ass." Then another bang and tinkling glass at the back of the house.

High school girls. No need to fear them nor them to fear me. I didn't want them to break their necks escaping, so I hurried through the sitting room to the kitchen and looked out. The secret access to the upstairs was an aluminum ladder that hadn't been there yesterday. I got a glimpse as the trespassers scuttled down: two skinny teens, one in coveralls, the other dressed bizarrely in an evening gown that had been shortened with scissors. Beneath it, black leggings with zebra stripes and cowboy boots.

Neither wore a red blouse, unlike the woman I had

photographed earlier. But that was okay. I smiled at the girl's costume until she turned and yelled, "Krissie—you asked for it, you *bitch*."

From above, a pitiful wail responded, a wail that soon turned shrill and familiar. Whatever friendliness I might have felt toward the two girls vanished when they abandoned their friend by jogging toward the river.

At least I had a name to work with when I found the girl they had left behind.

I circled back and inhaled a gulp of air at the door, which was open. Then went up the stairs, calling, "Kris . . . Krissie? There's no need to be afraid." Several times I repeated soothing variations while I panned the flashlight across the landing. Soon, I heard a cooing, whimpering noise that seemed to come from the music room, where one French door hung loose on its hinges.

"Don't be afraid," I said, then followed the flashlight inside, where the piano had also been adorned with white streamers and beer cans. Something else I recognized: seeds from a mimosa pod littered the floor. They were flat and shiny, as brown as miniature cow chips. Some had been powdered and heated in a pan. The pan showed scorch marks from a flame.

Smoking drugs, I thought. *The same smoke from the fireplace . . . That's why I feel so odd.*

The mix of giddiness and despondence I'd experienced earlier was curling its way into my brain. Not strong, but noticeable. Thankfully, my awareness produced a counter-emotion: anger. How reckless, I thought, and how cruel, to poison unsuspecting people by filling this house with their smoke. It made me more determined to help the girl.

I did a slow search of the music room. On the far wall was a poster that had been left behind. The lettering was big and easy to read despite its toilet paper adornments:

MEET CHUMAN
Love Child of Woman & Ape
(As seen on *National Geographic*)

It was an oversized photo—not a drawing—of a man who was as hairy as a werewolf. He had a flat simian face and wore a restraining collar as if he were a Rottweiler. Snarling, too, canines bared, and a metallic glint in his eyes—compliments of Photoshop and a promoter's imagination.

The poster struck me as repugnant. Then I remembered that Tyrone, a real person who lived alone in a trailer, had probably posed for the photo. That made me feel even worse. Because of an affliction, the man had no other way to make a living, yet tonight teenagers had mocked him, had added obscene graffiti, then toilet paper streamers—more Halloween decorations to set the mood. A lewd drawing, too: a snake with fangs and a smile protruded from Tyrone's mouth like an extended tongue.

I wondered if the girl they'd left behind had also found the image disturbing. She wasn't in the music room—I even looked under the piano. Her crying had stopped and started again. Now it seemed to float down the hall from the other side of the house.

Strange. Usually my ears are as sharp as my eyesight and it's exceptional, if Loretta's doctor is to be believed. Was I hallucinating? No . . . my mind was struggling with the smoke but okay. Her crying was real. Somewhere in this house a frightened girl was hiding or . . . or *she was being held against her will.*

That gave me a jolt. The possibility was real, not paranoia. And the most likely suspect was Theo.

I stopped, opened the camera bag. The pistol was right there, if needed, but not ready. I shucked a round into the chamber, used the de-cocker as a safety precaution, then returned the weapon to my bag, the bag over my left shoulder.

Exiting into the hall, I called the girl's name a few times and swept the area with the flashlight. Her weeping was continuous but impossible to pinpoint. An empty house echoes. But in the Cadence house, with its tin roof and domed cupola, Krissie's sobs followed the rafters like a conduit and vibrated off the walls. Finding her was like searching for speakers in a theater. I paused at every room and closet. I also kept an eye on the spiral staircase.

Finally I narrowed it down to the cupola because its door was ajar. The door was a half-sized access that opened into a room that was circular and barely big enough to fit four people. The previous evening, Birdy and I had explored it. Inside, wooden rungs scaled the wall to where a school bell had once hung. A peaked roof and grates protected the interior from rain but not wind, which spiraled downward into the house. As I approached, a steady breeze streamed through the doorway, cool on my face. The air was cleaner here. It made sense that a girl who was hallucinating might take refuge in a spot where she could breathe.

Yes . . . the girl was inside. Her weeping ceased when the flashlight pierced the entrance. I switched off the light and said, "Krissie, no one is going to hurt you. Can I come in?"

"No! Who are you?"

She was panicky. I feared she'd climb the cupola's ladder and try to escape by crawling onto the roof, so I took my time. "My name's Hannah. I don't know about you, but this smoke is making me sick. Can we go outside to talk?"

"Stay away. Where did Gail and Frieda go? They promised not to leave me."

Girls—I don't care the age—are not easily fooled, so I told her the truth. "You'd be smart to never trust that pair again. They ran off." Quietly, I moved toward the door.

"Ran where? I don't believe you. The other party?"

"The river. Or someplace close. Is that where they parked their car?"

"They wouldn't do that."

"You heard what that girl called you, Krissie. We both heard the word she used."

The girl sobbed when I said that. "Gail promised I'd have fun. They never invited me to their parties before.

That's all I wanted—to be with them and have fun. Why would they be so mean?"

"Because that's the way some girls are," I said and couldn't but help sharing her hurt. Without seeing Krissie, I knew what she would look like: gawky or chubby and too plain-faced to be anything but the easy target of jokes and mindless cruelty.

And I was right. Before I ducked through the door, I flicked on the flashlight and took a look. She was a scrawny little thing with mousy hair and earrings she had probably spent an hour fussing with in front of a mirror. Wearing her best clothes, too, pleated skirt and a blouse that was lavender, not lipstick red—and too flat-chested to have been the woman in the photo.

I switched off the light and entered, saying, "No one's going to hurt you now," then knelt beside the girl. "Tell me what happened. Or . . . it's probably better if we go outside first. This smoke will only make you sicker if we stay." I reached to touch her shoulder but withdrew my hand when she lurched away.

"Don't touch me. I can only close my eyes if I'm alone. And that's what I want—just me, alone." The girl's muddled reasoning, as much as her hysteria, gave me a chill. Alcohol—the smell wasn't strong, but she been drinking, too.

"I think we should get you home. Do you have a cell phone? How about we call your parents."

That was the wrong thing to say. She shoved me and scrambled to her feet. "Don't you dare tell my mom. Where did Gail and Frieda go? Gail wouldn't leave me.

You're lying about that." She braced herself against the wall and began to slide away as if balanced on a ledge.

It was darker in here. I was a looming gray shadow to the girl. She was a shadowy stick figure. Soon she would feel the ladder rungs against her back and might climb to the roof. So I retreated to the door and ducked outside, hoping she would calm down. Gave it a few seconds, then said, "Kris, I'll do whatever you want me to do. I can stand here while we talk. Or I'll sit outside on the porch and wait until you feel better. But I can't leave you, sweetie. Not until I know you're safe."

There was silence, then a shuddering sob. "You mean it?"

"Whatever you tell me to do, yes."

"My mom can't know. I think something bad happened inside my head. The things . . . what I see inside my head . . . *they* keep coming back. Snakes . . . Gail wouldn't stop talking about snakes. Scorpions, too. And another party—she said we'd have so much fun."

I didn't want the girl to focus on snakes and scorpions. "There's nothing wrong with your mind, sweetie. It's the smoke, some kind of drug they tricked you with. Once we get outside, you'll feel better. Krissie? I promise you'll be okay if you trust me."

I put the camera bag on the floor and continued to talk to her. It took another minute of soothing and cajoling, but the girl finally crawled out and joined me in the hall. Stood there, undecided, looking up, as if trying to determine if I was real or imaginary, a safe companion or a threat. She hadn't actually seen me. It was darker inside the cupola, but dark out here, too. So I attempted to put her at ease, saying, "My hair's probably a mess, so don't be shocked when I turn on this flashlight."

I pointed the light at the floor . . . then toward the ceiling to illuminate the hall. I was half a foot taller than Krissie. She was reluctant to make eye contact but finally did. She looked up, a girl whose face was as plain as my own. Puffy lips, eyes glassy, she stared at me for a moment with interest. Then her expression changed and she began to back toward the stairs, frightened by what she saw.

It wasn't easy to force a smile but I did. "What's wrong? My earrings aren't nearly as nice as yours. Is that it?"

Krissie appeared to be having trouble breathing. "You're her," she whispered. "You tricked me."

I wondered if the light had sparked another hallucination, but also feared she would fall down the stairs if I switched the light off. She had yet to look behind her and the steps were only a few yards away. "Sweetie, you're going to be just fine once we get outside." I held my hand out as an invitation to stop.

"No—Gail told me the stories. You're her, that woman." Then she hollered, "I saw you! Stay away from me. You're dead . . . You're a witch."

Did she mean Lucia? I wondered. Krissie was only a few steps from the stairwell. If she didn't fall, she would soon run—her wild eyes guaranteed it. So I shined the light on the landing and made sure she saw the steps by asking, "What woman? Is that her on the stairs?"

Thank god, she turned. But it cost me the little bit of trust I had earned. "You lied to me again. You . . . You're evil." Then Krissie reached for the missing banister and nearly fell anyway, but recovered, while I stood frozen holding the light so she could see.

"You don't have to run," I said gently. "Just get downstairs in one piece, that's all I ask."

The girl realized she'd scared me and hesitated. "If you're not her, why is your shirt soaked with blood?"

Blood? I looked down at my copper red blouse and finally understood. She was definitely hallucinating. Krissie had convinced herself I was the ghost of Irene Cadence. Terrifying for her, but a possible opening if I used it right. "The woman you saw wasn't me," I said. "I have a picture of her, though. If you wait for me outside, I'll let you see it. Truth is, I'd like your opinion." I reached for the camera bag. "Do you remember meeting a woman named Lucia?"

"I don't believe you. Your hair . . . you've got black hair, too. And you're beautiful just like Gail said."

I had to smile at that. "When I was your age—this is true, I swear—I thought I was the ugliest, clumsiest person on earth. Maybe you can relate." I left the bag where it was and stood. "How about we go outside? I've got a cooler in the car with drinks. Just you and me, we'll talk about how awful high school can be."

Krissie jerked away when I offered her my hand. "You're lying. Stop pretending you're nice."

"It's true I have to pretend sometimes. But, Kris—I'm

not the one who ran off and left you." Once again, I extended my hand.

The girl couldn't let herself believe the truth. She shook her head, threw her scrawny shoulders back. "Go to hell!" she hollered, "I'm going to the party and find Gail," then ran down the stairs and out the door.

I followed, but first had to retrieve the camera bag. By the time I got outside, she was almost to the trees, where there were car lights and the rumble of motorcycles, too. To me, though, it looked like Krissie was angling toward the old railroad bridge when she disappeared.

That's the second thing I told the 911 dispatcher after I had explained the bare basics.

"She might be headed to the RV park," I said, "looking for her so-called friends."

15

THE *THIRD* THING I SAID TO THE 911 DISPATCHER was, "I told you there was a girl in trouble. You didn't believe me. So I expect you to believe this: we need to find that girl before she hurts herself. And send extra deputies because drugs are being sold from this house. A dangerous drug. And I know who's doing it."

That wasn't exactly true—Theo, Lucia, and/or Carmelo could be responsible—but I wanted all the uniformed cops I could summon before I went after Krissie. And that's what I intended to do instead of standing on the porch, talking on a phone, in the wind and beneath stars and a rising full moon. Which was the *fourth* thing I told the dispatcher.

"Have you been drinking?" she asked when I was done. From the tone of her voice, I could tell I had pushed too hard or was rambling. And she was right. My anger had caused me to say too much and with too little respect.

"Sorry, I got carried away. But you can't go inside that house without inhaling smoke."

"Then you *are* under the influence," the dispatcher said. "Smoking what? And how do you know it's dangerous?"

"I'm not sure of the name. It's from a type of mimosa tree. The dealer burns the seeds in the fireplace but grinds them into a powder first. Maybe to get kids started, but probably because he has a sick sense of humor. Or could be . . ." A more devious reason had popped into my mind and I had to sort it out.

"Could be what?"

"I hope I'm wrong but it might be his way of taking advantage of women. Young girls would be easy targets."

"The man you buy drugs from," she said, "can you spell his name for me? I should warn you, everything you say is being recorded."

I was already impatient but that made me mad. "Buy it? Lady, I don't even smoke," then caught myself before saying anything stronger. Instead, I kept it simple. "I'm going to look for Krissie. Have the deputies call when they get here."

I hung up, fuming, furious because the dispatcher had ordered me to stay put and wait for an officer to arrive, which had given the girl a long head start. Now the question was, should I drive to the campground or save ten minutes by walking?

Because I was anxious and angry, the answer seemed

obvious, but I couldn't decide. Either way, the camera
gear needed to be locked in the trunk, so I hurried to my
SUV while I argued back and forth. I hid the bag under
a towel but removed the pistol first. It was too big for my
purse—a clutch wallet, actually, by Kate Spade—so I
zipped the gun into the little backpack I had carried on
Carmelo's boat. The few supplies it contained weren't
heavy. The gun added only a pound.

When I shouldered the bag, I remembered that I was
supposed to meet Belton between eight and eight-thirty.
It was nearly eight now, which was another reason to take
the shortcut across the railroad bridge. With the flashlight, if I jogged most of the way I could be at the campground entrance in a few minutes. Belton, I felt sure,
would be willing to help search for Krissie. Then he
could drive me back to my car when I was ready.

I wasn't a coward and I was armed—taking the bridge
made perfect sense.

Don't do it. Deep, deep in my mind, the persistent
voice of reason demanded to be heard. *You're not thinking straight. You've been drugged.*

But I had already wasted a lot of time. Krissie was in
no shape to be roaming alone. I had to find her before
her friends—or an even crueler man—hurt her more.
Take the shortcut, urged the reckless woman inside me.

That's what I decided to do.

My SUV is equipped with a keypad on the driver's-
side door and only I know the five-digit code. It's a nice
feature that eliminates the possibility of locking the keys

inside and reduces the risk of theft. So I touched the keypad to engage the locks.

Don't do it. That voice again. This time, it added a mental image: me standing alone at the entrance to the serpentarium where Theo lived. I would have to pass that driveway to get to the campground.

Suddenly, I was convinced.

Using the keypad, I got into my SUV and did a fast U-turn on the gravel road.

THE REASON it was faster to walk to the RV park was because I had to drive four miles north to a bridge that crossed the Telegraph River, then east for a mile to a macadam road, where I turned right. That road doubled back southwest, four miles again, and wasn't wide enough to dodge all the potholes. Until then, I hadn't realized how remote the spot was.

Four miles? The repetition sparked a detail that didn't surface immediately. Gradually, it came back: Birdy had said the weather girl's car, and the car of another missing person, had been found in a woods four miles from the Cadence property. Not the same place but similar.

Four miles on either road, if driving north, would intersect with a spot near the highway bridge. No doubt police had considered the significance, yet that didn't relieve my anxiety. This was lonely country. Occasionally, an eighteen-wheeler roared past, slapped me with a wall of wind, then left me alone. The moon was up, orange and smoky, its size distorted by an October horizon. It showed cypress trees on both sides of the road and vacant land that had to be swamp or open range for cattle. Mist pooled in my headlights, the tang of brushfires bespoke a land that might yield to hard work but would never be subdued.

Men like Brit and Joey Egret—and Capt. Ben Summerlin, too—would do fine out here, sleeping rough and traveling by foot or on horseback. The same was true of my distant aunts, Sarah and Hannah Smith. But this was no place for a modern girl. Especially one like Krissie who was lost and alone, her brain hallucinating.

My thoughts shifted to the three missing people, then to the Florida State cheerleader who'd become a TV weather girl. Why had she stopped her car in a place like this? Whatever indignities she had suffered, however feverish her fear, the truth had not vanished with her. *Someone* knew. Someone who had traveled this same narrow road. A man, most likely. A man who was a beast— or whose inner beast lived just beneath the skin and had a taste for the unspeakable.

Both hands on the wheel, I kept the speedometer at seventy-five, hoping a sheriff's deputy would stop me for speeding. That's what I was thinking about, what I would say to the officer, when my phone rang. The noise so startled me, I jumped and crossed the center line, then overcorrected and swerved toward a ditch. I got the car under control, slowed to sixty, then engaged cruise control, before I finally answered.

Too late. Belton Matás, according to caller ID, had

hung up. But then the phone pinged with his voice
message:

"Hannah, dear, I assume you're on your way. But, the
thing is—and there's no reason to worry, so don't—but I
think a mutual acquaintance of ours *knows*. I'm talking
about what you found today. And he's acting very damn
strange. So I'm in my RV now and I'll meet you—"

A sustained metallic screech, possibly static, ended the
message. Or maybe that was all Belton had to say. But
why guess? I touched *Call Back*. Six rings . . . Seven . . .
Then a message said the subscriber was not set up for
voice mail.

I tried again. No answer.

Ahead, the road forked. To the left was a tiny concrete
church, Calvary Baptist, lights off, parking lot empty. On
the right, a sign read *Slew RV Park 1 Mile*. I slowed, followed the arrow to the right, then pulled over into the
weeds. I rechecked the door locks and listened to the
message again.

. . . *a mutual acquaintance of ours knows . . . And he's
acting very damn strange.* Belton surely meant Carmelo
and hadn't said his name in case Carmelo was eavesdropping. That made sense. But why end the message so
abruptly?

So I'm in my RV now and I'll meet you—

Meet me where? If Belton had added a location, his
voice had been obliterated by the metallic noise that
overpowered the speaker in my phone.

It didn't matter.

Belton was a smart man. If he wanted to intercept me

before I got to the campground, he would know where
to park. Probably somewhere on this road—I was only a
mile away. If not, he would soon call. When he did, I
would explain that Krissie was a priority. And what could
it matter if Carmelo knew I'd found a sunken canoe?

That all seemed reasonable, but I double-checked my
line of reasoning anyway. Rather than lessening its hold
on me, the drug in my system had branched deeper.
Headlights of passing cars were painful to my eyes. The
Halloween moon, bright as it was, pulled at the darkest
fears within. As a defense mechanism, my anger exerted
a thrumming pressure on my temples. It made me irri-
table; even eager for a fight.

You're not yourself, the voice of reason warned. *Don't
be reckless. If you lose, the drug wins.*

Lose what? A scrawny teenage girl was the person who
had something to lose, not me. I was a grown woman,
belted safely in the steel confines of her car. I had my cell
phone *and* a gun.

Reckless thinking, the voice countered. Then proved it
by stressing an uncomfortable fact: *You don't know Belton Matás any better than you know Theo . . . or the others
you've met in the last two days.*

My lord . . . that was true. I sat there a moment, wondering if I should return to the Cadence property and
wait for police as the dispatcher had ordered.

No . . . I couldn't do that. If someone organized all
the women in the world who had been plain-looking and
unpopular as teens, life would offer more hope for girls
like Krissie. But here, on this night of wind and moon, I

was an organization of one. And, by god, I was not going to leave that girl out there alone.

I wouldn't search recklessly, though—a concession to the nagging voice inside. First, I sent a text to Birdy that included my location and a few details regarding plans to meet Belton and search for a runaway girl. Then, because I wanted to hear a voice I trusted, I left the same information on the biologist's machine. Even though he was out of the country, I knew that Tomlinson, his best friend, checks messages daily after pilfering a few beers.

There! It was eight-fifteen on a Saturday night, a busy, sociable hour even in an isolated spot like the campground. Someone might be hosting a party and there was a chance Krissie would join her "friends" there. If Belton wasn't waiting for me around the bend, there would be enough activity to shield me from Carmelo or anyone else too smart to risk witnesses.

The backpack containing the Devel pistol was on the floor, passenger side. I hauled it onto the seat beside me, checked my rearview mirror, and drove on.

I ROUNDED A CURVE onto a gravel straightaway and, in the distance, my headlights found what I had been hoping to avoid:

SLEW VACCINE AND HERPETILE

TRESPASSERS RISK ENVENOMATION

The warning sign near the gate where Birdy and I had seen a strange muscular little man and heard something stranger escape into the trees.

Still no call from Belton. And no chance he had slipped past me in his rental RV. The road was too narrow. Oaks and mimosas fenced both sides, their canopy interlaced so only a strip of moonlight glazed the road and a serpentine path along the river.

Serpentine . . . The word jarred a sensitive nerve in my brain, causing it to twitch, then spark. My full attention was demanded. This was not a normal reaction. I knew it. I braked to a stop and told myself, *Breathe slowly, the feeling will pass.* It had been thirty minutes since I'd exited the smoky confines of the Cadence house. The effects of the drug would gradually wane, not get stronger. That's what I wanted to believe.

But was it true? Aside from a few puffs on a joint, I didn't know anything about drugs, especially hallucinogenics—except for what Tomlinson had told me about an uncommon mimosa tree. In South America, native people smoked or inhaled the resin to go on what he called vision quests, a sort of trance that lasted hours, even days. The mimosas of Brazil were massive compared to Florida's variety. As I could see through the window, the same was true of trees that bordered the road.

The fact was, my symptoms might worsen. Why was I lying to myself?

Serpentine . . . The word continued to annoy me. It had something to do with Krissie. She had sobbed about *things* in her head, then mentioned snakes—*Gail wouldn't stop talking about snakes.* Gail had also promised to take Krissie to a party. No . . . *another* party that was nearby.

From a distance, the sign taunted me—*Slew Vaccine and Herpetile.* Then the carnival poster of Chuman, the man-beast, tried to force its way into my mind, fangs bared to frame a lewd drawing of a snake. Repugnant. I banged at the steering wheel to banish the image. The message was obvious, yet I wouldn't allow my imagination to wander into a subject so dark.

"Theo, you bastard."

Aloud, I said those words. Then pulled the backpack onto my lap and opened it. The Devel pistol was there atop mosquito netting and other emergency supplies. I cracked the slide an inch—yes, the chamber was loaded. I laid the pistol on the seat, lowered my window, and drove ahead.

I was sick and tired of being afraid.

The gate was open. If there was a party, there might be music, so I stopped and listened. Trees harbored a screaming chorus of frogs, but that's all. I had no idea how far back the buildings were. A long way, no doubt. I angled into the mouth of the drive, my headlights showing a glittering swirl of insects and waxen foliage.

I was so focused on the driveway, I almost missed what happened an instant later: fifty yards down the road, a hunched figure stumbled from the shadows. It ducked my lights, then vanished into shadows on the other side. A second person followed, but much faster, running with an odd loping gate.

I only got a glimpse and was so startled that I sat there

dumbly for a moment. I wasn't imagining things but didn't understand what I'd just seen.

Two drunks, I told myself.

No, that was wrong. The first person might be drunk but might also be hurt—and was being pursued by a second person who was faster.

Krissie?

Male or female, I couldn't be sure. But the person who'd stumbled had appeared too bulky to be a teenage girl. More likely, it was a sizable, overweight man.

Belton.

I shifted into reverse, spun the tires, then kicked gravel again when I put my car into drive.

16

IF I HADN'T BEEN SEARCHING, I WOULDN'T HAVE noticed Belton's RV hidden by trees on a utility easement that sliced cross-country from the road to the river. At first I saw only red taillight reflectors, so I backed up, jammed the SUV into gear, and turned toward the ditch.

There it was: a cream-colored camper, the driver's door open, the vehicle canted to the left on uneven ground. The easement didn't look drivable and Belton was too smart to try even if he'd had a reason. It was possible he'd suffered a stroke and gone off the road—which would also explain the person I'd seen stumble. If Carmelo had been involved, he had been running away, not in pursuit.

My window was still down. Twice, I yelled Belton's name, then put the car in park. I didn't want to get out without first calling 911 and wouldn't have, but Belton answered me, calling, "Hannah . . . ? I need help, Hannah." He sounded weak and confused.

My reaction was to act, not think. I threw the door open, grabbed my phone, and ran; jumped the ditch, weeds knee-high. "Are you hurt?" I yelled. "Where are you?" His voice had seemed to come from near the camper, but now I wasn't sure.

"Here . . . Can you see me?"

No. My headlights showed the RV in full frame and oak trees that separated it from the road, but all else was moonlight and shadows. "Keep talking, I'll find you."

"To your left a bit, dear. My god . . . I have no idea how this happened."

"Are you hurt?"

"I . . . I'm not sure. They got me so drunk or stoned." *Drunk?* I didn't believe him.

"We have to get out of here, Hannah."

"Hang on. Everything will be okay," I said. But I was starting to panic because I was almost to the RV and still couldn't see him.

"A bit to your right, dear, then keep walking straight."

I did, taking long strides. The RV, with its door open, was directly ahead but with no dome light on to show what was inside. I had to kick my way through palmettos to step up on the running board . . . then nearly fell back because of the smell—a fecal musk I instantly associated with sickness. Yes . . . the old man had suffered a stroke and lost control of his bodily functions. I forced myself to confirm the cab was empty, then pushed away.

"Say something, Belton. I might have to go back to my car for a flashlight."

"I'm feeling . . . woozy."

His voice seemed to trickle down from the trees—impossible, but sound plays tricks in the woods, especially at night.

"Shake the bushes, if you can. Am I getting closer?" I assumed he had collapsed on the ground so was tromping a slow circle around the camper.

"My son was here," Belton replied in a dreamy way. "I keep hoping." Then he mumbled something else.

"You have a son? Tell me about your son. What's his name?"

More mumbling, which my ears locked onto. I turned toward the lights of the SUV and slowly, very slowly, allowed my eyes to drift upward from the ground to the moon-bright branches of an oak tree—and there was Belton Matás, his shirt ripped off, sprawled over a limb that was eight feet off the ground.

I yelled, "Belton!" and ran toward him. Maybe I screamed, too. I'm not sure, but something I did caused an explosion of movement high, high in the oak tree. I looked up. Three stories above, blackened by the full moon, a man-sized creature stared down at me. Hanging from his distended arm was something that resembled a life-sized rag doll.

This time, I definitely did not scream. But I did yell with all the fear and anger in me, "Get the hell away or I'll shoot you!" It was an empty threat, the gun was in my SUV. But the creature responded, replied with a metallic screech that threatened me even while it retreated. At the same instant, I heard the snare drum crackle of limbs shattering and something heavy falling toward me from above.

Instinctively, I threw my hands up . . . then was knocked sideways by a weight that numbed my shoulder before it thudded to earth. The sound alone was enough to sicken me—a gaseous thump, like hitting a pumpkin with a sledge. There was sticky residue, too, a sheen of black on my arm. Dazed, I tested with my fingers and sniffed—it smelled of brass.

Blood. I was bleeding. I explored my face, forearms, my shoulder, yet found no wounds.

What had happened? It took me a moment to figure out I was on my knees. I got up, eyes automatically seeking the creature in the tree. The thing was gone. A crashing noise told me it was traveling fast through the oak canopy toward the river. That was good . . . But there was still something very wrong. Something missing from the sounds and odors I had become accustomed to. *What?* I couldn't think straight.

"Are you hurt, Hannah dear?"

Belton's voice. He was several yards away, still in the tree but making an effort to swing down. Then he yelled, "Watch out!" just before he fell and landed hard on his side.

I ran and knelt, then helped to steady him when he sat up. "Don't try to stand," I said. "Don't do anything until the police get here." I was trying to make sense of events and also trying to remember what I had done with my phone. I'd had it in my hand until . . . ?

"It's too bad about the child," Belton said. "I swear, an animal that strong, there was nothing I could do."

"What child?" I replied, but shushed him before he could answer. Suddenly, I understood what was troubling me. My SUV—the headlights were still on, but someone had switched off the engine. Captain Summerlin's journal, the gun, everything except my phone, was in there. I said, "Shit," and started toward the road . . . but only got a few steps before I stopped and whispered, "Oh my god."

It was because of what I saw at my feet. Illuminated by headlights was the rag doll body of a girl who had fallen through tree limbs before knocking me down. Nothing identifiable left of her face. But the lavender blouse told me the blood on my arm was Krissie's.

Belton startled me by hollering to someone, "Figured I was dead, didn't you? *Idiot*."

I looked up. A man crossed the ditch into the headlights, coming toward us. It was Theo, not the simpleton guide. I found out for certain when I tried to run—Carmelo had exited the camper, aiming a shotgun.

THERE WAS A PARTY under way in Theo's garage apartment, but no one saw him bully me into the building of tile and neon with steel doors that protected the reptiles housed inside. Shelves of acrylic trays and large terrariums in a space that smelled of lab rats and Clorox.

No windows, only air-conditioning ducts, so the stink of snakes mixed with decades of mold.

"This is all her fault," Theo reasoned, talking to himself. "She got nosy. Now she won't cooperate—there's no choice when some mark acts like a hick." He swung me around by the shoulders and stood close enough that I felt his breath on my face. "Last time I'm going to ask . . . Where's the Civil War journal?" He waited for pressure to build inside his head, then screamed, "I know you're lying about that book being in the car!"

I had ceased trying to fight—couldn't, the way my hands and ankles were bound—but I wasn't going to beg. Several times he had accused me of lying about the backpack, which was missing. At first I thought it was to distance himself from the theft. But now, half an hour later, I was convinced someone had beaten him to my SUV and stolen the backpack. Carmelo, I assumed, until Carmelo—that bastard—had slapped me while demanding the same information.

Except for a brief meltdown, I had managed to maintain control. Or at least sound calm, which was evident when I replied, "Birdy is a deputy sheriff, Theo. How many times do I have to say this? She knows where I am. A dozen squad cars will be here soon, so why make it worse? I'll be your witness by telling the truth: they can't blame you for a murder your chimpanzee did—even if he is *your* responsibility."

I was too mad not to add that last barb. And too late to take it back. Theo, his cheeks coloring, sputtered, "Don't call him that. Oliver isn't a chimp. He's part ape—a Bondo. Get that through your thick skull. He makes one little mistake and it's like the end of the world."

I started to say *One little mistake?* but caught myself in time, while Theo jabbered on. "Don't you dare blame him. That . . . *teenybopper* was an idiot to be out there alone, probably taunted the poor guy. Then you showed up. If anyone's to blame, it's you and that stupid little redneck twat."

"Don't call her that. *Krissie*—she has a name."

I thought Theo was going to slap me as he loomed over me, six inches taller. "You threatened to kill Oliver, didn't you? I heard you. Screamed you'd shoot him. So it's no wonder he did what he did. Scared the hell out of the poor guy—Carmelo was there and he heard you, too. Ollie's sensitive, him and Savvy both. And intelligent— they'll know it was you. If you keep lying, I'll stick you in one of the cages for a night to prove it." He looked across the room to another door, a door that had outer bars and what looked like a mail slot. "Maybe I will. Then you'd *understand*."

I should have grasped the significance of the bars on the door but was stunned by what I'd just heard. Two chimpanzees—Oliver and Savvy—and at least one was a killer. I dipped my head toward the floor. Theo waited, expecting me to apologize, but I couldn't force such a sickening lie. I had seen what one of those animals had done to a frightened, innocent girl. All I could manage was, "I don't know much about chimps. Sorry if you took it the wrong way."

He found my stubbornness infuriating. "Well, now!

Lucia won't put up with your bullshit. I warn you right now."

I wasn't surprised the woman was on the property, but his deference to Lucia took me aback.

Again, he waited. "Is that all you have to say?"

It should've been, but I couldn't keep my mouth shut. "Where's Belton? I want to see him." The old man had been lying on the floor, Carmelo as guard, when Theo had dragged me from the RV.

"If he's smart," Theo said, "he's telling the truth about why he came here."

"That's not what I meant. Belton has a heart condition. I don't know how much alcohol or drugs you poured down him, but letting him die is a mistake. When the police get here, the more Belton and I can say in your favor, the better off you'll be." Then the anger boiling in me had to add, "*Pretending* to be smart isn't going to save you this time, Theo."

He called me the foulest of names while I winced, expecting to be slapped again. He didn't, but banged me against a stack of terrariums, then forced me to the floor. Behind my ears, a sizzling hum of rattles warned that only glass separated me from the snakes within. I didn't turn to look. Nor could I stomach the craziness in Theo's eyes. So I continued staring at the floor until he finished his rant.

It took a while. He raged about the chimps, alternating between anger and his eagerness to dodge blame. Oliver was thirty years old, Savvy was a younger female, but both could outsmart the electric collars they always wore. It wasn't Theo's fault. "Accidents" happened.

"People underestimate their intelligence. Not me. Oliver helped me with math homework up to about third grade—oh, he's brilliant in many ways. Do the research: a Bondo's short-term memory is off the charts compared to humans. Same with chimps. Their analytical skill, in some areas, is far superior. And their eyesight, their sense of smell—my god, Oliver's nose is as good as any bloodhound's." Theo squatted in front of me to ask, "Do you know what the *real* difference is between them and us?"

My anger got the best of me. "I don't kill and eat children. I'd prefer not to guess about you."

He rocketed to his feet. "That's disgusting. I won't tolerate it. You don't know what the word *loyalty* means, do you?" The subject seemed to flip a switch in his head. Tears began to well. "Ollie practically raised me after Mother died. Fed me with a spoon until I was old enough to feed him. Every day, we played together. Slept together, even swam and took baths together. Twenty-seven years we've been like brothers. Our father never gave a shit. Oliver was the first person ever to stand up to that old bastard—*finally*. Now you expect me to turn him over to the cops?"

I didn't trust myself to speak. *Our* father? But Theo's tears scared me more than his craziness and threats. I didn't look forward to dealing with Lucia but was hoping she would come into the room.

"Think about it!" Theo yelled and began to pace. Soon his mood took another sharp turn. As he paced, he talked about how misunderstood he was and said abusive things about me and "Bertie." If I really was a descendant of Sarah and Hannah Smith, they had to be white trash. Then he became a tour guide. I had to sit there while he went on and on about snakes and how important his work was to medical science.

Finally he wheeled around as if to leave but had to stop one last time and say, "This is all *your* fault. Finding that canoe, then the girl—I didn't ask you to come here. So don't blame me for what happens next."

He left, slammed the door, fiddled with a padlock outside and jammed the dead bolt to seal me in.

I felt like bawling. My hands were bound behind me with plastic-coated wire called a tie wrap. My ankles were joined with two loops of the stuff so, even if I managed to get to my feet, I would have to take short shuffling steps to walk. Theo had found my cell phone, too, while Carmelo went through my pockets—just thinking about the incident made me cringe. The way his hands had lingered, Carmelo's sickening leer while his fingers explored my blouse. This was after he had slapped me, but it was the humiliation of his hands on me that had finally caused a meltdown of tears.

I was too mad to cry now. Escape and contact the police—that's what I had to do. Even so, my mind wandered to my stolen backpack.

Who took it?

Then moved on to the pistol, a chrome-plated weight in my imagination but steady in both hands when I squeezed the trigger.

Three times I pictured myself firing yet couldn't decide *Who will I shoot first?*

17

As if wearing clogs, I shuffled around the room searching for a way out. Old 1960s fixtures dated the construction. On a desk was a modern touch: two large computer screens monitored a dozen cameras around the property.

Every ten seconds the checkerboard images changed. The parking area, with the old Land Rover Theo had mentioned, a couple of other cars there, but no sign of the camper or my SUV. An interior shot of a withered little man sleeping in a rocker, a blanket tucked around his shoulders—Theo's father, I assumed—sitting motionless as a painting while an antique TV set flickered. Next, three shots from what had to be Theo's apartment. Theo hadn't returned to his party yet, but I recognized some of the people. A voyeur's view of the bathroom, where a girl sat on the toilet, her zebra-striped tights at her feet—it was Krissie's friend, Gail, in her outlandish costume. In the kitchen, Lucia held a bamboo tube and tilted it toward the face of one of her witch friends.

I had to wait for the images to cycle to see why: now Lucia had her lips on the tube and appeared to blow powder up the woman's nose, the overweight witch reeling back as if stunned. Soundless laughter—no audio—which made it appear as if it was all happening underwater.

I moved away and continued to search. All around me were terrariums and shelves of acrylic trays that contained snakes. More than a hundred pit vipers, Theo had bragged. Diamondbacks and pigmy rattlers, bushmasters, moccasins and copperheads. Banded kraits and cobras were spaced along the far wall. As I passed by, a cobra flattened its head in warning and watched me with satanic eyes.

The prize specimens, though, were two dozen coral snakes that shared a terrarium in the center of the room. Nearby was a milking table. I shuffled over for a closer look, but not too close—if I fell, I would crash face-first because my hands were behind me. Mounted on the glass was a plaque. It bore an inscription, which I had to scrunch down to read:

In Memory of My Loving Mother
Lydia Rom Slew
Artist, Actress, Showman, Historian,
&
Descendant of Egyptian Queens

Theo, even when not in the room, had something to say. The serpentarium had been named for his mother, who, before dying of snakebite, had passed down her interests to her son, along with her out-of-control ego.

Egyptian royalty. Bizarre. But her middle name, Rom, tugged at a recent memory—something Birdy had said regarding Gypsies.

It didn't matter.

My attention shifted to the coral snakes. Their bodies were slim, a couple of feet long, with skin as colorful as jelly beans—red and black segments separated by yellow in Life Savers bands. Under any other circumstances, I would have marveled at their beauty. Now, though, I only considered their possible usefulness.

I'm not terrified of snakes, but I avoid them and have never had the desire to handle a venomous reptile. If I *had to*, though, I would choose a coral snake. Only once had I seen one in the wild—actually, it was under my mother's house. The snake had been so docile, it was no surprise when I'd read that corals seldom coil and strike. The few people bitten usually made the mistake of surprising them or handling them roughly. A dangerous mistake because their tiny fangs inject a neurotoxin far more powerful than any snake in North America. Slow-acting—almost a full day before the human nervous system shuts down—but deadly.

"It takes two years and fifty thousand milkings to produce a pint of venom," Theo had claimed. "And if bite victims don't get antivenom within twenty-four hours, they die. Any wonder why I'm a rich man?"

A deranged egocentric, more like it. It was weird to be in this space while, at the same time, Theo appeared on one of the computer screens and reached for the bamboo tube Lucia had offered.

Snorting more drugs, I thought. *Good. More time to get my hands and ankles free before he comes back.*

Chin-high near the milking table, I noticed, was a shelf full of equipment: heavy gloves as long as my forearms, a catch pole with pincers hanging near an aluminum pole—a snake hook—and something Theo had forgotten about, a box cutter lying in plain sight.

Did the box cutter contain a razor blade?

I'm no stranger to the strengths and weaknesses of tie wraps. I keep a pack on my boat. They bind like steel under pressure, but a nick and sudden snap will pop them like string. Using my mouth, I dropped the box cutter on the table, then backed against it, hoping it had a razor. My fingers fumbled around until they became familiar with the case and sliding blade. Minutes later, my hands, then my legs, were free.

The first thing I did was confirm that Theo was still at the party. Then I rushed to the sink and washed myself clean of Krissie's blood. The sight and smell of the red swirl spinning down the drain almost caused me to retch.

There's no time for that. Weakness can wait, staying alive can't.

Talking to myself helped. I washed my face, too, while I wondered, *How do I escape from a windowless room made of concrete? Well . . . maybe through the air-conditioning ducts.*

I took a look. I'm a large woman, with shoulders from years of swimming. The ducts weren't wide enough. I had heard a dead bolt slam on the main entrance but tried the front door anyway. It was locked.

The second door caught my attention—two doors, actually: an outer door of steel, the inner door all bars like a jail cell. The next room, possibly, was where valuable snake venom was stored. I wanted to believe that. But then remembered Theo staring as he threatened to put me in a cage with the chimps. That worried me. Something else: what looked like a mail slot was actually a hinged pass-through large enough to fit a tray stacked with food.

I didn't want to believe *that*.

Why house adult chimpanzees next to a room full of snakes? It makes no sense.

It was a high-security room, I reasoned. Had to be. Probably refrigerated. I pictured a big stand-up safe inside, too. The prospect didn't offer much hope as an escape route, but I went to the door and turned the latch anyway.

Surprise. The bars swung open on rusty hinges. I caught the frame before it banged the wall. A brass lever controlled the next door, which would also open inward. I reached to try it but stopped myself. There was no dead bolt on my side. And no way of knowing if the internal lock was engaged. If I turned the lever, the door might open. But the same was true if someone, or some *thing*, opened the latch from the other side.

The thought of what awaited me was unsettling. The

image of Krissie's mangled body appeared in memory: faceless, her flesh gnawed to the bone. Oliver and Savvy—one of the chimps was a monster, maybe both. What if they were on the other side of the door?

I stood for several seconds. My eyes shifted from the lever . . . to a fist-sized dent above it . . . and finally focused on the pass-through. The opening was covered by a metal flap. Lift the flap, I could look through to confirm what was in the next room. Caution demanded that I do it. So I knelt and leaned one hand against the metal sheeting. When I did, the door settled into its frame with a soft *click-click*.

Instantly, from the other side, I heard *tap-tap . . . tap* as if in reply.

The space around me, already quiet, began to hum with a dense and dreadful silence. I'd been too overwhelmed to worry about paranoia or the effects of the drug. But now told myself, *You're imagining things. Open the flap and look.*

I did. Lifted the little metal lid, which was light and loose to the touch. I leaned my face to the opening . . . then exhaled, relieved. Almost smiled because in the next room all I saw was a wedge of tile flooring and a desk where books were stacked near a lamp that was on but not bright. A couple of dog toys, too—a retrieving bumper, a chunk of rope—and something else: a window. The window was closed, but it was a *glass* window. No bars. Force the door open, my freedom lay on the other side.

I stood and caught my breath. Rather than act in

haste, I decided to check on Theo one last time. As I stepped away, though, I heard it again: *tap-tap . . . tap*.

Three distinct sounds. Like a fingernail signaling from the next room. I cocked my head and listened. Heard the compressor whine of air-conditioning . . . an October wind in the trees outside.

Wind. That might explain the noise. Even so, I tiptoed to the door . . . knelt, and was again reaching for the metal flap when a more familiar sound stopped me—a dead bolt snap at the front door, the door yet to open because there was still a padlock to deal with.

Theo had returned.

I swung the bars closed, then moved in a rapid animated silence. I wanted the room to appear as if nothing had changed.

It was Lucia at the door, not Theo. When she entered, I was on a folding chair facing her, my hands behind my back. Tie wraps were looped around my ankles. Hopefully, she wouldn't notice how precariously the ties hung there.

Not to worry—the woman was too stoned to do anything but gloat, then get down to business. The bamboo tube she carried, though, was a constant worry. It was longer than expected, tipped with a wisp of a mouthpiece.

"Hannah-Hannah, the man killer," Lucia chided as she approached, voice syrupy. A shapeless black dress— no, it was a robe that caught air near her sandals. "You don't really think I'll let them hurt you, do you, dearie?"

I said, "That's a wise choice. Police will go easier if you don't."

"Quite the tough little lady, aren't we?" Her smile vanished. "That's not the reason. I'm protecting you because we're going to make a deal, just you and me . . . *dearie*." She stopped several steps away and gripped the bamboo, her fingernails glossy red. "Theo's a total nutcase, no argument. But he's pretty good in bed. And I've got enough tapes and video to send him to the electric chair, if I want. Do you understand the power that gives me?" She reached to lean against the desk . . . misjudged the distance but finally found the desk with her hand.

I asked, "What do you have in mind?" but was wondering, *Where did she put the key?* Lucia had locked the front door before crossing the room. No purse, no visible pockets, and she hadn't left the key in the lock. It had to be on her somewhere.

Stoned or not, the woman was shrewd. She noticed me eyeing her robe with its waist belt and hood, a white peasant blouse beneath. "What are you looking at?"

I said, "Truthfully? I'm scared to death. But it's the same thing I wondered about last night when we met: how a woman your age stays in such good shape. Weird to be thinking that now, I know, but you asked."

"A little manipulator," she decided, but sounded pleased nonetheless. "What I'm telling you is, Theo is not going to jail over some little redneck tramp. What's it matter that she died tonight instead of next year in some bar or truck stop? I don't give a shit about his filthy monkeys either. Are you kidding? With their fleas and constant jacking off, and that female with her disgusting pink bows and collar. I'd love to see them dead. Hmm. Maybe we can work that into our deal."

I held my tongue while Lucia paused to realize, *Yes, that's a possibility.* Then said, "Theo is useful. When I tell him to do something, he does it. And that includes favors that would make you blush—you're such a pious little creature, aren't you? What I would miss a lot more is the ten thousand a month he pays me not to turn him over to the law. Young cocks don't grow on trees and I *own* his."

I said, "You don't have to worry about me. I won't—"

"Shut up. Theo's very upset that you and the old man found the boat or whatever it is. So you're going to give him the journal, explain the code or whatever bullshit he keeps babbling on about. You see, honey, all men are just boys and boys like to hunt for treasure. Do that—and a few other favors—and he'll have no reason to argue when I tell him not to kill you."

I wasn't going to ask why a sunken canoe was important, yet she held up a hand to silence me anyway. When she did, I let my anger slip. "Sheriff's deputies should be here any minute. Take your time."

"No, dearie, they won't. I have your phone. Twenty minutes ago, you called nine-one-one and canceled the emergency call you made. Then you sent a text to our little friend, Liberty Tupplemeyer. Want to guess what you wrote? Oh—and I happen to know that Liberty works in the morning. Between now and tomorrow night, all sorts of ugly things could happen to you.

Carmelo, for instance. Or the monkeys. Theo says you saw what his big bastard—Ollie, for christ's sakes—what he did to the girl. Was it bad?"

I felt my ears coloring.

"Yes," Lucia said, "I can see that it was. Lucky for her it wasn't that disgusting female chimp—females, we're always tougher on our own sex. I read a study. First thing a chimp does is bite off a woman's nose, then her lips. The genitals go next. You know—eliminate the competition." The woman sweetened her threat with a knowing smile while her fingers massaged the bamboo tube.

Her superior tone was grating. It matched the expression on her face. I wanted to lunge from the chair and grab her. I might have done it, but then what? If she didn't club me unconscious with the bamboo, I'd have to tie her before I searched for the key—or risk that the second door was unlocked.

That was my excuse. But the real reason was fear. So far, I believed Lucia's claims: Theo and Carmelo were under her control. She alone could spare my life. I didn't want to die. It was wiser to listen.

"What do you want me to do?"

"Work with me. You'll make more money than you ever imagined and here's how." Lucia checked the security screens—Theo was still in the kitchen—then moved closer. "Liberty's aunt, Bunny Tupplemeyer—the old lady's worth two hundred million dollars. Possibly more. And she's very fond of you both."

My theory about Bunny's *astrologician* had just been

verified. Yet I had to ask an obvious question to appear confused. "Do you know her?"

"I link paranormally to special people," she reminded me, "and Bunny's money makes her *very* special. She's a sad old woman dying of lung cancer. Did you know? No . . . of course not. Well, here's the thing: Bunny believes you came into her life for a reason. That you might be her rescuing star. The zodiacal term is *a transect connection*. It offers the hope of soul migration, which I don't expect you to understand. Think of it this way: the old lady is hoping your spirits have so much in common that she'll hitch a ride into your future."

"After she's dead, you mean?" I asked the question well aware that Lucia, the witch, might also be Mrs. Tupplemeyer's astrologician. "What happens to her soul isn't up to me or our horoscopes. You believe what you want."

Lucia's reaction: *How sweet.* "Offend your Sunday school convictions, did I? A star chart is just number crunching and numbers don't lie. The trans connection thing is true. Bunny *knows* it's true. She's a self-important old bitch, but she's not stupid. That's where you come in, Hannah-Hannah. You're going to convince Bunny not to back out of the real estate deal. Instead of putting her million dollars in escrow, she's going to sign a check. And keep right on signing them." Lucia's green eyes brightened, she stood a little taller and fluffed her robe, while her attitude dared me to refuse.

A lot of things went through my mind: Mrs. Tupple-

meyer's attorney saying, *She took advice from the wrong
people.* At the very least, Lucia and others were skimming
money from investors. More likely, the whole investment
scheme was a fraud. I couldn't put it all together now.
But if playing along saved my life, I would do it. Giving
in too easily, though, would be a mistake.

"I'm not in the habit of cheating people," I replied.
"If I do this—I'm not saying I will—how much are we
talking?"

Lucia liked that. *"Greed."* A nod of approval. "Any
other vices you're willing to share with me tonight?
Don't answer. If Bunny comes through with the million,
let's say . . . well, how does a hundred thousand sound?"

She was lying. I knew it but managed to appear interested. "That's a lot of money."

"Isn't that what I said? But there's something else you
have to do before you get paid. Are you ready for this?"
Her smile was that of a mean drunk. "What I want is all
the dirt you can bring me on your buddy. That's right,
dear little Liberty, the deputy sheriff." She paused, disappointed by my response. "You're not shocked?"

"Liberty and I haven't been friends that long. Even if
I was willing, I don't know much about her. Nothing bad
anyway."

"Put your mind to it, dearie, you will. There's not a
woman on this earth who doesn't have a guilty conscience or some dirty little secret. Photos are good, but
video is better. I'll give you some microrecorders to
plant here and there. Have duplicates made of her apartment keys, too. I want her hard drive copied, her texts

and e-mails, everything. There's not enough time to get my hands on all two hundred million before Bunny dies, but her niece is going to inherit a bundle. By then Liberty and I—you, too, of course—will have what's called a special relationship."

I tried to disguise my disgust but couldn't. Lucia waved the bamboo as a warning and came closer. "You'll drop all this holier-than-thou bullshit when I tell you the alternative. You'll go to state prison on a murder charge—sound fun? A big attractive girl like you might actually enjoy herself."

My hands, crossed behind my back, began to fidget. "Get away from me. You're crazy."

"No, I'm *methodical*. Guess who the last person was to see that little redneck girl alive? Honey . . . it was you. I've got audio of you both in the Cadence mansion. Her screaming at you, 'Don't touch me . . . Stay away from me.' Heartbreaking, the way she pleaded. The girl called you evil, as I remember. Your voice records nicely, Hannah. I loved the part where you said, 'Sometimes I have to fake being nice to people.'"

"I never said that."

"Oh, but you did. In so many words anyway."

My mouth was so dry, I couldn't swallow. Pretending my hands were tied seemed a cowardly retreat from Lucia's lies. Yet I sat there and tolerated them.

From a safe distance—or so she thought—the woman hiked her dress and knelt so we were eye to eye. "Why wouldn't you leave that poor child alone? It was sickening the way you kept after her. Push, push, push. What are you, twenty-eight . . . thirty? Too old to invite a teenage girl into your car for a drink. But you did. Just the two of you alone. That's how you lured her outside, isn't it? It all came out quite clear on the audio. God only knows how drunk the little tramp was when you dumped her at the side of the road—or wherever you left her. I'll flesh out the details after I've edited the tape."

Lucia, with her smug certainty, smirked and attempted to stare me into submission. I stared back. She had liquid green eyes set deep into the hollows of a face that was stamped with crow's-feet—smoky parties and whatever poisons that had scarred her from within. I don't know what the woman saw in my eyes. Rage, no doubt. But something darker, too—or unfamiliar—because her expression gradually changed. I watched Lucia gulp and stand, her balance wobbly. Then she stepped back while her ego and her eyes sought a graceful excuse to look away.

She found it. "Who the hell opened that?"

My vision was so tunneled, I didn't know what she meant until I followed her gaze to the opposite wall. The barred doorframe had swung open. I had closed it. I knew I had closed it. But to protest my innocence was, in fact, an admission that I had moved around the room.

"It was like that," I said.

"It *was not*," she snapped and walked toward the door. "That's the room where Theo's mother sent him when he was bad. He never opens it. *Ever*."

I didn't reply, just watched. Among the equipment near the milking table was a snake hook—not sharp, but on a five-foot aluminum pole. If I sat patiently until Lucia got to the door, I could have the thing in my hands and be ready when she turned around.

So I waited. The woman kept glancing over her shoulder to check on me. Maddening to pretend helplessness, but I did. Finally—*finally*—when she reached for the door, she looked away, but then spun around to surprise me.

I had just started to get up but stopped in time. Lucia continued to glare, one hand on the bars, her back to the door into the next room. I shrugged innocence and looked at the floor—which is when I saw what she had noticed: the tie wraps I had placed around my ankles were gone. They were several feet away where I had kicked them when I'd tried to stand.

Lucia raised the bamboo tube as if it were a flute. "You sneaky little bitch—show me your hands. You needed your hands to open this door."

No more pretending for me. I stood and kicked the chair back—a metal chair that clattered across the tile. I was already moving toward the snake hook. "Call the police if you've got a complaint," I said. "An ambulance, too, if you get in my way."

I meant it. I didn't waste a glance at the woman until I'd pocketed the box cutter and had the aluminum pole in my hands. Then I turned . . . but wasn't prepared for the scene before me: Lucia had the bamboo tube to her lips and was zeroing in on me as if the thing were a blowgun.

A blowgun . . . ?

Yes, a blowgun. I hadn't believed Theo when he said Lucia had studied with an Amazon tribe. But it was true. Extra darts, thin as needles, were visible in her right hand.

I yelled something, I'm not sure what, and hurled the pole at her, which clanged off the bars. Almost simultaneously, a wasp stung my left wrist. I looked down—not a wasp, a bamboo sliver three inches long. Lucia, her back pressed to the door, was loading the tube again as I twisted the needle out, careful not to snap off the point.

"Bet it burns like hell, doesn't it?" She didn't scream the question, instead sounded hopeful and eager, a woman whose pleasure would be delayed until I had experienced pain.

I picked up the folding chair to use as a shield. "What's on those darts?"

Lucia was in no rush now. She had the tube loaded again. Twitched her nose in a way she thought was cute. "You're bigger than most, so I'll use five to make sure. Attractive girls"—a wicked smile—"usually only need two." She braced her shoulder against the doorframe and raised the blowgun to her lips.

I ducked behind the chair and found a crack to peek through. Then I stood straight and forgot about everything else. "Get away from that door," I told her.

Behind Lucia, through the hinged flap, a hand with freakishly long fingers had appeared. It was attached to an arm furred with auburn hair that glistened and snaked longer and longer as if squeezed from a tube or controlled by a contortionist. A fecal stink pushed ahead of it.

I started toward Lucia and yelled, "Get away from that door!"

Too late.

Long hairy fingers explored the hem of the woman's robe, then sensed body heat. Lucia's reaction was to turn and look. Then she opened her mouth to scream but instead made only a high-pitched choking noise.

It took a confusing moment before I understood: Lucia hadn't lowered the blowgun. While screaming, she had inhaled one of her own darts.

18

By watching Lucia during the next few seconds, I learned something that would take time to understand: when panic transitions to horror in human beings, God frees us from our bodies—an act of the greatest kindness. The sufferer is replaced by a mindless creature who is left to struggle and endure pain in the hope of escape.

For Lucia, there was no escape—unless I went to her aid. And I did go to her, although I'm not sure why. My reaction, however, was delayed by my own horror. The chimpanzee's fingers, after burying themselves in her flesh, found her collar and tried to pull her through a slot no larger than a mailbox. Bones snapped. More bones snapped when he tried again. Finally Lucia fell after the robe ripped away. The chimp's hand was searching for Lucia's hair when I at last took action.

A moment later, I had the aluminum pole overhead, ready to strike. Lucia saw me, stared up with glassy eyes, and once again made a whistling noise because she couldn't scream. Perhaps she feared I intended to hit her. That's exactly what I didn't want. So I waited for the chimp to extend his arm before I slammed the pole down. Unlike my distant aunts, Hannah and Sarah, I've never chopped wood for a living. But I have used an axe. I swung so hard, my feet came off the floor—and was rewarded by a screech from the other side of the door, then a furious baritone chatter that warned of revenge. Yet the chimp refused to let go of the woman's hair.

I swung again . . . and again—finally, the animal's hand retreated. Stupidly, I tossed the pole away and used both hands to grab Lucia's waist and tried to push her out of danger. The smart thing to do would have been to reposition myself and *pull*, but I didn't. Nor did I consider the length of a chimpanzee's arms.

When I believed we were safe, I started to say, "I've got to roll you on your stomach because—"

That's as far as I got. On my buttocks, I felt a tentative weight, then the chimp latched onto my belt. With my left hand, I reached back and clawed at his hairy wrist while I searched my right pocket for the box cutter. Before I could use it, I was yanked backward; I sledded across the tile and slammed into the door. My tailbone absorbed most of the impact. Pain radiated into my spine and caused the box cutter to spin to the floor. I was dazed, but the razor was still within reach. I grabbed it and slashed blindly. The chimp shrieked . . . Then I was free, lying on my side.

I rolled, and kept rolling, until I knew I was safe. When I looked up, Lucia was still in danger, so I lunged, grabbed her ankle, and pulled her away, too.

"Open your mouth!" I yelled. "Wider."

She made a gagging noise but did it. I couldn't see, but my fingers soon found the dart lodged in her throat. Gently, I jockeyed it free. It came out as two slivers. The point was sharpened like a needle, blackened as if it had been scorched.

"Did I get it all? Swallow. Open your mouth again— let me see."

"He . . . would have killed me." Her voice was raspy, but at least she could speak. "Why . . . why did you . . . ?"

I steadied her head with my hands and for the first time noticed the pendant hidden beneath her dress: a silver ram's head mounted on a pentagram. I knew its meaning but let it go. "We both need a doctor. What kind of poison is on those darts?"

Lucia shook her head. "Can't move. Am I bleeding?"

Her spine was broken, I realized. "I need the key to the front door. I'll call an ambulance. Tell me about the poison while I look for the key."

The woman's eyes glazed, but deep, deep within was a glittering awareness. *"No,"* she said.

I felt like shaking her. "I need to know what kind of poison. If I die, you're going to die, too."

Lucia's eyelids fluttered to beckon me closer. "Go to

hell . . . stupid girl." Those were her last words before she died.

I tried CPR. Her lips smelled of moss when I blew air into her lungs. Out of a sense of duty, I kept at it, but was preoccupied with my own fear. Had the poison killed her or a broken neck? The spot on my wrist was red but no longer burned. If poison was circulating through my system, the effects were mild. A mild euphoric edge, if anything. Unlike Lucia, I had pulled the dart free instantly.

She's beyond help, I decided. *Find the key—run.*

But where was the key? In Lucia's robe—had to be—but the robe had been ripped off and was piled at the foot of the door. Before risking that, I hoped the key was somewhere on her body. As I searched, the metal slot opened. The chimp's eyes peered through: two oyster-sized orbs of glowing amber. They swept the room . . . found the dead woman, then focused on me. Intelligent eyes. Eyes that noted details of my face, the color and size of me.

Oliver is brilliant, Theo had bragged. Or was I dealing with the female chimp? The snake pole and bamboo tube were within my reach. I grabbed the bamboo, yelled, "Get away—Savvy!" and hurled the thing.

It wasn't the female chimp. The metal lid slammed shut, then levered upward. The chimp thrust his hand through and flipped a middle finger in reply. He grunted—*UNT . . . UNT . . . ITCH!*—a series of baritone belches intended to be understood. Then added, *"OWL-A-BER!"* to correct me. He glared at me for several seconds and then went to work on the door's hinges, prying and pounding with a tool of some kind.

I understood more than the foul names he'd called me. I had to escape or a killer that Theo claimed was half chimp, half ape would soon force his way into the room.

The key . . . Where is that key?

My eyes settled on the robe piled within easy reach of the door.

THE GLOVES near the milking table were made of leather and wire mesh. They extended above my elbows. I wore them to cross the room, even though the bucket I carried was hooked to the end of the snake pole.

The door had been loosened by the chimp's pounding. It crossed my mind that he was so busy, he might not notice if I tiptoed close enough to snatch the robe. I didn't have the courage to try, though, couldn't bear the thought of his hands on me again, so I stuck with my plan. It was a variation of something I'd thought about earlier, a way to surprise Theo.

When I was closer, I lowered the bucket to the floor and removed my left glove. I dropped the glove into the bucket, then watched and waited.

Coral snakes are shy. They live underground. Even when hunting, they prefer cover, which is why they are seldom seen. The snake I had captured used its tongue to find the glove's opening. Soon, two feet of segmented colors—black, yellow, and red—disappeared inside as if slurped down a drain.

Now came the dangerous part. Using my right hand, I lifted the glove from the bucket and folded the wristlet closed. At the same time, I slipped my left hand under the glove to provide support, but also to appear as if I was wearing it. I took a big breath . . . then walked toward the door and pretended to have courage. "Hey . . . Hey, you—Oliver! I heard those names you called me."

The silence on the other side was abrupt. The metal lid opened. Amber eyes blinked with what resembled surprise. I hollered, "I'll shoot you if you cross me again!" then extended the left glove as if it were a weapon.

Never have I seen anything move so fast as the hand that snatched the glove from me. I had intended to offer brief resistance. Impossible. The glove disappeared through the slot before I could jump back. Then I did jump back and immediately grabbed the aluminum pole with its dull hook.

I heard a series of sniffs and guttural belches . . . then a grunt of surprise. After a beat came a roar that would have sent me running if I'd had someplace to run. While Oliver thrashed and roared, I rushed the door and used the hook to snag Lucia's robe.

I didn't look back until I was near the computer screens. My attention seesawed between the robe and the chaotic noise in the next room and the security cameras. In the kitchen, Gail and her skinny teenage friend laughed while the plump witch gestured—but Theo was gone. Nor was he in view of the other cameras stationed around the property. Most likely he was returning to the serpentarium.

The key . . . Lucia had to have hidden it somewhere.

The robe contained several pockets. I found a bamboo quiver with a few darts left, a cigarette lighter, and a quarter-sized bag of powder. I placed it all near the box cutter, then turned the robe inside out, my hands shaking.

I was running out of time. The chimp had refocused his rage on the door. Over and over he slammed his body against it—two hundred pounds of sinew and muscle. After another violent collision, the top hinge exploded, throwing shrapnel across the room. It created an opening through which the chimp's fingers appeared. When Oliver had a handhold, he began to rock the door back and forth. The opening at the top grew incrementally wider. Very soon, the bottom hinge would snap.

The robe's hood revealed a hidden pocket, something hard inside. I struggled with it, then gave up. I wouldn't have time to unlock the door even if it was the key. I had to do something . . . anything to buy time.

What?

Snakes. I was in a room filled with venomous snakes. Deploying weapons that might also kill me was a reckless act. But recklessness was my only hope. Shelves were stacked with shallow trays. I ran across the room, pulled a tray free, and spun it toward the door. Impact jarred the lid off. I watched long enough to see a rattlesnake as thick as my arm appear, then reached for another tray. As I did, I heard a slavering growl. I turned. Oliver's long arm was draped over the door. His head would soon follow.

Don't panic—fight back.

I did. Freeing one snake at a time was useless, so I squared my shoulders and grabbed the closest section of shelving. Back and forth I rocked the frame until an entire stack of trays crashed to the floor. Amid the buzz and hum of reptiles sliding across tile, I hurdled the mess, dodged Lucia's body, and ran to the robe.

"Please, God, let the key be here." I whispered those words before opening the hidden pocket.

It was.

OUTSIDE WAS moonlight and clean air, but I tarried only long enough to bolt the door behind me, then ran. I had to get to the RV park and find help. That's what I intended to do, but soon had to stop because Theo and Carmelo blocked my path.

Fortunately, I saw them before they saw me, so I ducked into bushes at the corner of the serpentarium. The men stood near the Land Rover beneath a moon that dimmed and brightened as clouds streamed past. Spoke in low voices—serious issues to discuss—while I tried to reorganize my options.

There weren't many. I could circle the property in the hope of finding my SUV. Or run to the river and hope Theo had told the truth about owning a canoe. If not, half a mile downriver there would be boats and canoes at the campground docks.

The safety of my own car was more appealing—punch the door code and use the key I keep hidden under the seat. Fire up the engine, spin the wheels, and go. I pictured Carmelo trying to stop me. Imagined him stepping out to face my headlights, then his expression of shock when I floored the accelerator. Too bad for either man if he got in my way.

One terrifying concern: *Oliver.* The room where Theo had once served detentions had windows and presumably a door. The chimp might be waiting if I retraced my steps. The property was big. He might also pick up my scent if I circled around the back or if I angled toward the gravel road.

Oliver's nose is as good as any bloodhound's. Theo's words.

Coral snake poison—if the snake had bitten him—was lethal but slow-acting. Victims had up to twenty-four hours—another of Theo's claims. Worse, I also had to worry about the younger chimp. I had no idea where she was caged or if she was caged. And, according to Lucia, Savvy was just as vicious or more so. My only weapons were in a paper sack: a few bamboo darts, a lighter, and the box cutter. They were no match for animals that could rip steel off its hinges.

Make up your mind, Hannah.

The dart's poison had caused a slight numbing of my left arm, and my lips, too. I couldn't waste more time peeking from bushes. I needed to move, but where? Concrete walls and a steel door had muffled the chimpanzee's chaos. It was blessed relief after what I'd been through, but now I strained to listen. Was Oliver still inside?

Above me were louvered windows. I touched fingers to the glass and waited. A series of tremors signaled that violence continued somewhere inside the building.

Yes. Now was the time to search for my SUV.

I took a last look at the men and reversed course. A distant row of trees marked the river to the west. It wasn't far, only half a football field away. Ahead was the entrance to the serpentarium. Beyond was the back side of the property, probably fenced, but that was a guess. Separating me from freedom was an expanse of mown lawn, where oak trees and moss created islands of gray on a frosted plain. If I tried to cross, there was nowhere to hide except for the trees and trees were a poor choice when fleeing a two-hundred-pound chimp. Krissie's death had proven that.

I took off running anyway. Jogged with long, silent strides until I neared the serpentarium door, which I sprinted past. Then I settled into a comfortable pace while my eyes searched. The dimensions of the snake facility were fixed in my mind. The adjoining room, where Theo had served detentions, was easy to pick out. I monitored it closely as I ran: a pair of lighted windows, glass unbroken . . . and no door until I came around the corner where light spilled onto the grass, which meant there was a door—and that the door was open.

I felt my breath catch. I nearly stopped. Had Oliver escaped? Or had he left the door open before entering the room to attack Lucia?

Possibly both.

I couldn't risk another change of plans. I ran faster,

every sense alert for sounds or movements of any kind. And there was movement—gray shapes furrowed the grass around me. Moon shadow, I thought, until an elongated shape materialized to my right. The object augered itself into a coil . . . its head blossomed wide and flat . . . then it pivoted to face me.

A cobra. That's what it was. And a cobra's hiss is actually a raspy roar. The sound was so loud and threatening, I stumbled when I swerved away and nearly fell. Luckily, I caught myself or would have sprawled atop several snakes that were all gliding westward toward the trees . . . or they smelled the river.

Panicking, I hurdled and high-stepped until I thought I was clear. Wrong. Every few strides I heard weeds move or a rattlesnake's buzz that warned the field was alive with snakes. The result was a zigzag course with my senses focused on the ground, not on what lay ahead.

The error could have been deadly. But my luck held. When I did shift my attention forward, a safe haven awaited: Belton's camper was parked in shadows under a tree. No lights showing, but that was okay. Even if Belton was gone, there was a chance they'd left the keys in the ignition . . . or that my car was parked on the other side, hidden by the camper's bulk.

Best of all, Carmelo and Theo were busy at the front of the property. I was on the back acreage, shielded by buildings, just me and the snakes.

With Lucia dead, what was there to fear?

19

I OPENED THE CAMPER DOOR BUT SNIFFED THE
air before entering. Forever imprinted on my memory was
the primal stink of Oliver, half ape, half chimp. Only reassuring odors greeted me, however—diesel and shower
soap—so I stepped inside, whispering, "Hello . . . ?"

In reply, a voice said, "Thank god, you're alive."

Belton's voice. I clicked the door shut. "Don't turn on
the lights. How do you lock this damn thing?"

"Carmelo broke the latch with a hammer. Did he follow you? Please tell me the police are coming."

I fiddled with the lock anyway but soon gave up.
Moonlight filtered through the curtains. I pulled them
back so I could see. The man was on his belly on the
couch, hands tied behind him—a needless cruelty that
revived my anger. "They left you tied up like this the
whole time?"

"Carmelo would have done worse, but I pretended to have a heart attack and pass out. Remember me saying he's not as dumb as he acts? In some ways, he's dumber because he's greedy. What about the police?"

"Theo took my phone," I said and went past him to check the ignition. "Do you have a key hidden?"

"Not in a rental vehicle. My hands . . . I lost feeling an hour ago. Untie me. I can't take much more. Oh—and my glasses. I need my glasses. They're somewhere on the counter."

"Any idea where they parked my SUV?"

"It's all a blur, dear."

I retrieved the box cutter from the sack and knelt. As I did, Belton added in a sheepish way, "Sorry about the mess. They blew some kind of drug up my nose. My bladder turned traitor. Nothing I could do."

Through the knees of my jeans, I could feel that the carpet was wet. "Hold still so I don't cut you," I said. They had used tie wraps on his wrists and ankles. *Snip-snip* and he was free. I helped him set up. "Can you walk?"

"Give me a second. What about my glasses?"

Two minutes later he got to his feet, hobbled from the back of the RV to the front but had to stop twice to steady himself. Then almost fell again when he pulled on a clean polo, even buttoned two buttons.

"I'm practically a cripple."

"You're better than when you started. It'll take a few minutes."

"No police, huh?"

"We need to get moving. Theo doesn't know I'm loose. But he will. In fact, he probably knows already."

"Then they'll come looking. I'll be fine now that I've got some blood circulating. The smart thing to do is, I stay here while you go get help."

"Not a chance," I said, although in truth that's exactly what I yearned to do—run for my life. If I made it to the river, I could swim if there wasn't a canoe or boat to steal. No point in telling him I'd been darted, that my mind was a jumble of fear, constantly scanning for new symptoms.

He sensed my distress and placed a hand on my shoulder. "Hannah, dear, I'll be eighty-one in December. My wife is dead and . . . and my only child is dead. So—"

"Stop that kind of talk right now. We're leaving together." I went toward the door and peered through the frosted window. "What about weapons? I don't suppose you have a gun or an axe or anything we could use?"

Up until then, the man had sounded coherent but feeble. My question changed that. "If I did, I'd send you on your way and kill both those sons of bitches."

When he added, "It's a long story," I thought, *He came here looking for revenge.*

True or not, his story would have to wait. "Come on. You can use my shoulder as a brace."

Belton, sheepish again, said, "I've got clean slacks if there's time."

There wasn't, which I was about to tell him when I saw in the frosted window someone approaching: a black silhouette, hunch-shouldered and moving with an odd loping gait.

No . . . not someone, *something*. Our visitor had distinctive ears, like two clamshells tacked to his head—chimpanzee ears. Oliver or the other one, Savvy, was tracking me but hadn't yet settled on the camper.

I whispered, "Don't make a sound," and stupidly felt for the broken latch on a door that couldn't be locked.

"Is it Carmelo?"

I hushed him with a hiss while I took the box cutter from the sack. Placed it beside me and got a firm grip on the doorknob using both hands.

I felt the camper shift with Belton's weight. "A fillet knife—I forgot. There's a knife in one of these drawers."

"Quiet."

Too late. Outside, the silhouette stopped . . . turned . . . listened. At the same instant, a drawer full of silverware clanged to the floor. I heard a grumbled *"Damn,"* then Belton made more noise by searching through the mess.

"Find that knife," I whispered. "You're going to need it."

I expected the chimp to sprint immediately toward us, but he approached warily, limping on one bad leg. Carrying something in his hands, too—a bag, possibly. The combination struck me as more humanlike than monkeylike, but it certainly wasn't Theo or Carmelo. And even if it was, there was no way I could hold the door closed if a man was determined to get in. We had to try something else.

"Go to the front of the camper," I told Belton and pushed him along. "Did you find the knife?"

"A steak knife. And not a very good one . . . Who's out there?"

"I'm not sure. We'll wait until he's inside the camper, then you jump out the driver's-side door and hide. I'll get him to follow me out the passenger side."

"That's crazy. How?"

"I don't know. I'll outrun him. Don't worry, I'm faster than most people."

"Hannah, I won't use you as bait—"

"Please don't argue." The RV's cab had twin captain's chairs that swiveled. I took Belton by the shoulders, backed him into his chair, and turned him so he was closer to the door. A fire extinguisher was mounted next to the console. I popped the straps and freed it.

He said, "I should have thought of that."

I hefted the canister—it was full—and removed the safety pin. "Don't do anything until I tell you. Then try to get to the river. Theo has a canoe. Or said he did. I'll meet you, but don't wait if I'm not there. Or go to the road, if it's easier, and flag someone down." As I whispered, my eyes were fixed on the camper door. In one hand, I held the box cutter, razor out. In the other, the fire extinguisher.

Belton started to protest, but I hushed him, saying, "He's coming in."

Not quite, but the chimp—or whoever it was—was close enough to blacken the frosted window that had been silver with moonlight. My hip was braced against a bulkhead while my heart pounded. "Get ready," I told Belton and walked toward the door.

"What are you *doing*?"

Watching the doorknob, is what I was doing. Watched the knob turn while something in me decided which was the better weapon, a razor blade or a pressurized steel canister? I slipped the box cutter into my jeans and backed away, the fire extinguisher in both hands. First I would blind our intruder with spray, then throw the empty canister. After that, run for my life—if I was able.

Slowly . . . slowly . . . the door swung open. A black silhouette spilled in with a gusting breeze. I sniffed the air, expecting the worst, while the RV shifted with our intruder's weight.

I took another step back and hollered, "I've got a gun and I'll use it."

A voice I didn't recognize responded, "No, Hannah, you don't. But I won't hurt you." More like a growl, the voice was so deep.

"Think what you want," I said, while Belton yelled, "We're both armed. Get the hell away."

The shadow retreated while the camper leveled itself. The door closed but then opened a moment later. Along with the breeze, the shadow reclaimed the room. "Stay away from the campground. The Gypsies will call Theo and they'll be watching the roads. Don't trust anyone."

I was stunned. "You're willing to help? Call the police, if you want to help us. Or tell me where my car is."

"I can't do that."

"Why? Who are you?" I stepped toward the door. "Come in before someone sees you."

The silhouette retreated. "No closer. And no lights. Head for the river. You'll have to climb the fence. There's a boat with a half a tank of gas. A little aluminum boat. Pull start with a kicker. Hike straight west if you can't find the path."

"How do you know my name?"

"Because I do. On the river, go north. The campground is south and Theo will find out. Remember— *north*. You saw what happened to that little girl?"

Krissie, he meant. "Then call the police," I said. "At least tell them what happened. If we go north, there's nothing for miles."

A long dark arm appeared and placed a bag on the floor. I got a glimpse of the man's jaw and his odd clamshell ears. "This is yours," he said and started to close the door, then remembered something. "I'm glad Lucia's dead. Did she dart you?"

"Yes."

"How many times?"

Belton asked, "What's he talking about?"

"Once," I said, "but I pulled it out right away."

"I think I saw Benadryl tablets in there."

Only then did I realize that it was my backpack on the floor. "What kind of poison did she use?"

"Lucia was a vicious, evil woman," the voice said. "I've always wanted to thank you, Hannah. Now I have."

The shadow retreated. The door closed.

Belton asked, "Who the hell was that?"

I stood there dumbly for a moment, then rushed to open my backpack. A box of Benadryl tablets had been placed strategically on top. The 9mm Devel pistol, still loaded, was beneath it.

"I think I know," I said, "but I hope I'm wrong."

Belton didn't have an opportunity to press. Outside the camper, security lights flashed on with the siren scream of the burglar alarm.

"Theo found Lucia's body," I told him. "We've got to run."

RUNNING IS something an eighty-one-year-old man with a bad heart cannot be asked to do, but there was nothing typical about Belton Matás. He jogged ahead of me with an odd wide-legged, arm-pumping gait that would have been humorous in a movie but wasn't funny under the circumstances. A Land Rover, lights blazing, had skidded around the side of the serpentarium, coming fast. Until then, we had been walking at a steady pace but were only halfway to the fence.

Belton ducked low. "Did they see us?"

"I don't think so," I said, removing the pistol from the backpack. "If they did, there's nothing we can do but make our stand here."

Wrong. That's when the man from Virginia decided he was spry enough to run. He took off at a pretty good clip, fast enough to worry me, although it was no struggle to keep up. "A heart attack isn't going to help our situation any. Belton? *Belton?*"

The man kept running. He was a big fellow, still had some power in his thighs, but was also carrying a lot of weight around the belly. Finally I grabbed his shoulder. "They're headed for your RV. Slow down. But be careful where you put your feet."

It was the second time I had warned him.

"Don't ever get old, Hannah, it's humiliating." Hands on knees, he sucked in air.

"I'd like to get a *little older*, if you don't mind, so keep moving."

"Why are you worried about snakes? At the homestead, you walked through weeds, muck, never a word. Totally fearless."

"I'll explain when we're in the boat. Would it help if I took your arm?"

Belton watched the Land Rover brake to a stop outside his RV. "Do you know how to use that pistol?" Carmelo had appeared in the headlights, carrying what I guessed was a sawed-off shotgun, then jogged toward the door, while Theo, the driver, stayed at the wheel.

I said, "He's going to be crazy mad when he sees you're gone. Please, Belton, we've got to get over the fence before they spot us."

"I did two tours in Vietnam, Army intelligence, and I still know how to shoot." He stood, eyes fixed on Carmelo, who ducked into the trailer. "Give me the pistol,

Hannah. You won't get very far towing my tired old ass. It's what *I* want."

"I'd prefer not to discuss your backside or your ailments until we're in the boat," I said and tugged at his arm while lights blinked on inside the RV. Soon, Carmelo, from the distance, yelled something in a language that wasn't English or Spanish—a guttural profanity, it sounded like.

"Stubborn girl," Belton grumbled. He pivoted and began to match my long strides, the two of us walking fast, hugging tree shadows, the fence a jumble of vines only twenty yards away. Yet it seemed to take hours to cross the last stretch of open ground. Every step, I expected a spotlight to find us or to hear a gunshot.

That didn't happen until Belton was straddling the chain-link fence where we'd found a break in the barbed wire. I had helped boost the man up and his shirt had snagged. As he tried to free himself, we heard grinding gears, then the whistling roar of a diesel engine. I didn't have to look to know they were coming because shadows were displaced by dazzling white lights. Belton, with his glasses and heavy chin, appeared to be glazed with frost. For the first time I saw that his arms had been gouged bloody by the chimpanzee Oliver.

I said, "I'll cut you loose," and pulled myself up onto the bar, but his shirt ripped away when he lost his balance. Belton landed hard and rolled. A second later, I was on the river side of the fence, helping him up. "Can you walk?"

He made a mewling sound so childlike, it was heart-breaking—frustration, indignity. But there was nothing he could do to change what had happened. Although he tried, saying, "I really wish you'd give me that damn pistol."

Behind us, the Land Rover was accelerating, not slowing: four bright fog lights mounted on the roof.

"You're going to get me killed, too, Belton. Please don't argue."

The man sputtered, "I give up!" He stumbled to his feet and went toward the river, crashing through bushes with his weight. A moment later, he called, "I found the path."

I stayed where I was and faced the Land Rover, the pistol level in both hands. I had never used the gun at night before and was surprised that its sights glowed like numerals on a watch: three intersecting green dots. The sights made it easier to draw a bead on the Land Rover's windshield. As an afterthought, I thumbed the hammer back, then touched my finger to the trigger and waited. Stood there in full view and didn't flinch even when a spotlight snapped on and found me.

Shoot Theo first through the driver's-side window. That's what I decided to do. *Shoot Carmelo next. And shoot him again if he exits carrying that shotgun.*

I wasn't afraid. Belton's childlike mewling had changed me in some cold and empty way. There was no indecision. No quibbling with my conscience. No labored breathing or panicky voice that urged me to flee.

It was as if a darkness had been set loose inside me. I felt free and focused and sure, as the Land Rover bore closer, speeding as if to crush me, bouncing tail-high over ruts.

Let them see you, I thought. *Make sure they know who is behind these bullets.*

I did . . . Then, when the vehicle suddenly braked to a halt, I felt a trickling disappointment—not relief. Fifty yards was a risky shot for a pistol that contained only seven bullets. I didn't shoot.

A shotgun appeared from the passenger's window. I ducked when Carmelo fired one blind shot but stood taller after pellets had rained down through the foliage. Fifty yards was also too far for a double-barreled shotgun.

Theo ground the gears. The vehicle crept closer. Once again, I took aim and placed my finger on the trigger while the spotlight illuminated what I was doing . . . possibly, even what I was thinking:

Shoot Theo first. One round. Then one for Carmelo. Maybe the bullets will pierce the windshield, maybe they won't—let God decide.

My thinking was so clear and sure.

The Land Rover stopped again. More grinding of gears, then Theo found reverse and backed away fast while the transmission whined. Carmelo yelled a profanity out the window just before the vehicle lurched forward, then kicked dirt toward the moon and sped away.

"Did you fire that shot?" Belton had returned to check on me.

"Cowards," I said, watching the Land Rover. "Both them just cowards. They ran away."

"You hit their car?"

I used the de-cocking lever so the pistol could ride safely in my backpack. It made a satisfying steel-on-steel click. "They didn't give me a chance." I walked past Belton toward the river. "You know where it is, so show me the path."

THE ALUMINUM BOAT that awaited was flat-bottomed, painted green, with a small outboard motor that coughed and sputtered but didn't fire the first few times I pulled the starter rope.

"Use those oars," I told Belton. "You row while I work on this. It's probably a bad fuel connection." I pushed the boat away from the bank and felt a weightless sense of freedom. The moon filled a crevice between the trees where wind gusted from the northwest, but the water was calm.

"Oarlocks," he said as if reminding himself what to do. "North, the guy told us, right? Is that north?" Belton pointed upriver with an oar.

I said, "If I get this engine started, maybe we should risk being seen by the campground people. There's nothing north of here but wild country and cattle. If we go south, the Caloosahatchee is only fifteen miles or so, then another few miles east to Labelle. We can call police from there." I looked up from the fuel tank. "You explored this river with Carmelo, what do you think?"

"That's the problem. Carmelo lives in a houseboat about three miles south of the RV park, and there are more houseboats where the river widens. I don't know if they're all buddy-buddy, but I doubt if we could get past without being seen. One phone call and he'd run us down with that Bass Cat of his." Belton fitted the second oar into the lock, then spun us around with an expertise that was encouraging. "We'll start north and see how it goes, okay?"

The gas tank was plastic with a heavy plastic screw top. I burped the tank, checked the fittings, and tried again. The little 15-horsepower engine was too simple to need computer chips yet still wouldn't start. "Why in the world would he loan us a bad engine?"

The aluminum boat surged forward, oars dripping. Belton replied, "He knew your name. Who is he?"

"We've never met, but . . . Well, I'm not sure. Tyrone, probably. I didn't get a close look at him."

"I wonder how he got your backpack."

"He must have beaten Theo to my SUV. I don't know why he'd want to help us—I just wish he had better judgment when it came to boats."

"Maybe it's because of what happened to Lucia."

I unclipped the fuel line from the engine and squeezed the rubber bulb until pressure built. "It was an ugly thing to see, Belton. Let's not talk about it."

"I met her and her friends my first night here. There was something nasty about those three. Or sinister. I'm not sure how to describe it. *Mean*, I guess." The boat skated ahead, the oarlocks creaked, while frogs and night birds trilled. "Hannah . . . if you killed Lucia, I'm sure you had no choice. We were kidnapped. The police will understand that."

"The chimp got his hands on her," I said. "It was . . . awful. He'll kill us, too, if we don't get away from here."

"You don't think that . . . *thing* is smart enough to come after us? He picked me up like I was nothing, could've ripped my arms off. I don't know why he didn't. Theo and Carmelo are bad enough."

"The chimp knows what I look like, knows my scent, too. I cut him pretty badly with a razor—"

"Good!"

"And I tricked him into grabbing a coral snake."

"A snake? Outstanding. Then he's dead by now."

"I'm not sure he was bitten. Even if he was, it's a slow poison. What I'm telling you is, Oliver the chimp has got his reasons to attack me. You should know that in advance."

"As if I'd leave you. He's just a damn animal. Short attention span and all that. No . . . Carmelo's the one we need to worry about."

"The girl Oliver killed, Krissie, she wouldn't agree."

Belton murmured, "Ah yes . . . poor little thing," then went silent and concentrated on the oars while I knelt in the boat's stern. It was possible the carburetor was flooded. I pulled the rope starter several times, then reconnected the fuel hose. In the microsilence that followed came the baffled roar from far downriver of an outboard motor starting.

Belton continued to row but now harder. "That's

Carmelo's Bass Cat. He'll come here first, thinking we're on foot." He started to say something else but then jerked around in his seat. "What the hell was that?" Oars out of the water, the man stared at the nearby shore.

"Did you see something?"

"You didn't hear it? Branches breaking, something high up in the trees, I could've sworn."

I crouched to get the pistol while my eyes searched, seeing stars above the river's gloom. The tree canopy was a ridge of gray that pulsated in the wind. "How far?"

"Just over there. But now . . . I don't know. Maybe I imagined it."

I said, "Cross your fingers and pray this works." I leaned over the motor and yanked the rope. After two failures, I opened the choke and tried again. Finally the engine caught, belched smoke, and fired to life. I slammed the choke closed and sat with the tiller in my left hand. "Get those oars in and move forward. Let's see if I can get this thing on plane."

Belton did it, but his eyes remained focused on trees that lined the shore, a silver tunnel of oak and moss that followed us as we snaked upriver in a boat that wasn't fast and plowed a wake.

20

CARMELO WAS FOLLOWING US. I COULD FEEL THE rumble of his engine through our hull despite the smoke and clatter of the little outboard. Nothing to see behind us, though, because we had rounded several bends, and another sharp turn lay ahead. I said, "He's following our motor slick."

"Our what?"

I motioned toward a trail of froth left by the outboard's exhaust. "He knows there's a boat ahead of him."

"But he can't be sure it's us. It could be anybody—unless Tyrone set us up."

"Tyrone wouldn't do that," I said, which came out sharper than intended. "We can't outrun him, we have to find a place to hide. Do you recognize this part of the river? We need a spot too shallow or too narrow for him to follow."

Belton sat facing me, looking aft, still fixated on the branches he'd heard breaking ten minutes before. "A spotlight. Carmelo just turned on a spotlight."

I glanced back to see a smoky beam ricochet off the clouds. "That's good. The moon's bright enough, he'd only use a light to search for us onshore. That means he's not sure we're in a boat. If he was sure, he'd be on us by now. Top end, that Bass Cat probably does sixty."

Belton said, "Then I was right," and allowed his eyes to explore ahead. "We never got more than a few miles north of the RV park. It gets narrow fast and Carmelo was worried about damaging his propeller. There was a little spot I wanted to see. I suggested we use his trolling motors, but he wouldn't give in. This was two days ago." He swung his legs around to face forward. "I remember a place where the river forks. Oh, and a couple of feeder creeks where Carmelo said the bass fishing was particularly good." His head swiveled like slow radar. "I don't know . . . it all looks so different at night."

I pivoted the tiller without slowing for the next turn and followed the concave bank. The current wasn't strong enough to abrade snags that lay beneath the surface, but shoals and sunken limbs were easy to spot because the moon was bright behind low sailing clouds. Around the next bend, trees funneled closer, a section of river so narrow it would be difficult for Carmelo to spin his twenty-foot Bass Cat around without coming to a stop. I asked, "Does this look familiar?"

"It's hard to see anything until we're past it. I wish we had a light."

"In my bag there's a flashlight, but I don't want to use it unless we have to." I craned my head forward. "There . . . to your left . . . does that look like an opening to a creek?"

It was, but I plowed past because there was another opening ahead and to our right—a pool of shadows like the mouth of a cave where low trees sealed the entrance. I slowed the boat and idled into the bushes after telling Belton, "Duck your head, then get the oars ready. Unless you want me to row."

"You're kidding. We'd need a machete to cut our way in here." He was fighting off leaves and spiderwebs.

I killed the engine, stood, and snapped a few limbs, letting them hang. As I did, the rumble of Carmelo's boat moved closer, no spotlight showing now. "Okay . . . help me push us back into the river. Once we're clear, I'll row."

"Row where?"

I waited until I had the boat moving, skating across the surface like a water spider. "He'll follow our motor slick and think we somehow disappeared into that cut. Or even get out to explore on foot. That'll give us time to find a hiding spot in the creek we just passed."

"Smart girl." Belton nodded, but then reconsidered. "I don't know . . . We'll be on the same side of the river as the serpentarium. Maybe we should keep going."

"There's no time," I said. "Open my bag. There's mosquito netting in there and spray. We'll need it."

Belton replied, "I still think the other side of the river is safer."

It wasn't snakes he was worried about.

. . .

CARMELO AND THEO were in the Bass Cat, close enough to hear their voices but impossible to see because we were twenty yards up a feeder creek, hidden under moss and limbs, when they stopped and used the spotlight.

Theo's voice: "Boats don't just disappear. See the broken branches?"

Carmelo: "Get that damn light out of my eyes. More likely, they went to the road and hitchhiked. Probably already talked to the cops. Fat old man, should'a broke his neck and taken all them maps and files. How you think he knows so much?"

"You're saying a boat can *disappear*? I don't see any slick upriver. Their trail ends here."

"That don't mean nothing if they run close to the bushes."

"Tree branches don't break themselves. Take the shotgun and get in the water. "

"Huh?"

"Hike in there and have a look."

"Why don't you?"

"Because you still owe me five grand for this goddamn boat, that's why. No . . . I'll hand you the gun *after* you're over the side. They can't be far."

Garbled complaints from Carmelo preceded the splash of a man lowering himself into the water.

"A motor slick don't mean nothing if she run close. The girl's a fishing guide. That's something a fishing guide would do. And not bad-lookin' neither, if you know what I mean." Laughter.

"Just do what I tell you."

"The boy genius, I keep forgetting. You don't think she's got a nice rack? Well, she does—I found out for sure when I patted her down. And them legs—long legs can be fun on a woman."

Theo replied with something too rude to repeat, then added, "Like a stork—she's all yours."

"I take you up on that one. Man . . . this muck . . . it like walking in shit." More splashing, then silence. "They'd've needed a chain saw to go any farther."

"Keep looking. They might have found a canoe. Maybe the one with the electric motor—that thing's fast. I told you to find out which boat's missing."

"Trolling motors don't leave a slick, man. Hell . . . there ain't nothing in here to see. Call the midget twins. You should have heard from them by now. We're wasting time."

"Only if someone tries to slip past the docks. That's what I told them. You're saying it's too narrow even for a Gheenoe? They could have taken the one with the kicker."

"Look for yourself."

"Well, someone broke these branches. Why would they bother?"

"While we're standing here jawing, that girl and old man could be getting away. Another mile or so north, it's too narrow for us. Depends on what they stole—*if* they're in a boat, which I doubt they are. You know what tickles me? Both them marks actually believed I was simple-minded."

"Yeah, well, you haven't convinced me. Come on. We'll take a look upriver."

Carmelo said to Theo, "How can I when you're blinding me with that damn light?"

The Bass Cat's engine slipped into reverse. The noise of cavitation cloaked the conversation that followed, Theo speaking in a low voice, Carmelo replying, "Well . . . if you say so."

Belton's hand found my shoulder and gave me a pat. "Good job."

I whispered, "They're not gone yet." We were scrunched low, both of us clinging to foliage to hold the boat steady. Seconds later I said, "Quiet. They're coming this way."

The bass boat was idling downriver, not upriver. That's what alerted me. Willow boughs formed an awning, a curtain I could part. Through a veil of leaves I saw the spotlight probe the entrance of the feeder creek . . . then the boat appeared, two cookie-cutter men standing behind the console in silhouette. The spotlight panned toward me. I ducked and leaned my shoulder against Belton as a warning. He understood. He got a better grip on the branch above, which allowed me a free hand to find the pistol. As the men idled closer, I raised the weapon and aimed it at the spotlight.

Carmelo's voice: "We're kicking mud. I don't want to fry another water pump. You know . . . I think that girl would'a pulled the trigger. I truly do. Back there in the Land Rover."

Theo's response was muffled.

"She could shoot us from the bushes, hide anywhere and wait for us to go by. *Bang-bang-bang*—just like that. That's why I don't like this poking-around crap."

Another muffled response but lengthier.

Carmelo disagreed. "That's one way. But it ain't the best way."

Theo spoke louder. "You leave the thinking to me, Einstein," then rambled on for a while before allowing Carmelo an opening.

"All I'm saying is, you take the shock collars off them monkeys, there's no telling who they attack. It's not like they fussy—I'll shoot that damn female, she charges me again. Don't think I won't. Liked to bit my arm off, that time."

"After what you did—*good*. And don't call them monkeys."

"You weren't even around. All I did was compliment her on her pretty pink—"

Theo hissed, "Shut up," then his voice softened. "Hey . . . what's that over there?"

I felt Belton squeeze my knee when the light found the overhang where we were hidden. A bright wafer of white that probed and expanded, steam rising off the water where moths collected, then the light swung away.

Carmelo continued talking. "As if that damn animal understood what I said. Shit, just crazy to let them two loose. You can hide a dead body every few years or so and get away with it. Fine. But more than two in one night, man, it's us they'll send to prison. You keep them damn monkeys on a leash or I'm done with this business. I mean it this time." He hacked, hacked again and spit. "That's not to say I won't find that gold and silver on my own."

Theo snapped, "Shut up. Just shut up," then got control of himself and spoke in a more careful way. "I think you're right. They're not in a boat. Let's head back."

"Say what?"

"You heard me."

"What's got into you? I thought you wanted to head upriver. Might as well since we're here."

"I'm worried about Oliver. He wasn't in his room and goddamn snakes everywhere. There's no telling what else that bitch did to him."

"Lucia—yeah, good riddance. Total bitch."

Theo said, "No, you idiot, that hick with the smart mouth. I'd like to see what Savvy does to her if Oliver's hurt. In fact, that's what I'll do—let Savvy handle it."

"I ain't got nothing to do with that, I just told you." The engine clanked into reverse. "Shit . . . Hang on . . . Sit yourself so I can see."

The creek was so narrow, the boat had to back all the way to the river. Several minutes later the engine revved and powered southward. It left a wake of squawking birds, a wash of waves that dissipated as the engine faded, then suddenly went silent. Belton waited to speak. "Theo wanted us to hear that."

"I know. I lost track of their engine. Did they stop?"

"He wasn't convinced we're here, though. More of a just-in-case thing. He's afraid you'll shoot. Me, I wouldn't hesitate. Are you sure you don't want me to take the gun?"

I said, "I'm wondering if he dropped Carmelo at the point, then stopped downriver to see what happens. What else explains why it took them so long to leave?"

Belton slapped a mosquito on his cheek and stretched his legs. "Stay here for a while and listen, I guess. What do you think? It's not quite ten-thirty."

I returned the pistol to the backpack and left the bag open. "I want to disinfect those cuts on your arms. We'll give it half an hour. If it was Theo who stayed behind, he can't keep quiet that long. Roll your sleeves up." I used the flashlight for a moment—several deep gouges beneath dried blood—then switched it off and went to work from memory.

He said, "Don't worry about me, how are you feeling?"

"The Benadryl pills made me a little sleepy. Otherwise, fine . . . Belton?"

"Yes, dear."

"I want to ask you something."

"Ask away."

"Now would be a good time to tell me that secret you've been holding back."

A FEW MINUTES after eleven I drifted the boat clear and paddled toward the river, the water shallow enough that I used an oar as a pole. For the first time in my life,

I despaired of moonlight, because the moon flung my shadow ahead like a warning to anyone who might await. Belton and I had agreed no talking, so we traveled in a hush of insects with a northwest breeze that tasted of smoke. He sat with his back to me, hollow-eyed, heavier for the history he had shared, me standing in the stern so I could use the tiller to rudder.

How do you comfort a man who, after four years' searching, is finally convinced his missing son was murdered? Worse, two men who at the very least had played a role in that murder were now chasing us.

"I was a poor excuse for a father and a worse husband. Kenneth was only twelve when we divorced, so he naturally sided with his mother. She remarried, so did I. That began a twenty-year estrangement." Belton, sitting in darkness, had kept his voice low, spoke matter-of-factly as if time had distanced him from events.

"After police notified me of Ken's disappearance— this was four years ago—I sat down and counted the times I'd made a serious effort to reconcile. There was once when he graduated from high school, then another after he got his master's. That's it. Both times, he refused. And, know what? Secretly, I was relieved. *Relieved.* Can you imagine? All the awkwardness, I guess, that comes with patching up a relationship, he spared me that. I was fixated on building my business, living the new life I'd planned. Selfish, an overachiever. It's strange how people like me rationalize the damage we do. We're convinced there's plenty of time to make amends, but that's a lie. It's a lie that postpones guilt and buys us freedom.

You won't be able to understand, Hannah. I've met damn few who are genuinely good and decent. People like you stand out."

Belton's story did not mesh with the person I had believed him to be, so I could only respond, "We all do mean things. You've changed or you wouldn't be here. When did you start looking for Kenneth?"

A year after police had tracked all leads to a dead end, Belton had sold his business and gone to work on the case on his own. As police knew, the son had an addiction problem—painkillers after a skiing accident, oxycodone his favorite. Because drugs were the focus of the investigation, the disappearance was dismissed as an unfortunate but all-too-common side effect. Belton was willing to believe what seemed obvious but wanted details.

Then everything changed. A year ago, he had found Kenneth's hidden hard drive and paid an electronics expert skilled enough to decrypt what it contained. Gleaning the names of more drug dealers was the objective, but Belton discovered something else. He was aware that his son had embraced a hobby while in rehab—metal detectors and the American Civil War—but until then did not realize the significance. Kenneth was as driven as his father. Florida, with its little-known and often untouched battlefields, soon became an obsession. He spent a month at the National Archives, where he accessed forgotten diaries and letters. By the next winter he had unique files on the Battle of Natural Bridge near Tallahassee and battles fought at Olustee and Santa Rosa Island and Fort Brooke, Tampa. He visited them all as a devoted hobbyist. So far, nothing to hide. What the hard drive revealed, though, was that Kenneth returned to those sites at night with his metal detector and dug for artifacts that he sold on the black market. It was criminal behavior that meshed with his addiction to unscripted drugs.

"Four months ago Ken's notes led me to a collector who lives outside Labelle. A nice guy, once I'd convinced him I was an artifact hound and knew a young collector from Virginia named Kenneth. He had no idea why I was really there, didn't even know that Ken had disappeared. It's the way that business works: don't ask, don't tell. Stick to dollar amounts and small talk. He gave me an e-mail address for Theo Ivanhoff—identified only as *T.I.* in my son's notes. And he said Ken had asked him where he could rent a motorboat to do some bass fishing on the Telegraph River."

"The canoe we found," I said, "which could have had a motor."

"I don't want to believe that, but I'm afraid so. Anyway, that was my big break. Know why?" Belton had to gather himself before he could explain, "Ken hated fishing. Too impatient. Like father, like son—my god, I wish I had gotten to know him better."

For some losses, there is no comfort. Even so, I tried by saying, "Once we're out of this mess, I'll help in any way I can. Promise."

Find the killer or killers of the missing Kenneth Matás, I meant, but felt certain we already had.

· · ·

The mouth of the feeder creek was deeper, but I waited until we had drifted into the river to use both oars and turn the boat north. It would have been just as safe to start the engine if Theo or Carmelo was watching from nearby—safer, probably—but that didn't dawn on me until Belton suddenly stirred and looked behind us. "Was that the wind?"

Oarlocks creaked when I folded the oars inboard and let the boat glide. To the southwest, the sky was a charcoal sketch of trees, moon, and a sky that boiled with slow-motion clouds. "There could be a squall building. Some of those look like they hold rain." I placed the pistol on the seat beside me. "Rowing's a waste of time. I should've started the engine to begin with." Then hollered toward the bank, "Carmelo . . . *Theo*. If you're here, let's get this over with. We're not going back, so if you've got something to say, say it."

Belton cupped hands to his ears and whispered, "Listen."

Far, far in the distance, I heard what sounded like a school of fish feeding. No . . . one big fish that crashed the surface, waited, then crashed the surface again. The rhythm varied but was so relentless I soon changed my mind. "Could be a waterspout. I heard a tornado once. It sounded like a waterfall coming through the trees until it got close, then it was more like a diesel truck. A loud, roaring noise."

"Trees," Belton repeated, thinking about it. "Yes . . . something coming through the trees. But still a long way off."

I cocked my head and concentrated. Gradually the roar of a waterfalls became the rhythmic crash of what might have been an animal swinging through the forest canopy, growing louder as it traveled toward us from the southwest.

I said, "Oh my lord," and got to my feet. "We've got to move." I started the engine and put the boat in gear.

Belton said, "We're imagining things—it's just the wind. Before a rain, the wind does that. You don't really think it could be—"

"Of course I don't," I said. "But there's no point in sitting here."

"It's because of Theo, the power of suggestion. That chimp is a damn monster—you don't have to tell me. Out here, though, he wouldn't know where to look. Animals will attack, sure, but they don't follow people for miles. The whole notion is absurd." Belton seemed satisfied yet soon added, "I'll watch behind us while you steer. Give me the gun."

I couldn't do that. He was an old man with a guilty conscience who believed he had nothing to live for, therefore nothing to lose—a dangerous combination. That's what I told myself anyway, although in truth my reasons were too personal, too complex, to understand, let alone explain. The Devel had been owned by my late Uncle Jake. Entrusting it to someone who was not afraid was an admission of my own self-doubt. Jake would not have approved.

I replied with an evasion. "If you see something I don't, the gun is all yours."

21

THE ALUMINUM BOAT'S TOP SPEED WAS 15 MPH, perhaps less, but over the range of a mile it was faster than the fastest man or animal. I wanted to believe that so argued the case in my head until I was satisfied.

Yes, it was true . . . on land anyway. In the ocean, it was possible that dolphins or killer whales or a fish that was all muscle, such as a tarpon, might be able to match our pace. But dolphins and killer whales weren't pursing us. Thinking this raised my spirits, so I shared my thoughts with Belton.

He didn't comment, instead kept his eyes fixed on the moonscape of trees as we carved our way through switchbacks that veered east or west, then straightened northward. Soon we came to the fork he had described. I asked, "Think we should go to the right?"

"Definitely," he answered.

We were both thinking what could not be said: a chimpanzee would have to cross the river to follow us if we veered right. It didn't worry me that Theo had mentioned swimming with Oliver as a child. Even if a chimp was pursing us—which was difficult to believe—it would be impossible for him to keep up if he had to take to the water. I said, "Good choice," and swung the boat northeast.

Like a funnel, the river narrowed. Shadows spattered the water with moonlight. Frogs trilled a seesaw chorus and fish boiled at our approach. After a few minutes, I began to relax a little. So did Belton. He said, "I think we're in the clear. They might watch the highways, but they can't catch us here."

I hefted the gas tank. It was half full, which I told him.

"Plenty of fuel," he said. "That's something else in our favor. How are you feeling? Still sleepy from the Benadryl?"

I had been stifling yawns, was desperate to close my eyes, but said, "We're not stopping until we run out of river. And if we do, I think we should hike north on foot. There's a road somewhere to the north." I wasn't sure that was true but tried to come across as confident.

Belton, sounding tired himself, said, "It's almost eleven-thirty."

"I'm fine," I replied. "The numbness in my arm is totally gone. It's doesn't seem that late to me."

His head drooped for a moment—no, it was a nod. "I was thinking about the spot I mentioned. The one Carmelo wouldn't risk his propeller to see? If memory serves, it should be a mile or so ahead. The remains of another homestead, although god knows if there's anything left. Google Earth doesn't show much, but people lived there. Kenneth found the spot on a map from 1858. I have no idea if he ever made it there to search."

"Who owns the property now?"

"It's part of a huge private tract. Cattle or sugarcane, something like fifty thousand acres. That much land, it's possible no one has been there for years. Just cows, maybe the odd boater. But no roads to it."

"Do you remember anything else from the maps? What about ranch houses? The road to Arcadia has to pass somewhere close to here." I motioned east. "Doesn't that look like cattle pasture through those trees? And the smoke is getting stronger. Most big ranches do controlled burns to avoid forest fires come summer. I'm guessing a ranch house can't be far."

"Hannah," he said gently, "I don't care what you say, you're exhausted. Why not curl up on the deck and let me steer for a while? I'll wake you if I see something."

I shook my head. "Not until we're out of this mess. I wish we had a chart or something. It's ridiculous how much I've come to depend on a GPS. I think it screws up a person's natural sense of direction. Our dependency, you know? The biologist I was dating, I don't know how many times he told me the same thing."

Belton looked at me. "You don't trust me with the gun or the boat, do you? Why?"

"I'm a decent shot and I'm not afraid to use it," I said. "It's not a matter of trust because—"

That's as far as I got. A boat length ahead, an animal surfaced—a manatee or alligator, its back a yard wide, glistening like tar. I shoved the tiller hard to the right but too late. The boat jolted beneath us while the outboard kicked itself free of the water, propeller screaming, and I was nearly thrown overboard. Belton shouted something and fell forward. He would have tumbled off if I hadn't grabbed his shirt. I jerked the tiller clear and held tight until the boat settled under us.

"What the hell was that?" The man got to his knees, a little dazed. "My glasses? Where'd they go? Damn it."

I shifted into neutral and studied the water. A series of oily swirls would have meant we'd hit a manatee, but the surface remained flat, pale. "An alligator," I said. "We must have hit a gator. That thing was huge." I took my flashlight from the bag. "I hope your glasses didn't go overboard. I don't want to blind you—watch your eyes."

"Are you hurt?"

"Move your feet," I said. "I don't see them." A second later, though, I did, the frame and lenses in good shape. I cleaned the glasses on my blouse and placed them in his hands.

Belton, after squinting experimentally, said, "Maybe it was a log. I damn near went over the side. Are you sure you're okay?"

"Logs don't surface, then submerge. Or maybe a manatee, but I doubt it. In a river this narrow, yeah . . . a gator, it had to be a big gator."

"Well, at least the engine's running. There can't be any serious damage."

I thought so, too, until I shifted into forward gear and twisted the throttle. The outboard revved with plenty of power yet we continued to drift sideways toward the bank. I switched the engine off.

"What's wrong?"

I said, "We must've sheared a cotter pin—the thing that holds the propeller to the hub. Sometimes people keep an extra pin taped under the cowling. Hang on, I'll check." I tried not to sound nervous but was. The ramifications hadn't hit me fully, but enough to realize we were in the middle of nowhere, nothing to drink, no food, and it would be a long hike out if I didn't get the boat running.

"Can you fix it? I mean, if there's not an extra whatever."

"Cotter pin," I said. I hunched over the engine and held the light under my chin while I removed the cowling. Nothing hidden inside but a spare starter rope. I reseated the cowling and locked it. "We'll have to row until we find a spot to land. Look around for a piece of wire. That'll sometimes work instead of a pin."

Belton muttered, "Damn, damn, damn."

"Or a fish hook that's the right size. I've got a few in my bag. But I'll have to snip off the barbs, then get out of the boat to see if one fits. That's why we need a place where we can pull onshore." I took another look around, seeing trees and clouds, the river milky white. "Otherwise, I'll have to get in the water—and I don't want to do that."

"Not if you're right about what we hit," he said, then helped me fit the oars into the oarlocks so we could take turns rowing. A few minutes later, I realized we had another problem: water sloshed from the stern forward with every stroke of the oars. I suspected the cause: aluminum boats are riveted and welded, the collision had opened a seam in the hull.

The difference between a leaking boat and sinking boat depends on how the people aboard respond. I didn't say a word even when my shoes were soaked.

IT WAS AFTER midnight before I found a spot where the bank, instead of being steeply wooded, angled gently onto a patch of sandbar. I used the oars to beach the boat engine first, then got out. Only then did Belton ask, "How'd all this water get in here?"

I said, "I'm sloppy when it comes to rowing, I guess. Help me pull up farther so I don't have to stand in water to fix the prop."

It wasn't easy because of the extra weight. Belton had once been a powerful man. His lack of strength frustrated him. Finally he said, "I'll see if I can find an old beer can or something to bail with," then tottered off in a way that told me he was stiff and sore. But he stopped when he got to the top of the bank and cupped his ears to listen. I pretended not to notice yet didn't move until he spoke. "I think Theo and Carmelo gave up," he said. "Your hearing's probably better. What do you think?"

I mimicked his technique. The silence of an autumn night in Florida is a riot of competing sounds, but on this night the silence was reassuring. Frogs, insects, and night birds were all I heard. No distant rumble of an engine, no crash of trees. I said, "They could have made up a lot of distance while I was rowing. And we've only come about half a mile. Take the flashlight and see what you can find—a container of some type would be better than a can. Oh, and you'll need bug spray."

I ran the light and mosquito repellent up to him, then returned to the boat and opened my bag. I knew what I'd packed, but I also knew we'd have to travel on foot if I couldn't get the boat fixed. That might mean walking all night over rough country. I didn't want to carry anything we didn't need, so I laid it all out in an orderly fashion. Captain Ben Summerlin's journal, which I knew I couldn't bear to leave behind, came out first. There was mosquito netting, clean shorts and a blouse, sunscreen, first-aid supplies, Calumet glow sticks, a little orange strobe light, fishing pliers, toilet paper and my personal items in a Ziploc, matches in a waterproof case, a tube of fire starter gel, a spool of thread plus a needle, fishing line, several hooks, and a tiny bottle of iodine tablets.

The iodine tablets reminded me that it had been hours since my last sip of iced tea and I was thirsty. Drop two tablets in a liter of rank water and the water would soon be safe to drink. Trouble was, I hadn't packed anything to drink from. I hadn't brought wire or an extra cotter pin either, but my failure to pack a simple drinking cup nearly pushed me over the edge. I drew my foot back as if to kick the boat, then looked at clouds streaming past the moon.

Hannah Smith—can't you do anything right? No wonder you're always in trouble and live alone.

I didn't say those things, but I thought them and came as close to crying as I had since my meltdown after Carmelo's hands had strayed down my blouse.

Carmelo—just thinking that name hardened my attitude. The man's face, his leer, his rude fumbling touch. Then Theo, pompous and delusional, came into my mind. I once read in a magazine about something called malignant narcissism. Theo's indifference about the horrible way Krissie had died proved the term fit. *One little mistake,* he had said of her murder, as if the girl's life was no more valuable than the life of an insect.

My self-pity vanished. It was displaced by the same coldness that had enveloped me when facing down the Land Rover.

"Fix the boat or start walking. You're not going to let them get away with this." This time I did speak aloud, said it as a vow that refused to tolerate more personal concessions to fear.

I repacked the bag, then turned to look for Belton. No sign of him or my flashlight. I started up the bank, backtracked to get the pistol, then went up the bank again. He appeared from the trees, calling, "You've got to see this."

I replied, "The only thing I want to see is a bailing can. Where've you been? I need that light to fix the propeller." I wasn't angry but knew I sounded angry. The truth was, I wasn't in the mood to fret over social niceties.

"Oh . . ." he said. "I got distracted—sorry. But come have a look."

I accepted the light from him and saw that his hands were empty. "Not even *a bottle*?" I said, then took a breath to calm myself. "Thing is, Belton, that boat's going to keep leaking if we don't find a bailing can. Might even sink. We can't waste time sightseeing."

"Sink?"

"If water leaks in faster than it goes out, that's what a boat does."

"You didn't say anything about sinking, dear." He stopped and faced me. "You've had a terrible night, you're upset, and god only knows what kind of drug that woman stuck in you. But we're safe now. Look"—he spread his arms to indicate a clearing in the trees—"I think this would be a good place to sleep for an hour or so. At the very least, rest and maybe drink some water." He motioned for me to follow. "Come see what I found."

I said, "We can't drink until we have something to *drink from*. Which brings us back to finding a container. Along the river is the place to look, not inland—unless there's been a hurricane I didn't read about." A gust of wind rattled trees to the south, another plowed streaks on the water. I reevaluated the clouds. "If that squall hits, we'll need more than just a bailing can. We should also think about how to hide the boat if I can't get it going. For all we know, they've used the trolling motor to follow us. Or canoes. Lord knows, we've given them plenty of time, the way we're fooling around here." I used my shoe to kick at a pile of leaves and wood. I walked farther, did it again, and knelt.

"What did you find?"

I tossed a crushed beer can aside, then held up what might have been a plastic milk jug. But the light showed it had contained water. I removed the top and sniffed. "This is exactly what we need. I've got iodine tablets on the boat. I doubt if they get rid of fertilizer and stuff like that, but we've got to drink something. I feel shaky, dry as sand. What about you?"

Another blast of wind tumbled through the trees. Belton slipped his arm around my shoulder. "That's what I want to show you. I found an artesian well, I think. Come look."

"A well?" There was nothing we needed more than drinking water, so I felt badly after accusing the man of wasting time. The urge to cry came over me again.

"You can't carry all the weight, dear. I want you to sit and rest for a minute. I'll get the iodine tablets after you're situated. They're in your bag?"

In a circle of oak trees, the earth was spongy with leaves too thick for weeds to grow. Where an old-fashioned pump might have once been, water bubbled from a rusty pipe and created a basin of sand. To the east was a silver plain of palmettos and an empty horizon beyond. Swamp possibly, but more likely I had been right about cattle pasture. That meant a ranch house *might* be within walking distance. But no sparkle of window lights to guarantee it.

There was something else Belton wanted to show me. "I probably wouldn't have noticed if the sun was up. The flashlight found it, happened to catch the edge of a brick—you'll see. The difference in color jumps out at you."

We were approaching a strangler fig, a tree that attaches itself to objects or other trees with a constrictor's grip and over decades gradually consumes them or appears to. It was a spiraling umbrella of branches that parachuted air roots to the ground. Even when Belton pointed at the trunk and used the light, I didn't understand until he dug the leaves away. "A gravestone," he said. "Underneath could be a little crypt made of bricks, although I'm guessing. But the shape—doesn't it look familiar? These bricks were part of the arch, I think."

There was no shape, only roots and leaves, but I knew what he wanted me to see. "Similar to the water cistern," I said. "Could be the same brick mason."

"Can you read the inscription on the stone? Even with my glasses, I couldn't make it out." He handed me the light.

I knelt by a marker made of rough cement and shells that was no bigger than a writing tablet. It lay half buried, covered with moss and lichens. I cleaned the surface, but only the top line was visible. It had been written in an elegant, feminine hand with a stylus or a stick before the cement had hardened. A name I read aloud:

Irene Jameson Cadence

Surprised, I got down on my knees. "But *why* . . . why was she buried here?" I began to dig at the base of the stone, eager to see if there was more writing underneath.

"It's what homesteaders did, buried their family on family land." Belton sounded puzzled by the question or my sudden interest, then realized there was more to it. "Yeah . . . the name's familiar. *Cadence* . . . probably related to the family that built the mansion. I don't find that unusual."

"I do, but we'll figure it out another day," I said. "We don't have time now." Yet I continued digging. "Get the iodine tablets. Oh—and fill the jug with water. *Please.* It'll be half an hour before it's safe to drink and by then I might have the propeller fixed. It's a small bottle, dark glass, near the top."

"The top of your backpack?"

"Of course."

I had snapped at him. "Hannah . . . you definitely need some rest—"

"Not until police know what they did to Krissie." I motioned him away without looking up. "I'll meet you at the boat in a minute." It was true I was determined to get moving, but in a secret part of me I wanted to be alone while I learned more about a woman with whom, in my imagination at least, I shared a family connection.

Belton left muttering about my stubbornness, which to some men is a substitute for the word *strength*. Seconds later, though, my strength vanished and I had to wipe away a single streaming tear.

The stone when fully exposed read:

Irene Jameson Cadence
Widow & Childless & Homeless
At Peace With the Lord
Born 3 June 1876   Died   19—

The blank date of her death hinted at what I suspected from the elegant penmanship: the woman on the balcony, Irene Cadence, had made her own gravestone and written her own epitaph. Perhaps had even taken her own life. No . . . that was an unfair guess. It was sad enough that she had recorded her loneliness in stone for eternity. A hint of self-pity, too, although I didn't allow myself to linger on a flaw so painfully familiar.

I got to my feet, switched off the light, and brushed leaves from my jeans while my eyes adjusted. I had just picked up the pistol when I heard a *smack-smack* sound like a fist hitting flesh. Then a man who wasn't Belton hollered from the river, "Girl! . . . Hey, *girl*! I'll shoot this old bastard. Show yourself."

Carmelo—he had found our boat.

I started to run away, but caught myself after only a few steps. I couldn't let him hurt Belton. Nor would I endure a moment as his prisoner. I was faster than Carmelo, I was smarter. But what if Theo had returned, too? He might be circling toward me from another direction. I couldn't just stand there and let it happen. I had to *think*.

My mind went to work while Belton yelled I should save myself, then Carmelo added more threats. "The old man says you got a flashlight. What you're gonna do is put that gun of yours in a place I can see it. Then back away ten or fifteen steps and use the light. When I get to the top of that bank, I'd best see that damn gun. I'm talking *first thing*. And you nowhere close. And I want your hands in the air." An impatient silence lapsed before he swore and yelled, "Better answer me, girl!"

Only one flimsy option came to mind. I hollered, "My ankle, I think I broke my ankle. You have to promise not to hurt us."

Belton, voice muffled, said something that was drowned out by Carmelo's laughter. "Bullshit. She's lying." Then called to me, "You're the only ones who can prove I never touched that young teenybopper. Or Lucia either—and good riddance, if you're the one what killed her. You can burn Theo, for all I care. All I want is for you to come back and tell the cops the truth."

Belton tried to yell *He's lying* but was punched or clubbed—something caused him to cry out—before Carmelo continued talking. "Oh, and one other little thing. Part of our deal is, you forget about finding that canoe. Ain't too much to ask, is it? Do what I say, I'll take you and the old man to a doctor. Anything you want. Hell"—more laughter—"why would I hurt a girl pretty as you?" Bushes rustled, a spotlight sought the top of the riverbank. "Have you put down that gun?"

I hollered, "No! I can barely crawl."

Carmelo wasn't taking chances. He had yet to poke his head above the embankment. "Do it now, damn you. I'll give you one minute, no more."

In a rush, I switched on the flashlight and painted a

few circles on the sky to confirm my intentions. Then balanced the light atop the gravestone and left it there, beam pointed at a chunk of wood that didn't resemble a pistol but would have to do. Nearby was an oak grove. I ran to it. Oak limbs were stouter, lower, less chaotic than the strangler fig. As I scouted, I thought about Capt. Ben Summerlin's ambush plans and recalled a passage from his journal: *Lure the enemy so close it's up to God to decide who lives or dies.*

Bait the trap . . . lay in wait . . . shoot to kill.

But did I have the courage? No . . . not courage— something darker was required. An absence of conscience; the unleashing of a quality so foreign I felt hollow. Self-doubt seemed to shut off my air—a haunting return of my old fears—yet I continued to search for a suitable spot.

Think, Hannah. Don't stand here shaking. Was it smarter to climb a tree and wait? Or surprise him near the river?

While I battled indecision, wind punched through the tree canopy. The gust tumbled limbs from oak to oak in synch with high, churning leaves, their sparks muted by the moon.

22

I circled downwind to a willow thicket, where I hid myself and watched from one knee. The beam from the flashlight I'd left was a dazzling tube that linked the riverbank with a chunk of wood and Irene Cadence's grave. I was midway between the grave and the river with a clear view of what lay between.

Carmelo was closer, easier to hear. He continued to call threats, saying I was almost out of time, he'd shoot Belton—just wound him, of course—or we could have some *fun* together. Nauseating, the oily way he phrased it. The man was drunk and talkative. On and on he went yet was afraid to poke his head above the embankment. Carmelo was, indeed, a coward . . . or buying time until Theo was in position.

Either way, I could do nothing but wait. Mosquitoes tracked my rapid breathing. They began to swarm. I

shifted the Devel pistol from one hand to the other, staying loose. In an attempt to still my brain, I focused my
senses outward: Carmelo's voice, Belton's voice, their
words often indecipherable. The scream of insects, bushes
alive with foraging rodents, and a squall breeze that went
suddenly still, then freshened, puffed and gusted from a
northern quarter of the sky.

The wind had shifted. Spend your childhood on the
water, you are aware of such things. The gusts frag-
mented, filtered down through the leaves, and explored
my face. It was warm, tropic air befouled by something
that fired a chill through the pores of my skin, up my
neck.

An odor . . . What was that disgusting odor? It
stunk of women's perfume . . . stale sweat . . . a canine
whiff of wet hair and rotten eggs. No . . . I was wrong.
My nose had been confused by the heavy perfume. Perfume so cloying, it cloaked a familiar musk—possibly as
intended. The fecal stench of a chimpanzee was otherwise unmistakable.

I got to my feet, the pistol ready. The stench laced
through willows from the northeast, the same direction
as the wind. That suggested the chimp could no longer
track my scent.

Oliver's nose is as good as any bloodhound's. Once again,
Theo's brag came to mind.

I no longer doubted it was true. I parted willow
branches until I could see the river and there it was only
fifteen yards away: an apish creature that had just climbed
onto the bank or dropped from a tree. It shook itself,

pearls of water flying, then stood upright . . . tilted its jaw skyward and sniffed the darkness.

I thought, *He's confused . . lost track of my scent,* the animal so close that its fur, saturated with perfume, stung my eyes. I raised the pistol, tried to frame the chimp's head with the V-sights while my hands shook. No doubt in my mind I would pull the trigger, but I had to make the first shot count.

Too late. The chimp put its fists on the ground, threw its feet forward, and loped away before I could recover. A moment later Carmelo called, "Who's there? Don't be stupid, girl. I got ears." The spotlight blinked on, illuminating trees above the sandbar where we had beached the boat.

Not thinking, I pushed my way clear of the willows and crept toward the spot where we had climbed the bank. To my left, bushes thrashed. Then I heard the trampoline recoil of tree limbs. Belton, thinking it was me, hollered, "Hannah, don't do it. Run!"

I wanted to run—sprint toward the open plain that I believed to be cattle pasture. My mind had already concocted enough excuses to satisfy police. Whether or not they were enough to satisfy my conscience was unimportant—not during this moment of indecision anyway.

But only a moment. I am no different than most: a durable thread runs through my weaknesses and doubt and that thread is me, the very core of who I am. It is not steel but might as well be because it will not allow me to stray far from what I believe to be right or wrong. I was armed, fast on my feet, and a strong swimmer. Those details didn't click in my head as thoughts but one simple truth did: abandoning an old man who had befriended me was wrong.

I walked faster, regretting the flashlight I'd left blazing on the gravestone. When I reached the riverbank, I would be silhouetted, easily seen by Carmelo or the animal that had been stalking me. I considered the merits of running to retrieve it, and might have, but I had lost track of the chimp. If he had circled downwind, his odor would not warn me before an attack.

The pistol barrel became my eyes. It steered my vision from left to right, to the trees that lined the river. The bright corridor created by my own flashlight lay just ahead. Rather than show myself, I turned early and started down the embankment in an eerie half-light of gray and green. Took my time, ears alert. Carmelo had been barking threats and orders all along, but there was something new in his tone when he said, "Hey . . you smell something weird?"

Belton, through foliage and shadows, replied, "When I knocked you on your ass, I didn't think you'd get up. Ten years ago you wouldn't've. This is pointless. Let the girl go and I'll tell you everything. Plus, you've got her journal. Don't believe me? Look in that bag."

When Carmelo snapped, "Shut up . . . *Perfume* . . . You don't smell that?" I stopped to listen. But also prepared to run by bracing a foot against an oak that was wider than my body, used it like a starting block. "Perfume," he repeated. "That sonuvabitch Theo. You got no idea what I mean, do you?" There was a silence. I pictured him looking at Belton. "A snake bit him when we went back for the Gheenoe. Got him bad. I *saw* it. But it had a weird name, this snake. He went to get antivenom, must'a freaked out and turned his goddamn monkey loose. You don't smell that French whore perfume?"

Belton said, "What's perfume have to do with—"

"*Quiet*—I'm trying to think. That strung-out fool doesn't give a damn about anyone. I told him I was done if he pulled this crap. Yeah . . . up in those trees, maybe. You don't smell that? Or the other side of the river. Those monkeys are meat-eaters, man. Screw it . . . Yeah, screw it. I'm out of here."

"But . . . then cut me loose first. And if Hannah's ankle is broken—"

"Tell the monkeys when they show up, *Mr.* Matás. Shit . . now what's wrong with this damn thing? Probably the battery."

I heard him bang at something. The spotlight came on again, a flooding beam. It moved among the treetops and swung toward me. I crouched low, didn't look up until Carmelo yelled, "Look . . . look'a there. That's her, the bitch!" A shotgun fired and the sky absorbed a furious inhuman shriek.

The shriek took form when I lifted my head. High above me was the chimp, mouth open wide, close enough it might have crushed me had it fallen, but the animal leaped toward the river instead. No . . . leaped toward Carmelo, who fired again—*BOOM*—then the howls of man and chimpanzee were indistinguishable from the searing thump of flesh on flesh.

Belton raised his voice above it all: "Damn animal . . . *Stay away!*"

I went down the embankment faster than was prudent. Made too much noise. Didn't slow until the spotlight showed familiar landmarks: the sandbar angling into the river, our aluminum boat and the Gheenoe with a trolling motor beached alongside. Carmelo's wailing and desperate profanities caused me to hesitate before exiting the bushes, but I finally did. The scene that awaited was nightmarish.

Belton was on his side, trying to worm his way up the embankment, his nose bloody. Closer to me, the chimpanzee's shoulders appeared to be melded into Carmelo's chest, Carmelo, on the ground, his clothes ripped, mouth open wide in a airless scream, while his body spasmed in surrender. The chimp had used its feet to pin the man's arms. Its hands cupped Carmelo's head like a chalice, tilting his neck to expose the throat, the chimp's face nestled close as if suckling but in fact had buried its teeth near the jugular. The animal was so focused on killing— or feeding—it did not react when Belton saw me and hollered, "Hannah . . . for god's sake, run." His voice broke like an adolescent.

My eyes followed the pistol into the clearing, at first seeing only the chimp's broad back but then realized that Belton was just beyond directly in the line of fire. The angle was all wrong, too risky to pull the trigger at a distance of thirty yards. I scuttled sideways without looking, unaware of the river until I was knee-deep in water and a slow current tugged at my jeans.

The sound of my clumsy splashing was too loud to ignore. The chimp sat straight, pivoted its head from side to side. Around its neck was a heavy pink collar with an electronic device. A remnant of pink ribbon, too, behind one ear, which meshed with the perfume.

Pink . . . Carmelo and Lucia had used the word like a profanity when describing the female chimp. So this was Savvy, not Oliver, the big male. She turned, searching, until her caramel eyes found me. She sniffed, tasted the air through lips glossy with blood—or lipstick—and chirped a soprano note of interest that transitioned into a growl. Eyes of caramel studied me . . . and blazed with recognition. Her fists became hammers. She pounded her chest—a hollow-coconut sound—then demonstrated her strength by grabbing Carmelo's arm and slinging his body several feet toward me. He landed as limp and boneless as a sack.

I fought the urge to flee, took a step back, and found firmer footing, then leveled the pistol and spoke. "Get the hell out of here or I'll shoot you." I was so scared, the words came automatically—a last warning to myself more than to an animal who could not understand.

Carmelo's spotlight lay in the sand, projecting monstrous shadows. Savvy made a chattering sound of indignation . . . flapped her outstretched arms like a child learning to walk, then started toward me.

I said it again: "I *will* shoot you."

The chimp kept coming, loping faster, then hunkered low and sprinted, fingers and feet kicking sand as she closed the distance.

Belton yelled something, yelled something else—a warning, no doubt—yet his words vaporized before they reached my ears. I heard only the metallic click of the pistol's hammer when I thumbed it back. I squared my shoulders and waited. Through a tunnel of light and consciousness, I saw only the chimpanzee's face . . . a glossy square of leather and teeth that radiated hatred and rage and mindless intent. The coldness that enveloped me was equally dispassionate, equally focused.

When the animal was fifteen yards away, still a long shot for a pistol, I pulled the trigger. Rather than an explosion, I heard a click. Stunned, I yanked the trigger again. *Click.*

A misfire, a bad cartridge. In my head, a teenage girl listened patiently while my Uncle Jake explained that misfires are not rare and easily cleared if you know what to do and stay calm.

Impossible to remain calm, but I managed not to freeze. I looked up while I shucked the cartridge free and slammed a fresh round in the chamber. Savvy was almost to the water, close enough that the stink of her body pushed wet air into my face.

Belton's voice broke through: "Shoot the damn thing!"

I raised the pistol and did exactly that a microsecond before the chimp vaulted toward the river. The gun bucked twice in my hands while Savvy was airborne, then her weight slammed into me. I fell backward and went under . . . and I stayed under, unsure if my shots had hit flesh. Using one hand, I crabbed along the bottom toward shore. Then got my feet under me and stood with my arms already outstretched, the pistol ready to aim and fire if needed while water poured down my face.

Belton's voice again: "Behind you. Shoot him!"

I spun, expecting to see the chimp. Instead, a boat was coasting silently toward me, a man on the bow who made a moaning noise and cried, "Oh my god . . . oh my god, where is she? I heard shots."

It was Theo. His lanky shape was unmistakable— steering a trolling motor with his feet, a flashlight in his hand. He switched on the light, blinded me for a second, then began to search the water's surface. "You tramp, you redneck tramp. You shot her, *didn't you?*"

I was furious. "You raise a hand to us, I'll shoot you, too. Don't think I won't."

"I knew it!" Theo, several boat lengths away, stomped his foot on the deck. "Oliver will eat you alive for this— I mean, *eat you alive.* Where is she?" Theo ranted on as the trolling motor spun him closer, then tilted his face toward the treetops and screamed, "OLI-VEEEEER! HERE SHE IS! COME TO DADDY!"

My finger was still on the trigger. If Theo had had a gun, I would have done it, would have shot him. I came close to squeezing the trigger anyway. Tell the police, *My life was in danger.* Tell police, *A teenage girl was butchered and this man laughed.* No . . . tell them, *I know what happened to those three missing people,* then read about Theo's arrest on the Internet.

A coldness still possessed me, but the steel cable within held fast. I didn't shoot. I lowered the pistol, turned and sloshed to our boat and grabbed my bag. Theo, vicious by nature, had slipped over the edge of his own canted world. He sounded feverish. Perhaps it was true he'd been bitten by a snake and given himself a shot of antivenom. I'd thought it was another of Carmelo's lies. No telling what the man would do if he had a gun aboard. And if we tried to escape in the rental Gheenoe, he would try to crush us with the Bass Cat. No doubt in my mind.

Bag over my shoulder, I jogged to Belton, whose nose was bloody and crooked. "Can you walk?"

He got up, eyes on Theo. "What happened to that damn monkey? You hit him. Stood your ground, by god, you did. How's your ankle? Or were you—"

"We've got to get out of here," I said, "but on foot. Where's that water jug? We need water." I started toward the boat, then saw the plastic container near Carmelo's spotlight, which burned brightly in the sand. The bottle of iodine tablets was open, pills scattered.

Belton touched his fingers to his nose, tested his right wrist, and grunted. "Now what's he doing?"

"You broke your hand, too?"

"Carmelo, I hit him a good one. Put him right on his ass." Belton couldn't hide his delight. "Damn . . . yeah, broken maybe."

"Theo might have a gun. Don't take your eyes off him. We'll need those pills."

Theo maintained a running commentary, his babbling mixed with lewd talk and threats. I stayed busy, ignoring him until he called, "There you are!" then spoke soothingly as if to a child. "Savvy . . . over here, girl, it's me. Oh shit . . . I was right, you *are* hurt."

The chimp was upriver, dog-paddling on the surface but struggling, using only one arm. I dropped iodine tablets in the jug and hurried to fill it with water while I watched. Theo kept the flashlight on the animal, Savvy blinking her caramel eyes until the trolling motor pulled the boat close enough. He placed the light on the deck, removed his shoes after calling me the foulest of names. A moment later, he slipped over the side. Repulsive, the cooing sounds he made while the chimp screeched and tried to swim away, slapping wildly at the water. Theo cursed me again and yelled to the trees, "OLI-VERRR! I NEED YOU!"

I spoke quietly to Belton. "If he lets the boat drift away, maybe I can swim out and start the engine before he notices. Can you shoot left-handed?" But I retracted the offer when a gust of wind—or a two-hundred-pound chimp—furrowed the oak canopy to our right. "We can't wait," I said. "There's one more thing I want to check."

I ran to pat Carmelo's pockets for a cell phone. Belton stooped, lifted the spotlight from the sand, and spoke. "I'll shoot Theo and you know it. Him and his damn chimp. That's why you don't trust me with the gun. Why not let me, Hannah? I'd confess to the police and we'd both be safe. Damn it . . . why not?"

He shined the light on Theo, then downriver, waiting for an answer while I knelt over Carmelo. Nothing but keys and a knife in his front pockets. I felt beneath him, turned my head away rather than focus on what was missing from Carmelo's face. That's why I happened to see what Belton did not see—what someone from Virginia wouldn't have recognized anyway: a pair of ruby red eyes gliding upriver toward the sound of splashing, those eyes set a foot apart, which told me the alligator we'd hit was at least twelve feet long and still healthy enough to feed.

Automatically, I started to call out a warning but caught myself. After a moment of self-inspection, I turned away and pretended ignorance . . . and an innocence that revealed the ugliest of truths: the beast within me was ready and waiting, but only when it suited my needs.

I took Belton's arm and pulled him toward the embankment. "How Theo dies," I said, "isn't for me to decide."

23

BELTON CARRIED THE SPOTLIGHT, BUT IT HAD A short or a bad battery and he soon tossed it aside. Moon shadow resumed dominance. I was so focused on sounds I expected to hear but had yet to hear—slashing water, Theo's wail of surprise—I was slow to notice something else: the flashlight I'd left on the gravestone was gone.

Belton asked, "Why are you stopping?"

I adjusted the bag on my shoulder. "Stay close and watch behind us. Are you sure that spotlight's no good?"

"You saw something. Do you think it's the other chimp? By god, I wish he'd show himself." The man put his hand on my back and gave a little push. "We've got to get away from these trees. We'll be fine once we're on open ground. You said there was pasture on the other side of the clearing. After that, all we have to worry about is cows." He laughed, but it was nervous laughter.

I was going through a checklist in my head. An almost new flashlight with fresh batteries. The wind might have knocked it to the ground, but the gravestone wasn't tall. The lens wouldn't have broken. The light should still be on.

I peered ahead, seeing only the circle of oaks and darkness. "Change of plans. We have to follow the river north a bit, then we'll turn inland. There's something wrong up ahead." When I started to explain, the river issued a single tumbling splash, then silence. Maybe the gator had taken Theo. I couldn't be sure unless I went back to check. Tempting, the prospect of jumping in a fast boat and leaving all this behind. I could not pass it up.

"Wait here," I said. "I won't be long."

"Where're you going? Not without me, you're not."

I retraced our path and Belton followed. Near the top of the embankment, I stopped and listened before exiting the bushes. A heavy thumping sound came from the river below . . . then a loud creak of rending metal. I peeked through: squatting on Theo's boat, which had drifted to the bank, was Oliver. Had to be Oliver—an ape-sized chimp with arms twice as long as a human's. Massive shoulders, a distended jaw that resembled a football, but a face that, by moonlight, might have been the face of a man wearing a costume. A rope or his broken collar dangled from his neck. Wearing shorts, too, or baggy cut-off pants belted at the waist, a comedic touch that was in fact grotesque.

Belton whispered, "Where's Theo?"

I shook my head and watched.

Oliver had ripped the steering wheel from the boat. A ring of stainless steel. He stared as if deep in thought . . . bent one of the spokes until it snapped and tossed it aside. Then grunted a bass drum *UHH-UHH* and duck-walked to the stern, where the engine had snagged bottom. He placed the wheel on the deck. The chimp appeared to be hurt, favored his left side like a person with arthritis. Squatted there while an arm unfurled and he dangled a hand in the water. A child playing: slap the surface, watch diamond droplets rain down. Oliver slapped and played, but now his baritone grunts resembled a man who contained his rage by growling.

I leaned close to Belton's ear. "I'm going to shoot him. Even with a broken steering wheel, I can steer that boat. He'll kill us. We both know that. But I have to get closer." Shooting downhill through bushes at a target fifty yards away was too dangerous.

Belton started to say, "Let me—" but then jerked his head downriver and whispered, "What the hell is that?"

The alligator had returned, attracted by Oliver's splashing, its tail carving a serpentine wake on the surface. The wake rocked our aluminum boat and whitecapped on sand. Only vague shapes were discernible. The gator carried a big chunk of something, an object that sank when its jaws slashed and released it.

Oliver saw the alligator, too, but continued to play his childish game. Splashed and waited until the gator was so close, it vanished from our view. There was a blur of movement, an explosion of water. The next thing I saw,

Oliver was hunched low, lifting mightily . . . the alligator's head was trapped inside the steering wheel. A snare . . . he had created a snare. Too much weight to lift clear of the water, so Oliver hammered at the gator's head with a fist until the animal slashed and rolled and finally broke free.

The chimp watched the thing submerge and went into a rage. Shattered the windshield, ripped a seat off its stanchion and hurled it at the gator's bubbles. Tilted his head back and yowled at the moon, a chalkboard screech that ended when Oliver suddenly stopped and sniffed the air. Settling back, he sniffed more thoughtfully and slowly, slowly turned to look in our direction.

Belton's shoulder touched mine. "He smells us."

"Maybe not. But get ready to run." Fifty yards, even over open ground, was a long shot, but I had the pistol up, ready to try. Only four bullets left.

Oliver squatted near the steering wheel, his big head and clamshell ears in silhouette. He massaged an elbow, peered at his left hand, which was swollen twice normal size. An injured athlete taking inventory, his behavior reminded me of that. The gun sights of my pistol were three glowing dots that framed Oliver's chest. I was thinking, *Get closer, he's hurt, just sitting there. You have time.*

I was wrong. Oliver exploded again, a blur of movement, and I stood hypnotized by a silver object that spun toward my face. The object sliced the air like a metal Frisbee, whapped through branches on a curving path, and hammered Belton to the ground.

The steering wheel, I realized.

From the river, a bass drum taunted. *UCKER . . . UUHM UCK.*

I knelt over Belton for just a moment, then stood. Oliver was on his feet, beating coconut sounds on his chest, his lips peeled back to show teeth. By the time I got the pistol up, he was still there but leaping toward shore. I fired twice . . . fired again after he stumbled and sprawled sideways into the river . . . the pistol spouting flames each time. Startling—I'd never shot a gun at night.

"Did you get him? Shit . . . I think my shoulder's busted. You must've shot me, too." Belton was dazed and on his side, trying to get to his feet.

"If you can, run to the clearing," I said. "I'll yell if it's okay." I rushed down the embankment, the whole time thinking, *I hit him, I know I hit him . . . But did I fire three shots or four?*

No . . . only three. The slide of a pistol locks back when empty. In darkness, I stopped and ran my fingers over the barrel to check. Just one bullet left, though. If Oliver wasn't badly wounded, one bullet might not be enough.

I thought about that. An animal of such freakish size and strength? Of course one bullet wasn't enough to stop him unless . . . unless I let Oliver charge me, waited until he was on top of me, too close to miss a shot to his heart or head.

So close it's up to God to decide. Captain Ben Summerlin's words flashed in memory, but so did Theo's threat: *Oliver will eat you alive.*

I told myself, *You can do this, you CAN do this.*

Ahead in moonlight, the sandbar and our aluminum boat were in plain view. Seconds earlier, I had heard the chimp thrashing toward shore. If I exited the trees, he would be to my right only ten or fifteen yards away. Not an easy shot, but at least some distance would separate us.

I started toward the river but could manage only a few steps.

No, I realized, I *could not* do it. First, a chimp bites off a woman's nose and lips, Lucia has said. I did not have the courage to risk that animal's teeth in me. Besides, I had Belton to think about. It was a handy excuse that wasn't a lie, but it felt like a lie when I scrambled up the embankment. Every few steps, I stopped to listen. Silence hinted that Oliver was dead. I became hopeful.

My hopefulness did not last. When I got to the top, I heard the rhythmic slosh of his legs kicking water. The animal walked unsteadily, fell once, but was on his feet. Then a tree limb buckled under a heavy weight and displaced leaves spun earthward into the river basin.

The shriek that came next spooked birds to flight. Through echoes, Oliver called a message to me:

UCK . . . UCK UN . . . ITCH!

I was already running when those bass drum grunts transitioned into a howl.

24

I FOUND BELTON AT THE ARTESIAN WELL, WHERE he had stopped to drink. His shoulder, if not broken, was in bad shape, and pain slowed everything he did. While he steadied himself on his feet, I kicked grass around the grave of Irene Cadence until I was convinced my flashlight was gone.

"If that animal's bleeding, he can't follow us far. You're sure you hit him? I need to know what we're dealing with."

Belton sounded shaky, too.

I said, "At least one shot. I don't know where, but it knocked him down. You shouldn't have drunk from that well. Better not to drink anything than get sick."

We'd left our jug of iodine water behind and I craved water. Scolding Belton strengthened my resolve. I held his elbow and hurried him along until he was okay on his own, then took the lead. Every few seconds I checked behind us: no sign of Oliver. But the squall had swung the wind around, the wind steady and stronger, which is what squalls do, siphon air like a blast furnace until the rain is spent. In the high limbs, a steady breeze masked sounds.

The oak grove funneled us into a clearing of weeds and palmettos, an undulant quarter mile that flattened into pines to the east. To the north, cypress trees formed domes of pewter and mist. It would be wet there, a chance of bogging down. Between the two, angling northeast, was a corridor of space and moonlight where the horizon showed an orange fringe—a fire. Open range, it appeared to be. Cattle pasture. The scent of woodsmoke came from there.

I pointed. "Someone's doing a controlled burn. It can't be more than two or three miles."

"Then which direction should we go?"

"Toward the fire. Out here, where there's fire, there are people to tend it. Usually. That tells me there's a ranch somewhere around." It was one a.m., but it was still possible someone was up.

Belton said, "Right hand busted, now my left shoulder. Knocking Carmelo on his ass was worth it. Don't get me wrong, I'm not complaining, but I'm not sure I can make three miles. Not without resting anyway. Don't ever get old, Hannah."

I replied, "I plan on living until tomorrow, at least. And, Belton, you're going to be right there with me."

That got a chuckle.

It was hard not to walk as fast as I wanted to walk. Impatience is among my failings. We exited the weeds into an area speckled with Brazilian pepper and palmetto bushes and sparse melaleucas. Paper trees, as they are also known, because they appear to be constructed of cardboard. The palmettos were waist-high, their leaves so dry, they rattled when disturbed. The sound reminded me that palmetto fields attract rattlesnakes. I'd seen several rattlers in places such as this. They liked the low shade and wealth of ambush opportunities. Unsettling. To calm myself and keep Belton moving, I didn't mention this, of course. Just the opposite. I emphasized the positive when I spoke.

I said, "Did you notice that chimpanzee's hand looked swollen? His left hand. The thing was huge. And he had to sort of drag his left leg. Well . . . except when he went crazy. He doesn't seem to feel pain when he goes crazy."

"I've known men who were the same. His hand . . . what about it?"

"Coral snake venom isn't as fast as some. That's what happened, I think. He got bit. All we have to do is put some distance between us and let the poison work. Plus, he's bleeding. I know darn well I put at least one bullet in him. A special sort of 9mm bullet. Federal Power-Shoks. They're hollow-points that expand when they hit something. He can't be in very good shape."

"How slow?"

"The poison?" I had to be careful. I couldn't tell him Oliver's nervous system would shut down within twenty-four hours. It might sap what little spirit the man had left. So I mixed in some gray lies with the truth. "He's already showing the effects. Gradually, he won't be able to use his arms or legs. Another hour or so, who knows? He won't be able to move."

"Is it painful? By god, I hope it's painful. I've never seen two more vicious animals in my life."

Strange. I felt the same anger but couldn't allow myself to admit it. "Don't be mean, Belton. What they've done is terrible, I know, but nothing in this world deserves more pain. The way Theo raised them might be to blame."

Belton bristled at that. "Sure. It's always someone else's fault."

I puzzled over his reaction for a while, then it came to me. "You're worried it was one of the chimps that killed your son."

"Goddamn right. After seeing what they did to that little girl? Carmelo, too. Sickening—they're monsters . . . *cannibals.* Can you imagine their teeth sinking in? The sound of something eating you. Terrifying. Drives me crazy even to think about." He stopped, put his hands on his hips, and tried to stretch like people do when their back hurts. The pain in his arms wouldn't allow it. "Damn, damn, damn," he murmured. "Just . . . sickening."

I've read about prairie dogs, colony animals that keep a sentry posted outside every hole. I played that role while Belton rested. I focused on the region behind us, turned a few degrees, then refocused. "Belton?"

"Do you see something?"

"No. But what I said was thoughtless. Worse, it was a

lie. The thing about Oliver, his being in pain—I feel the same as you and should have said so. But it *is* wrong. I know it's wrong and I apologize for that."

The man had his hands on his knees. He chuckled toward the ground. "Hannah . . . dear, dear Hannah . . . I've never met anyone like you. While we're being honest, maybe for the first time in my life I should, well . . . maybe I should just say thanks."

"No need. You would've done the same."

"Fair-minded—always so damn fair. Now I feel like a total shit."

"That wasn't my intention."

He laughed again in a weary sort of way. "Dear, I am not the kindly, sweet old gentleman I pretend to be. I took you in, Hannah. It was all an act. Just like Carmelo's idiot act. No different. What I told you about Kenneth, that much is mostly true. But I used you. I wanted to find that gold shipment just as much as I wanted to find his killer. I thought your distant uncle's journal might be the key. So I was sweet and charming—all an act, and I've got it down pat. The truth is, I'm actually a fairly ruthless con man. Well, self-interested anyway. Fifty years, nearly sixty, that's how I've made my living. When I said I'd sold my business? It was actually hard to keep a straight face."

Under other circumstances, I might have been angry, but I felt drained. "We all make our way as best we can, Belton. As far as I'm concerned, you've treated me—" Midsentence, I halted. "Wait a minute. How do you know it was my uncle's journal?"

The man stood upright and tested his broken hand. "Kenneth and his mother were right to disown me. I'm a fraud. That's all I meant. I figured you've earned the right to know."

"Thank you. Now answer my question."

"Guess I should have kept my mouth shut."

"Too late. How? Did you sneak a peek on the boat yesterday?"

"Your stubborn streak, I forgot. Okay . . . I know Ben Summerlin was your uncle because I read the journal. All the pages Theo could open and photograph anyway. He told me about the family connection. The whole journal, diagrams, everything, it's on my computer."

I said, "Good lord," and distanced myself by a step.

"Like I said, a con man. The award I supposedly brought Theo? It was a box of oxycodone tablets. Pharmacy-grade. Earlier tonight, Theo had quite a laugh thinking you'd never figure out the Masonic connection. That led to an argument. No sense going into why."

I didn't understand the Masonic reference but took my eyes off the horizon long enough to say, "Yes, they were. Your son and wife were both right. And I feel like a fool. Have you rested long enough? Or maybe I should just jog on ahead and leave you."

I located the fire's orange thread and started toward it. The last thing I expected Belton to say was "I think that's a good idea. But leave the pistol. If the chimp follows you, I'll kill it."

I faced him. "Noble. Is that part of your act, too?"

"Actually, yes. One of my best bits, but this time I

mean it. Not the noble part. I can't go any farther, Hannah. I would love to put a bullet in that son of a bitch."

Once again, under different circumstances, I would have been furious. All the anger in me, though, had to remain focused on escape. I walked back, took the man's elbow, and said, "Come along, Belton—before you really piss me off."

WE WERE MIDWAY through a stand of palmettos, heartened by the sound of distant bawling cattle, when the water Belton had drunk caused a stomach cramp that bent him over. The cramps worsened. Soon he requested privacy to deal with his gurgling stomach. Walking had been difficult—thick brush and hidden stumps in what had once been pine forest. Palmettos resemble Japanese fans with fingers and their roots are a relentless series of snares. Belton and his bad heart needed a break.

I said, "There are plenty of bushes to choose from," and stepped away. My joke didn't quell my anxiety. Diarrhea for a person his age, in a place so far from help and as waterless as sand, was serious. A raging chimpanzee, even if alive, became a secondary problem.

Or so I believed until I saw the light. It moved toward us from the south, a few hundred yards away. The light blinked off, then blinked on and stayed on just long enough for me to gauge a slow, loping rhythm.

Belton saw it, too, but didn't understand. "Thank god. I hope it's the police. I don't care as long as they have water. Out here in hell's half acre, who else could it be?"

I controlled my breathing and said, "Let me know when you've finished your business. It wouldn't hurt to hurry, if you can."

He was wary of my tone. "What's wrong?"

"We shouldn't linger in one spot too long, that's all. Those cattle we hear belong to a ranch and the ranch can't be far." I had my back to him, of course. Hopefully, he didn't see me slip the pistol from my pocket. My bag was on the ground. I knelt to open it.

"A rancher, then. Good. Try to get his attention."

"Not coming from that direction. If there's a ranch, it'll be somewhere north of here."

"I don't care who it is. They might hear if you yell. Hannah . . . ? Hannah! Why don't you yell something? Christ, don't let them get away before they see you." After several seconds, bushes rattled and I heard the jingle of his belt. "Okay, I'm done. Damn it, tell me what's wrong."

I picked up the bag . . . thought for a moment and put it down again. Placed it on a tree stump that smelled of pine. It was one of many stumps amid a few old-growth survivors scattered across the field, trees as tall and straight as power poles. On this milky blue night they resembled the masts of schooners that had struck a reef and sunk in shallow water.

Belton, striding toward me, said, "That was a flashlight. Who else would be out here with a flashlight?"

Then surprised me by waving his arms and hollering, "Hey . . . over here. We're over here!"

I grabbed the man's sleeve but let go when the light blinked on. It searched through two hundred yards of darkness for the source of the human voice. Too far even for a dazzling little LED, my gift from the biologist. I waited until the light was out and kept my voice low. "He would've found us anyway. It's not your fault." Said it in a comforting way, I hope, then patted Belton's shoulder and got busy.

"Are you afraid it's Theo? Hell, I'd be happy to see Theo. Crazy as he is, trust me, I'll work out some sort of deal."

I was kicking among the palmettos and gathering wood while a plan organized itself in my head. Not a last-minute plan either. We'd been walking for half an hour and I'd spent every quiet moment calculating a way to deal with Oliver if he caught us in open country. Now here we were. What I feared, though, was Belton's heart, how it would react to more stress or even gathering wood.

I talked while I tossed splinters and chunks of lighter pine into a pile. "The best thing for you is to rest while you can. I can't do this alone. I need you ready." I looked south to where a small, vague darkness was now occasionally visible. It appeared and disappeared like a bear humping through tall grass, the grass silver because of the moon. Not fast but steady, although an occasional pause as if resting.

"He's hurt. I'm surprised he made it this far. Maybe

it's the craziness driving him. We both know what that means."

Belton, following at my shoulder, didn't want to believe it. "Please tell me you're not starting a fire. What if it's Theo? He wouldn't just go off and leave his boat. Think about it—chimpanzees *don't carry flashlights*."

"They aren't supposed to wear sandals either, but some do. And pants. The flashlight's been on my mind since it went missing. Ask yourself why he switches it on and off like that instead of using it to see. Trust me, Theo's not out there—unless that big gator carried him all this way."

"Are you saying the alligator got—"

"Pretty sure. Now's not the time to talk about it."

I stood and checked Oliver's progress, decided I needed help after all. Facing the animal, I extended my arms to create a forty-five-degree angle as Belton grabbed his stomach and winced but paid attention. "I've got fire starter and lighters. On this line and this line, we'll light pieces of wood, get a bush burning, then walk five or six steps and do it again. Sort of a reversed arrow shape, if it burns the way I hope."

I resumed hunting wood. "The wind's behind us— what ranchers call a head fire. Nothing burns as hot and fast as a head fire. Ranchers avoid it, but it's just what we need. This was pine forest years ago. I noticed as we were walking. Sap wood doesn't rot and these palmettos are so dry they'll burn. Maybe not like gasoline, but the wind will get them going and the wind's blowing right into his face."

"If it really is the chimp, he'll outrun it. He's not going to stand there and burn."

"I'm not sure what he'll do, but at least it will give us some time. Can your shoulder handle a little work? How's your stomach?"

Belton, on his toes, saw Oliver poke his head up. He made a whistling sound, finally convinced. "Hannah, if I were you—being the type of person I am?—I'd run like hell and never look back." He wasn't smiling. "I know what you're doing—straight from your uncle's journal— but your uncle had more than one bullet. Leave the gun, Hannah. I'll stay here and kill that thing."

I kicked a pine root free. "You're not the reason he's dying, Belton. Oliver won't stop until he gets me."

25

A SOBERING AWARENESS: I HAD PLACED THE flashlight on the grave of Irene Cadence as bait. Now Oliver was using it the same way—he continued to flick the switch on, then off for long periods, hoping to lure me closer. Terrifying, when I thought it through. Oliver had *watched* me balance that light on the gravestone. He had *watched* me find a hiding place to ambush Carmelo. No other explanation. The chimp had been closing in, ready to crush me from behind or above, when he'd heard the rolling splash of the alligator. Instead of attacking, he had rushed to protect Theo and Savvy. The only reason I was still alive was because of the chimp's superior senses.

No . . . two reasons. Theo had said to me, *You don't know what the word* loyalty *means.*

Now that I *did* understand, I couldn't bear to ponder

this admirable quality in an animal that intended to kill and eat me.

Words from America's bloodiest war also grated at my conscience: *For them who runs, the fat pine is strung at every fence row. The Gerillas has been loosed & hells flames is ready.*

I had felt shamed by Ben Summerlin's callousness. I'd condemned his behavior as "inhuman," yet here I was stealing his plan of attack because I did not possess his resolve or war-hardened cunning. If anyone had a right to feel shame, it was the women who anchored my family history, Hannah and Sarah Smith. Unlike them, I was a modern girl. I had been pampered by current times and was unprepared for the realities of survival in this hard land.

All sobering, all too true, but these negative tangents did not address the task at hand.

Better to think about a cozy houseboat where, over coffee, Joey Egret had made up for his shyness by discussing his class on hazard reduction burning. He'd used terms like *drip torch*, *fuel load*, *wet line*, and *flank fire*. Lots of others that went over my head, but the basics stuck with me. I grew up in a house that had only a fireplace for heat, so fire-building skills are always of interest.

My aunts Hannah and Sarah might have at least smiled at that.

When Belton and I were ready, we started the palmettos burning in such a rush, I can't claim skill was involved. Sap pine dabbed with combustible gel will blaze no matter who strikes the match—or Lucia's lighter, which I chose not to use. Belton went one way, I went the other. I'd found a root so rock hard with sap I needed only a match to start it burning. That gnarled fork became my torch, which I used to light more pine fragments as I hurried along, starting a new fire every ten yards or so, palmetto leaves crackling with heat and rising flames as the wind tunneled beneath.

A factor I hadn't considered was what fire does to a person's night vision. I couldn't see beyond the torch, but details near my feet were as crisp as noon. This saved me from stepping on a rattlesnake that hadn't bothered to coil, but it also cloaked Oliver's movements. My response was to extend the fire line only a little farther before I tossed the torch away and jogged back to find Belton.

He, too, was finished. Stomach cramps had forced him into the bushes, so I allowed the man privacy. Stood there, my bag at my feet, and for the first time got an overview of what we had done: a hundred yards of burning palmettos, some only sparking while other sections blazed. It was because of the vagaries of wind—another factor I hadn't considered. I had hoped my inverted arrow design would lure and then trap Oliver by funneling him into the very heart of the flames. The wind, however, shifted and ricocheted and fueled random designs of its own.

I began to worry, but there was nothing to do but stand back and watch. To the east was higher, drier ground. The waist-high fire we'd started had already jumped a distance and become a separate entity, a ravenous wall that shot sparks into the sky while it pushed toward a lone pine tree far away. Those sparks sailed and tumbled in the wind. Some landed in a meteorite arc and generated small blazes of their own. Most sputtered and died. A few did not.

To the west was cypress swamp and the river basin, cooler areas that stirred breezy subcurrents. Those currents nudged flames northward despite a gusting northeast wind. Patches of fire appeared to leapfrog, desperate to dodge the cooler air. They moved in a counterflow and were soon feeding on brittle palmettos behind us.

Belton stepped from the bushes, his jingling belt muted by the seesaw gusting flames. "We've got to get out of here. This whole damn field's going up."

I had already shouldered my backpack, ready to move, but I didn't move or respond because of what I saw gliding toward us: a flashlight, maybe a quarter mile away, a white mushroom glow that searched the ground, then went out. It angled from the northeast, our only corridor of escape.

"That can't be Oliver," Belton said. He had to raise his voice to be heard. "Just a minute ago, he was south of us. Nothing on earth can move that fast. Maybe it's a rancher who saw the fire." Sick as he was, the man was nervous enough to finally address the creature by name.

I noticed the slip, even while Ben Summerlin's words gnawed at me, but from the aspect of the quarry, not the predator. *For them who runs, the fat pine is strung at every fence row.*

I shook my head. "That's what he wants us to do, go

running toward that light for help. He's upwind now. That means his nose is no help, so he'll lie flat in the palmettos and use his ears. Or climb a tree and track us by sight. With all this smoke, we won't know he's close until he's on us. Probably from behind. First me, then you."

Belton started to say, "You give that damn thing too much credit"—a statement that ended with a wince and a groan. He bent with another spasm, face pale. "There's nothing left in my stomach, but it just gets worse." He grimaced again before looking at me, help-less. "Take the gun, I understand. Save yourself, dear. *Please*." He staggered toward the bushes while he undid his belt.

The fire hadn't encircled us but soon would. Wind whistled through palmettos with the rhythm of waves, each brown fan vibrating, while flames responded with a choral roar. The chorus oscillated with ascending and de-scending notes: a snoring giant, a waterfall. The voice of fire assumed many forms.

Hypnotic. It was a seesaw melody that stilled a place inside me. As scared as I was, it allowed me to think. On the houseboat, Joey Egret had explained the dangers of setting a head fire. Head fires were impossible to control. It was better to start a blaze that crept slowly upwind—a burn back, he'd called it. The term was familiar. I had used it in a general way, but didn't understand the subtle-ties until now.

I put down my bag and called to Belton. "We're not going anywhere."

Because of the noise, I had to repeat myself twice. Then explained, "The fire can't reach us if there's nothing left to burn. That's what we're going to do—clear a big, safe space and stay right in the middle. We'll sleep here, for all I care. The important thing is, Oliver will have to walk through fire to get to us."

Before Belton could argue, I told him, "Say good-bye to those bushes and start collecting wood."

THE HEAD FIRE we'd started charged southward, a gelatin wave that gained speed and width but also provided a space to retreat to when I torched the bushes behind us. Our retreat wasn't hurried. No need. This was a different breed of fire. It sputtered and sparked, seeking fuel downwind, but there was no fuel, only scorched and smoking palmettos that refused to burn twice. So the flames I nursed stayed low and crept north at an angle. They reminded me of sailboats running close to the wind, pointing hard into the wind, before coming about and tacking. Fresh flames sparked a windward course. The mating of air and fire produced much softer choral notes: rain on asphalt, a woman's sleepy laughter.

Smoke was our only enemy . . . our only natural enemy, at least. We backed away, pulled our shirts over our mouths, and waited while the earth smoldered, the fire behind us a searing heat that I truly believed was our protector. We scanned the northern horizon and tried to see beyond the flames. In the distance, cows bawled— dark specks on a plain of milky blue. Smoke spun itself into dust devils, mini-tornadoes that sometimes charged us before levitating toward the moon.

After a while, Belton asked to use my backpack as a seat. The man was exhausted yet felt the need to talk. Something was nagging at him—some lie he had told about my great-uncle's journal, was my suspicion. But after he had circled the subject without getting to it, I told him, "Tomorrow, after you've slept and had a shower, we'll talk. Or write it down, if your conscience is bothering you, and I'll read it when you buy me dinner." Then I made a joke, saying he had so much soot on his face, he was invisible, so he had nothing to worry about. Like a commando.

The man didn't respond for a moment. Stared straight ahead, kept his eyes fixed, while he got to his feet and said, "There he is."

The flashlight again: a white mushroom glow to the northeast. Much closer, although distance is hard to judge when distorted by heat. A football field away? No . . . closer. My hand found the gun in my back pocket, but only for reassurance. For the same reason, I turned to inspect the fire protecting us to the south. Only twenty strides separated us from boiling flames, heat so intense it stung my face.

Belton, voice low, said, "He's coming."

Oliver, he meant.

The mushroom glow had become a hard white eye. The light painted vertical brushstrokes as if carried by a man who was walking. The beam flattened, lifted, and suddenly loped toward us . . . or toward an opening in the flames—a corridor of smoke and seared grass cleared by the wind. It was the only safe entrance.

I stepped toward the opening and drew the pistol. For the hundredth time, I confirmed that my last bullet was chambered, then attempted a deep breath, but heat—or fear—was a constricting weight. When several shallow breaths hadn't helped, I retreated into that quiet space in my head. Choral notes of wind and flame mimicked a woman's weepy laughter, but a bass-chord mantra dominated: *Weakness can wait. Weakness can wait . . .*

I found a moment's peace there. My long-dead aunts had survived this hard land. Irene Cadence, too, in her way, but with an end so empty of triumph that her loss and her loneliness hardened my resolve.

Half a mile away, the lone pine tree exploded in flames. A beat later, the sound of the explosion pushed by me in a wave and changed the wind's own cadence into a sustained wail. For an instant, just an instant, the tree blazed like a candle. It illuminated every shape and living thing outside the circle of flames, but I took an extra moment to analyze the flashlight's source. Only then did I realize we had been terribly wrong.

I wheeled around to warn Belton, *That's not Oliver!*

Too late. I didn't speak because Oliver was there. He was breathing heavy, standing erect, thick-jawed, his fur smoking after an upwind passage through the flames. Stared with amber oyster eyes that saw me, only me, indifferent to the man he was suffocating and Belton's attempts to pry one massive paw from his face.

I yelled, "Let him go!" and everything I saw after that was framed by the pistol's gun sights.

Oliver put a fist on the ground and vaulted closer, dragging Belton with him.

A shield, I realized. First, a snare from a steering wheel. Now Oliver had devised a human shield.

I backed a step while the stench of burning hair and sulfur found me. My eyes followed the pistol to Oliver's exposed knees . . . tracked upward to where his circus-sized pants smoldered on blistered thighs. Only the space of a few inches separated Belton's head from Oliver's face. And there, on his neck, instead of a collar or a rope, a snake had anchored its fangs and held fast. A ribbon of scales still dangled.

Tyrone's carnival poster. The image appeared in my mind but was rejected. This was a man-ape, not Tyrone who had endured deformity since our school days.

I wondered, *What is keeping him alive?*

Loyalty . . . rage . . . hatred—none explained such relentless behavior. But what Oliver did next hinted at the truth and the truth was darker than any word I know. He grunted—*ITCH!*—and lunged at me with a sweeping arm. I dodged his hand and got the gun up while he opened his jaws wide, then posed for a microsecond over Belton's exposed neck—a look that threatened, *Surrender or I'll do it.*

That's when I shot him. Squared the sights on Oliver's forehead and didn't remember squeezing the trigger or even the sound of the gun blast. The only thought in my mind was, *Shoot low, you'll kill Belton. Shoot high, Oliver's teeth will find you.*

I shot to the right but low, which underlined a reality, not a threat: caged or uncaged, Oliver was a predator, a blood killer without soul or conscience. He would have feasted on me, feasted on all humanity, if I'd missed. So I had risked Belton's life to save my own by lowering my aim.

I didn't miss. The bullet hit Oliver beneath the cheek, severed one clamshell ear, and tumbled him backward toward the flames. He didn't move when I helped Belton to his feet, a man who was too angry to go into shock.

"Is he dead? That son of a bitch!" Belton charged toward the creature—possibly to kick him—but collapsed after a step, groaning, "Damn . . . my leg." Sat there and embraced his knee while I studied Oliver, who was on his belly and still breathing.

I looked back at the opening in the flames, hollered, "We need help!" then placed myself between Belton and Oliver. His pelt smoldered while his ribs expanded and contracted. I watched ten bare toes flex as if testing mobility. His right hand moved, then his left arm. "Crawl away," I told Belton.

He did. I slid sideways, following.

Because the pistol was empty, the slide had locked back to show its empty chamber. I thought, *He can count, but he can't see through metal,* and I slammed the slide closed as if I'd just shucked a bullet.

Oliver's head tilted to focus his only ear. An amber eye

opened. It fluttered as if fighting sleep, or death, and rotated toward me.

I walked at him with the pistol. "I'll shoot you again if you move."

Oliver exhaled a low growl and lay still, but his eye continued to track me.

From behind, Belton sounded a note of surprise. "Hey . . . *Hey*, someone's coming. Is that a horse?"

I took a quick look: blurred by heat and flames, a man wearing a cowboy hat had dismounted. He hunkered low to summon his nerve, then charged through the smoke, calling, "Are you the idiots who started this fire? By damn, I'll leave you here to burn if it was you." He switched off his flashlight and pocketed the thing. A bandy-legged man in his sixties.

Mild disappointment. I had hoped it was Joey Egret I'd seen approaching on horseback. Worse, the man was not carrying a rifle as cow hunters often do.

Belton tried to stand. "Call the police—that thing's a goddamn killer. I'll explain, but not while it's still alive. Do you have a gun? We need a gun if he's not dead." Talking too fast, Belton's tone communicating fear.

Oliver's brain processed the words, his eye absorbed details. He got a knee under him and was positioning a hand when I leaned with both arms extended. "This pistol is all we need—now lay still, damn you."

The man said, "Hey, now!" and his boots clomped him closer. He removed his hat, slapped it clean of ashes while his eyes adjusted, looking from Belton to me, and then saw the heap of smoldering fur. "What the hell's going on here? That one of my calves? Y'all going to jail if you kilt one of my—" He stopped a few steps from Oliver. "Good lord, this here's a damn monkey. Why'd anybody want to hurt a monkey?"

Oliver's eye fluttered to consciousness and glared at me while he appealed for help by imitating the mewling of an injured puppy. The man said, "This ol' boy's in bad shape," and reached to stroke Oliver's shoulder but was unnerved when Belton and I both yelled out warnings.

A low growl and one dulling amber eye tracked me while I backed the man a safe distance, far enough to say into his ear, "Is there a rifle scabbard on your saddle?"

Cow hunters are prone to stubbornness. "I'm not known as a monkey killer," he replied. "The way you keep that handgun pointed, why do you need my rifle? Poor thing's about dead anyway. A veterinarian is what he needs, then we'll let the law sort this out."

"Police will be more interested in a corpse you'll find down by the river—most of his face missing," I said.

That got the man's attention. I told him my name, and added, "I'm a friend of Joey Egret and probably a dozen other people you know. My uncle was Jake Smith, and I'm related to the Summerlins. I'm not asking for your blessings, sir. Just the loan of one bullet."

In rural areas, surnames are tribal and carry weight. Instantly, the man's sympathies shifted and I was granted temporary rank in his cavalry of one. Mr. Harney—that was his name—kept my Devel pistol trained on the monkey but first wanted a question answered. "The other woman, where is she?"

I assumed he had mistaken the wailing cry of fire and wind for a human voice.

"No," he insisted. "When that big pine went up, she waved for me to come. Sort of looked like you, but longer hair and wearing a bright red shirt. She ain't here? Or . . . or maybe it *was* you."

In the fire's heat, I felt a chill and could not answer until I'd returned with the rifle, a Winchester .30-30. I said, "Mr. Harney, in my SUV—if we find it—I've got a picture I'd like you to see."

Then I shucked a round and finished the job.